MURDER OFFSTAGE

A POSIE PARKER MYSTERY

L. B. HATHAWAY

D1530279

WHITEHAVEN

WHITEHAVEN MAN PRESS

London

First published in Great Britain in 2014 by
Whitehaven Man Press, London

A CIP catalogue record for this book is available
from the British Library.

ISBN (Mobi:) 978-0-9929254-0-6
ISBN (ePub:) 978-0-9929254-1-3
ISBN (paperback:) 978-0-9929254-2-0

Jacket illustration by Red Gate Arts.

Formatting and design by J.D. Smith.

For Marco

Monday 14th February, 1921
(Valentine's Day)

One

The man's body lay exactly where it had fallen, his head quite shot off.

He was dressed in a carefully pressed black tuxedo, and a sticky puddle of his blood oozed out over the smart tiled entrance hall of London's Ritz Hotel.

If you had looked very closely you would have seen that the cuffs of the man's black jacket were just a little too shiny and threadbare for him to have been a regular hotel guest, and a snob would have said with a sharp intake of breath that the cut of the dinner suit was not quite *the thing* anymore. It was at least twenty years out of date, in fact. Posie Parker noticed all this and more.

'Get out! This is a murder scene,' shrieked the nervy Hotel Manager, flapping his hands ineffectually at the small mob of newspaper journalists who threatened to engulf him. Policemen were dancing around too, adding to the confusion. All the way up the Grand Staircase guests stared down, clutching their sour-apple Martinis in disbelief. A flashbulb went off suddenly, blinding them all. The tang from the flash was strong and it wafted heavily in the air like a poisonous chalky fog.

'OUT! OUT!'

'Who is he, guv'nor? Give us a name!' shouted one of

the journalists, a stocky fellow with an insistent manner. But the Hotel Manager could only shrug, for no-one knew who the dead man was.

In all of the chaos no-one noticed a slim, well-dressed brunette in her very late twenties push her way through the revolving glass door and step inside, out of the whirling February snow-storm.

She looked around with the eye of an expert and located her target.

'Rufus!' she called brightly. Tucking her enormous carpet bag under her arm, she hitched up her pencil skirt and stepped calmly over the headless body, judging it correctly as the quickest way to get to her old friend. She made for the crowded Grand Staircase, floating upwards on a cloud of parma violet.

She found him at the very top, leaning theatrically over the bannister, cigar balanced precariously in one hand, emerald-coloured drink in the other, surveying the scene below. She tapped him on the shoulder.

'You called me. And here I am!' Posie declared, in as enthusiastic a manner as she could muster.

'You didn't tell me it was going to be a full-blown murder! A professional job too, by the look of things; a very good shot. I thought you said something about a diamond in the message. Perhaps the messenger-boy got it wrong?'

Rufus turned to her at last, and Posie saw at once that he must have been drinking all day, perhaps all of the previous night too. He seemed to have terrible trouble focusing on her.

'Ah! Nosy Parker. What ho! Good of you to come.'

Posie swallowed down her anger – she hated this old nickname – but Rufus was her elder brother Richard's best friend from Eton, and her only link to her brother since he had been killed in the Great War three years earlier. Besides, Rufus was rich, and she hadn't had a paid job at the Detective Agency in more than three weeks. Better take anything, she'd said to herself as she changed into her heavy black boots and made herself ready for the snow, setting off at a brisk half-run from her office in Bloomsbury twenty minutes earlier.

Gently she prised the vicious-looking green drink from his hand.

'By jove, it's all my fault. All of this,' Rufus was motioning to the floor below him. 'A fella's dead, and all because of my girl.'

Posie led him to a comfy-looking red velvet armchair tucked into a shallow recess on the landing. She squatted down next to him, moving a potted aspidistra out of the way first.

'*What* girl? Last time we met you were bemoaning the lack of a good woman in your life – and that was only about a month ago. We met at the theatre, remember? That silly play with all those poor girls dressed as dancing caterpillars? You invited me. Remember?'

A look of fondness spread over Rufus' face briefly like a warm fug.

'How can I forget, Nosy? That was where I met her! Afterwards, in the Circle Bar. You dashed off to feed your cat or something. Minsky? Minky?'

'Mr Minks.'

'Mnnn.' Rufus flicked his long fair fringe from his eyes and seemed lost in another world for a minute. He took a drag on his cigar. Posie gave him a short sharp dig in the ribs.

'Anyway, it was love at first sight, Nosy. The most beautiful girl I've ever clapped eyes on. We've been living here in my rooms at the Ritz ever since. I got her to give up the caterpillar job at once. Demeaning stuff for a clever girl. *My* girl.'

Posie stared at Rufus in horror.

'Obviously it was all top secret,' and here Rufus tapped his nose and gave Posie a wink. 'You know, *hush hush* and all that. We were having a fine old time. I was buying her clothes every day on Bond Street, jewels too; taking her to all the best places. I wanted her to be in the best possible state before she met my father.'

Posie gulped, a sickening fear spreading over her. She remembered the Earl of Cardigeon of old, his temper was the stuff of legends. He was known to be a real old monster.

'Your father, Rufey? Was that a good idea? Why on earth?'

Rufus looked at Posie in sheer amazement.

'She was going to be my wife, you idiot! I thought I'd get the old buffoon used to the idea in good time.'

Posie cursed. This all spelled disaster. She'd never normally have thought of Rufus as a sitting duck, ripe for the picking by any pretty girl who fancied a free ride for a while. But, well, things had changed. Rufus had never been quite the same man since the Great War, and what with his infernal drinking…she'd been a bad friend, she should have looked out for him better.

'What happened? Today? What happened with the girl?'

Rufus held his head in his hands a moment before answering.

'I proposed, of course. At lunchtime. Over a bucket of champagne in the Palm Court.'

'Why?' wailed Posie.

'Call yourself a detective?' snapped Rufus nastily. 'It's Valentine's Day, you noddle! A perfect day for it. Dash it all, I don't know why I bothered to call you here if you're so slow.'

Posie sighed: it was all too clear what had happened.

'You called me because she's run off. Let me guess: you gave her some priceless engagement bauble you had bought on Bond Street, and then she disappeared for a while to powder her nose. You thought she had been gone a long time and when you went to look for her in your rooms you found she had miraculously disappeared. Including the ring! No note. She had disappeared out of a back exit. Am I correct?'

Rufus squirmed beneath her gaze.

'*Almost* correct. Sorry for being mean just now, Nosy. I'm just rather strung out.'

'I'd say,' nodded Posie calmly. 'So what did I get wrong then?' She hated being wrong. Even in the middle of a crisis.

Out of the corner of her eye she noticed an elderly Butler in the hotel's smart livery approaching them. He shuffled to a stop, and presented a silver tray to Rufus, on which two cream-coloured telegrams rested. Rufus ripped them open half-heartedly. He groaned and turned his face into the velvet of the armchair. Posie grabbed the two telegrams from his quivering hand and read them quickly.

The first read:

GOT YOUR TELEGRAM. COMING TO LONDON ON NEXT TRAIN. IDIOT BOY - THAT DIA-MOND IS A FAMILY HEIRLOOM. IT WAS YOUR RESPONSIBILITY TO KEEP IT INSURED AND IN THE SAFE AT THE BANK. IT HAS A CURSE ON IT; I'LL DO MORE THAN CURSE YOU WHEN I GET TO YOU TONIGHT, I'M WARNING YOU.

YOUR (DEEPLY UNHAPPY) FATHER.

P.S. THANK GOODNESS FOR BRIGG & BROOKS. AT LEAST WE MIGHT GET SOME INSURANCE MONEY OUT OF THIS DAMNED MESS. PERHAPS I'LL GET THE ROOF FIXED AT REBBURN NOW.

Posie sank back on her haunches and wrapped her arms around herself. She whistled softly under her breath. She stared at Rufus in amazement.

'I know, I know! Don't tell me. I was an idiot! A fool. She took me for everything.'

She flicked to the second telegram quickly. It read:

BRIGG & BROOKS OF LONDON CONFIRM THE VALUE OF THE MAHARAJAH DIAMOND IS LISTED AS SEVEN HUNDRED THOUSAND POUNDS. IT IS UNINSURED. AS YOU WILL RECALL YOU HAVE NOT KEPT UP WITH THE ANNUAL PREMIUMS FOR THE LAST 2 YEARS, DESPITE FREQUENT REMINDERS.
BEST OF LUCK.

She looked up at Rufus, gobsmacked:

'What happened? I thought you had plenty of money. Why didn't you keep up the premiums, Rufey?'

'I forgot! I just forgot! There was so much else going on!' he wailed through splayed fingers, covering his face.

Posie chewed her lip worriedly: more likely Rufus was so addled by drink over the last two years he hadn't got a clue what was going on in many aspects of his life.

'But why on earth did you want to give her that *particular* diamond? A family heirloom? Surely a girl like that would want something newer – something flashier – in a modern style?'

'I told her about the Maharajah diamond when we first met,' Rufus groaned. 'She was fascinated by it. She kept asking me about its history, its story. It has quite a scandalous tale behind it, you know. Eventually I took her to see it at the bank. Got them to open up the safe specially and she held it, and held it, as if it were magical or something. As if she were under a spell.'

'Almost a million pounds' worth of diamond can do that to a girl,' Posie muttered.

'In the end we went every day to see the stone. She couldn't get enough of it. You know, I think the Bank Manager thought I was touched in the head or something.'

Posie declined from commenting, and waved him on in encouragement.

'Eventually I got the idea of having it mounted into a ring, and giving it to her as an engagement gift. I kept imagining the pure pleasure on her little face! The Maharajah diamond glittering away on her finger! I never thought for a minute this would happen. I'm in for it now, Nosy. Uninsured, and my father coming down here to boot! Be a brick – tell me, what should I do?'

Posie was just summoning up the energy to speak when she caught sight of a number of people heading along the narrow landing in their direction. Several policemen were bobbing along subserviently behind a tall important-looking man in a homburg hat and a beige trench coat. He looked like he meant business.

'Heigh-ho, Rufey,' Posie muttered, and got to her feet. 'Looks like Scotland Yard have sent their finest. That was quick! Did *you* contact them? Perhaps it was your father?'

Rufus just curled up even more into the armchair and started a low, steady groaning sound.

'Lord Rufus Cardigeon, I presume?' the Inspector addressed the armchair in a loud, carrying sort of growly voice which made Posie immediately feel guilty of something, but of what she couldn't say. The groaning continued. A crowd of guests had now turned from watching the gory murder scene below and were edging around them in a tight circle.

'I am Miss Parker, sir.' Posie stood as tall as she could, and squared up to the man, extending her gloved hand.

The Inspector looked bemused for a minute, then took it gingerly.

'Inspector Oats, Miss. From Scotland Yard.'

'I thought as much. Have you come about the missing Maharajah diamond? Lord Cardigeon here is very shaken by it, sir. It seems he has been duped by a chorus girl who stole the diamond not more than an hour ago. Thank you for coming so quickly.'

'A diamond? What diamond? And who is this Maharajah you're talking about? Some foreign chappie, is he?'

The Inspector stared at Posie with a look of total incomprehension in his trouty pale blue eyes. She stared back.

'Report it to one of my men if there's been a theft. I'm here on serious business.'

With this the Inspector turned to one of his men, nodded and shouted in a dramatic fashion: 'All right, boys, let's be 'avin''im.'

Two burly policemen jumped on Rufus and sat on him in the armchair while a third came forwards brandishing glittering silver handcuffs. There was a sharp dramatic intake of breath from the crowd. The handcuffs were snapped on and Rufus, from underneath the two policemen, could be heard wailing.

'Lord Cardigeon, I am arresting you on suspicion of being an accomplice to the murder of the as – yet – unidentified gentleman lying in the hallway downstairs. You do not have to say anything, but what you do say may be taken in evidence…'

'Hang on, hang on a minute,' Posie jumped in front of Inspector Oats. 'You've got this all wrong. My friend here is the victim of a crime, a THEFT! He's certainly not involved with the murder here.'

'Come on, lads,' said the Inspector, and the policemen dragged Rufus to his feet. The Inspector turned to Posie, and said in his carrying voice:

'I'm afraid it is *you* who have this wrong, Miss. I have a hotel full of guests willing to swear on their lives that your friend Lord Cardigeon has been living in sin here for the last few weeks with a well-known gangster's moll. She's called Lucky Lucy Gibson. She's on the most-wanted list of criminals in London. She's famous. It was her who took a pot-shot at our dead friend in the hall here and was last seen jumping into a black cab outside with a smoking gun. What with all the snow, she's disappeared! Vanished! *Why* she killed the chap downstairs is what I want to ask your pal here about – I think he may have been in on it too.'

'Lucy?' Rufus mumbled. 'I don't know anyone of that name. My fiancée was called Georgie. Georgie le Pomme.'

Posie groaned in exasperation. She wanted to slap Rufus.

'That must have been her stage-name,' she hissed at him. 'But is it true – what the Inspector said – that Lucy, Georgie, *whatever* her name was, killed the man downstairs?'

Rufus turned a deep ruby red and nodded slowly.

'I said you *almost* had the story correct, Nosy. I didn't have time to tell you the truth. After she disappeared, I went looking for Georgie up in our rooms, and as I was about to come back downstairs, defeated, I saw her in the entrance hall arguing with an elderly foreign-looking fellow in a tux. Next thing I knew she was taking out a revolver and shooting the chappie! I called out her name – I thought she was in trouble – but she ignored me and ran off! The Maharajah diamond was glittering away on her finger as she left! I swear it! I had nothing to do with *any* of this shooting story.'

'We'll see about that,' said the Inspector and gave some special signal for the policemen to frogmarch Rufus down the stairs. He twisted backwards and gave Posie an imploring look:

'Tell my father what's happened, Nosy. And tell him

about Brigg & Brooks. Please?'

Posie sank into the red armchair, flabbergasted.

'What did you say about a *stage-name*, Miss?' asked the Inspector unexpectedly, lingering on. He had his leather-clad notebook out and his pencil quivered in the air hopefully.

'Lord Cardigeon met this chorus girl at the theatre; the Athenaeum Theatre in Piccadilly, to be precise. I was with him that night.'

'Really?' asked the Inspector quizzically. 'How curious. I've never known Lucky Lucy tread the boards before. Did you actually *see* her on stage?'

Posie shook her head. 'No. Strangely enough I did not. She was dressed as a caterpillar.' Posie realised immediately how silly she sounded, and then added in a quiet, subdued voice, '*If* she was there at all, that is.'

The Inspector snorted. 'What nonsense! Now I really have heard it all,' he muttered, angrily putting his notebook away. He swung off down the corridor.

Poor old Rufey, Posie thought to herself. What a day: one mess after another.

And it would be up to her to sort it all out.

* * * *

Two

It had started to snow thickly again by the time Posie reached her office on Grape Street. The flakes were falling fast and it was a relief to close the door on the cold, wintry world.

The Detective Agency was on the second floor, up a narrow blue-carpeted staircase, which had, like everything else in the building, seen better days. But when choosing it two years earlier, Posie had decided the location of the office was perfect. It sat in a shabby triangle enclosed on three sides by Covent Garden, the glittering Theatre District and musty old Bloomsbury. The looming silhouette of the British Museum, like the prow of a great ship, was just visible from the office window. Posie *had* hoped that clients from all walks of life, from all the worlds that the triangle quietly intersected, would approach her and use her Detective Agency to solve their unsolvable mysteries, unravel their unfathomable secrets.

But, as with many things in life, it had not worked out like that...

* * * *

When she had first opened, Posie had sat solemnly waiting for her first client to arrive, day after day. She had been flooded with disappointment when no-one came, despite the bright new bronze plaque outside on the street which had cost her the earth and which read:

THE GRAPE STREET BUREAU.
P. PARKER & ASSOCIATES.
Mysteries and Problems Solved.
No case too big or small!
(2nd Floor)

She had not dared have 'Detective Agency' inscribed on the plaque – it had seemed too presumptuous somehow. After all, she was just starting out. And likewise, she had not dared reveal the fact it was *just her*. She *was* the Detective Agency. She reasoned to herself that a small white lie never hurt anyone: sometimes you needed to be extravagant with the truth.

After two months of absolutely no clients, Posie was on the point of shutting up forever, desperately calculating when *exactly* her money would run out, when into her office walked her saviour. In the shape of one Mr Irving.

He had presented himself in her office one morning around coffee-time, a small startled-looking man in his mid-fifties, in brown tweedy clothes and a dented homburg hat. There was something ferrety about his manner – he was the sort of man you forgot instantly, which was, as it turned out, his business.

'Nice place you've got here,' he remarked casually, almost sniffing the air as if to check on its suitability. Posie had simply nodded, it *was* nice, she knew that, but when she had taken on the lease it had been dank and dirty. With the last of the small capital sum she had received under her father's Will she had bought a few sticks of good furniture to furnish the bare rooms and enough tins of emulsion from the Army & Navy Stores to keep her busy painting the place singlehanded for a week.

Mr Irving had thrust his cheaply printed card across the desk at her as he cast an appraising eye around Posie's neat cream office.

She read:

IRVING & SON.
PRIVATE DETECTIVE AGENCY.
For all your legal and personal needs.
33B, Lincoln's Inn West.

'Posie Parker, at your service. How can I help you, Mr Irving?' she had asked in as confident a manner as she could, fearful he would read in her every move that he was the very first person to ever sit opposite her in the woefully unused client's chair.

He tore his eyes away from the only decoration in the room, a small and delicately painted watercolour of the Cap d'Antibes in France above Posie's desk; a riot of bright sunshades and azure sea. It had been painted by Posie's father when he was a young man.

'Nice bit of seaside you've got up there. Fancy. Not much like Margate, is it?'

Posie coughed politely and pointed to Mr Irving's card enquiringly.

'Not a small talk kind of gal, are you? Very well. I'm here to see if we can *help each other*. Come to an arrangement, sort of thing. This could be your lucky day.'

'Go on.' Posie looked at the man curiously, and with a smidgen of mistrust.

'I've got a nice little practice going, just ten minutes from here. In Lincoln's Inn. See on the card? Not a high-level shindig, more your *everyday* sort of business. But it pays the bills nicely.'

'What is it you do?' Posie asked bluntly, interested.

'Spy on folks,' laughed Mr Irving, rubbing his hands together gleefully. 'In the trade we're known as *shadowers*. We get a tip-off from a lawyer and then we follow people; mainly rich toffs or businessmen having affairs, or keeping mistresses. Rum-doings. We take photos, and then the lawyer uses the snaps as evidence in divorce proceedings for their clients. It's lucrative work; we get referrals from more than twenty lawyers in all. Keeps me and my boy going nicely.'

What horrid work, Posie thought, trying not to visibly shudder. Dirty work, somehow; almost akin to blackmail.

'But I don't see how our interests coincide, Mr Irving? You sound as if you are doing well enough already without my help.'

'Look at the address on the card, Miss. What do you notice?'

She faltered for a minute. 'Why! Your address is just a basement! 33 *B*. Is that what you mean?'

'Yep. Good girl.' Mr Irving nodded. '*Just* a basement, as you say. Only, at the end of this week we won't even have that. We're being thrown out. The basement is being turned over for this newfangled telephone equipment for the lawyers' offices.'

A flash of understanding hit Posie.

'You want to buy me out?' she asked quietly in a meas-ured voice. She didn't know whether she felt happy or sad at this prospect.

'No,' Mr Irving shook his head firmly. He was gazing at the Cap d'Antibes again with a look of longing.

'I've decided to retire. It's about time. Go some place nice, perhaps. Grab a bit of sunshine, mebbe. But my boy

Len, he needs a job. He survived the war, thank goodness. He's a good lad, but he needs a *chance*. He can carry on just as well as we both did before, using everything he's learnt from me. I walked past your sign this morning and I just wondered…perhaps you need some help too. An assistant? A good detective? Just you, is it, Miss, working here?'

Mr Irving looked at Posie squarely with his eagle-eyes and his many years of experience of the very worst aspects of human nature. Posie held onto the business card tightly. The print had rubbed off all over her scarlet-manicured hands. No point trying to hide the truth now, she thought to herself. She nodded:

'Yes. It's just me. But I don't have enough work, even for myself.'

'That's what we'd bring to the table,' Mr Irving went on hopefully. 'Work. Masses of it. Len's one of the best shadowers in London. We've got cases coming out of our ears, and enough lawyers on our books to fill your empty bookcases. And more. You'll never need to worry about paying the rent here again.'

Posie swallowed. This was all very surprising.

'But what do you want from me? This is *my* Detective Agency!' Posie squeaked, and immediately realised she sounded childish.

'Don't worry,' Mr Irving said reassuringly. 'Just let Len come and work for you. The location here is perfect. No need to change your sign outside, or the name. In our game discretion is key, anyhow. All profits, after costs, to be split 50/50, between you and Len. How does that sound?'

It had sounded good, dirty work or not, and Posie had put her scruples quickly aside.

And now, two years down the line, Posie looked back fondly on that day as indeed being her lucky day. Mr Irving had proved some sort of ministering angel from heaven, in fact.

Len's shadowing work alone had kept them afloat for

many, many months. Through it all, and especially at the beginning, dear, good-hearted Len had never once questioned Posie about her lack of work; never complained about the days he spent chasing errant husbands all over town while she sat in the office at Grape Street reading *The Lady* and drinking sugared china tea, waiting for a suitable case to come in. They covered the bills and split the profits 50/50 and that was that.

It had only been in the last year that Posie had finally started to gain some cases of her own: a missing wife here, a Belgravia cook gone astray there, a minor insurance fraud.

Most recently and importantly, however, she had helped track down a gang of clever jewellery robbers dressed as choristers who had burgled a shop at Christmas in the exclusive Burlington Arcade (in what had come to be known as 'The Carino Affair', after the Italian Countess, Faustina Carino, whose jewellery, in for repairs and cleaning, had been the main target of the heist).

Posie was relieved she was finally able to bring some bacon to the table, and glad too that she was finally making a name for herself and for the Detective Agency. The Carino Affair had landed the Grape Street Bureau some good press – a small article in *The Times* which was nicely written – and perhaps more importantly, a friend and supporter in the form of one Detective Inspector Lovelace, of New Scotland Yard.

Posie firmly believed that you couldn't underestimate the importance of knowing good people in the right places, especially at sticky times.

Times such as now, perhaps…

* * * *

Plodding up the stairs and unwrapping her frozen layers of damp scarf, Posie was jolted sharply back to the present by the sound of loud, high-pitched laughter coming from the office. She opened the glass-stencilled front door and peered in.

The little waiting room was bright and warm. The fire was blazing merrily in the hearth and Len was sprawled all over the sofa. Babe Sinclair, their glamorous American secretary from New York, sat cosily to Len's right, nearest the fire. Her impossibly shiny black hair glinted beautifully and her sumptuous glittery jade necklace threw off beams of reflected light from the fire. On the coffee-table next to Len's beloved camera was a crumpled green-and-white striped bag from Lyons Cornerhouse.

'Crumpet?' Len asked cheerfully. Posie saw that he had improvised with a stoking iron and that he had been toasting the cakes over the fire. Posie nodded and slumped down into one of the armchairs. She kicked off her wet snow-boots and sat in her damp stockinged feet; the likelihood of any clients wandering in off the street without an appointment on a foul day like today was very small. She took the crumpet Len handed her gratefully, she hadn't realised how hungry she was.

Babe had begun to look at Posie resentfully, for she had been having a good time alone with Len, who never took anything too seriously. Babe knew too that she owed her job to Len, who had taken a shine to her at interview, rather than to Posie, who had only ever been frostily polite. She had only been working at the Grape Street Bureau for a few weeks, since just after Christmas, and she was still in her probation period. She realised that Posie's return meant she would now have to do some *actual* work, and she picked up her blue notebook from the floor with an exaggerated weary gesture.

Through mouthfuls of hot crumpet Posie gave Babe brisk instructions to send three important telegrams.

She dictated the exact contents, which Babe wrote down in a fancy American shorthand which Posie had never encountered before. Posie gulped the last crumbs down gratefully and licked her buttery fingers. She noticed that the secretary was still sitting in her chair, pouting slightly.

Posie sighed to herself: *Was it just possible that they had managed to hire the worst secretary in the world, ever?*

'What are you waiting for? Please, Babe. It's urgent. Send the telegrams now. Take the money from the strong-box on my desk.'

'But, gee, Miss,' drawled Babe, 'it's kinda snowing badly outside.'

'Hang it all! Don't you have snow in New York every winter? I would have thought this was nothing compared to that! Now, off you go. And when you come back I want you to go into your office and start the typing. If there isn't any to do, I want you to do the filing. If anything's not clear, come and find me. I don't want you disturbing Mr Irving out here. He's very busy.'

Babe gave a *moue* of dislike and then went through to Posie's office where she could be heard jangling coins together, and then she flounced out of the office, wrapping her shorn-black head in several woolly scarves. Len and Posie listened to her heavy, cross footsteps thumping down the stairs, followed by the violent slam of the front door onto the street below.

Len gave Posie one of his *I-can't-believe-you-just-did-that* looks.

'What?'

He smouldered at her. She felt her insides melting.

'I'm *not* being mean sending her out into the snow. That's her job! Anyway, she should be working, not shilly-shallying around with you out here, eating cakes. What do we pay her for, after all? We can only just afford it. As well you know.'

Len raised his eyebrow at Posie and smiled gently.

'We're sitting out here as our own offices are freezing. I thought we'd economise and light just one fire. Give her a break – I know you don't like her, Po. And anyway, I'm not busy. I don't have another case on until tomorrow.'

Posie glowered back at him. Len always had her sussed out, and he was right; she *didn't* like Babe, didn't trust her somehow. It was just a gut feeling she had.

To lighten the mood he started to skim through a sheaf of his freshly developed photos on the coffee-table, offering comments as he flicked through. Len looked at one in particular and threw back his head, laughing aloud, and the sound of it caught at Posie's throat, tugging at her heart, making her look away quickly into the roaring flames of the fire.

She was, simply and inconveniently, madly in love with him.

He was totally unsuitable, and totally out of her league. But he was a man with whom she felt a tense, thrilling crackle of electricity every single time he looked her way. And she could have sworn he felt it too.

Dashingly handsome, Len was tall and loose-limbed with dark curly hair and green eyes that crinkled up at the corners when he laughed, which was often. Sometimes Posie couldn't believe that the original Mr Irving, that ferrety little man, and the magnificent Len, with whom she had the good fortune to work with on a daily basis, were actually *related* to each other.

When she had suspected she might be falling in love with Len, right at the start, she had talked herself sternly out of it. It wouldn't do at all: Captain Harry Briskow, her fiancé, was newly dead, lying out on a battlefield in northern France somewhere, buried with no name and no grave for her to mourn at. Her only remembrance of kind, loyal Harry was one photo, and a little gold-and-silver ring with six diamond chips which he had given her the night before he had left.

A ring which she had now taken off and put to rest at the back of a drawer in her bedside cabinet. Besides, it wasn't just the memory of Harry either. It was more complicated than that.

Len was attached. He had a girl he had been seeing down Leytonstone way for years, a childhood sweetheart. An unnamed girl whom Posie had never met and who wasn't spoken about by Len, but whose presence could be felt sometimes hanging between them like a hardy, unforgiving ghost: a new knitted tie worn loyally just after Christmas; an unexplained bouquet of fresh freesias bought at lunchtime in the market at Covent Garden. Bridges which had not yet been burnt: which Posie could not *expect* to be burnt.

Posie leant casually in and looked at the photograph Len was laughing at now. It showed a well-known and particularly odious Member of Parliament, often in the newspapers, in a state of total undress. He was trying to frantically close the curtains on a scene he would rather Len had not been photographing. Posie couldn't help but smile.

Len went out and made some tea. When he came back with it he asked Posie about her day.

'Something about a jewel robbery? Babe heard the messenger-boy telling you.'

Posie nodded, noting to herself to be more discreet in the future. She described her afternoon.

Len whistled. 'Coo-ee! What are you going to do now?' he asked, curiously.

'Well, I'm not going to let the grass grow under my feet, that's for sure. I'll do everything possible. But a word of warning – you may have to help me out in the next few days. Is that okay? I'm not sure I can do it alone.'

Len nodded and his eyes twinkled in the light of the fire. 'Anything, Po. Just let me know when you need me. You know I'd do anything for you.'

If only, Posie thought to herself, and cursed him for being so totally and utterly lovely. She headed off to her freezing office to collect her thoughts.

'Happy Valentine's Day!' called out Len cheerfully.

* * * *

It was almost dark. Posie sat motionless at her desk in the failing light, her head in her hands. Mr Minks, the cream-and-brown Siamese, rubbed himself purposefully around her ankles. He wanted feeding.

He was a spoilt cat, Posie knew. A terribly haughty cat, too. And he really preferred the company of men to ladies, especially Len's company. But Posie loved him with all her heart and he was the only link to her past, to her father's Vicarage in Norfolk, where Mr Minks had spent his glory days happily climbing the red velvet curtains in the Reverend Parker's study. Mr Minks had been her father's pride and joy.

Since her father's sudden death two years ago, when Posie and Mr Minks had both found themselves unexpectedly homeless, Posie had felt perpetually guilty at uprooting the Siamese and installing him in the dingy London office. But Posie wasn't allowed pets at her digs on the top floor of the Mews House she lodged at in South Kensington, and so Mr Minks had to live alone at Grape Street. Posie had tried to make it homely for him by installing old velvet curtains for him to climb up in the tiny back kitchen, and by spending far too much of her salary on fresh cuts of chicken for him, which she cooked on the primus stove twice a day.

'I know, I know. Dinner time. Come on, your Lordship.'

After retrieving a bit of chicken in greased paper from

the outside windowsill of the kitchen, she fried it absently, forgetting to turn it half way and blackening it badly all down one side. Posie was miles away in her thoughts, thinking about her busy evening ahead: she had three interviews lined up for that night, and she realised that she was going to be slightly hampered by limits of time.

Posie put down the burnt chicken for the cat, who sniffed at it disdainfully in complaint. She hurried back into her office.

From a small locked cupboard by her desk she grabbed her evening kit, which Len jokingly called 'the glamour attack', but which in reality consisted rather boringly of a black velvet flapper dress, a feathered headband, crimson lipstick and a small bottle of violet scent. In two seconds flat, Posie had changed.

Posie could never be called a beauty, and she knew it. Her face was just too square for a start, lending her a wholesome rather than a romantic air, and her eyes were a rather commonplace English blue, but she knew too that she scrubbed up rather well, and even drew a few wolf-whistles when she tried her very best. She kicked around under her desk for a pair of heels and flicked the buckles closed. She smudged her eyes with a dash of kohl pencil and squirted herself liberally with perfume.

'Night night, Mr Minks!' she called. She could hear him attacking the chicken with gusto now in the kitchen. Beggars couldn't always be choosers.

She snatched up some change from the office strong-box and ran out, locking the door behind her. Too late she realised she should have taken a coat or a stole, and she felt briefly nostalgic for her beautiful silver fox fur, given to her by Harry years before and sold when the Grape Street Bureau was just starting up.

'Taxi!' called Posie out on the street, trying not to shiver too much, and a cab mercifully pulled up alongside her on the slushy pavement.

'Where we off to then, Miss?' asked the driver, setting his timer.

'The Athenaeum Theatre, please. Fast as you can. Stage Door!'

* * * *

Three

The show was due to start in half an hour.

Posie lingered for a minute outside the Stage Door of the theatre, studying the brightly coloured posters, the reviews. She had seen this show only one month previously with Rufus but she had totally forgotten its title.

Yes, there it was: *Showtime Madness!* It was billed as an 'all-singing, all-dancing night of entertainment', but all Posie could remember were the girls dressed in their heavy, bulky caterpillar costumes, legs and arms straining for freedom. So many girls, all in a green caterpillary line.

Which one had been Lucy? Or Georgie, as Rufus had known her as? Had she really been on stage at all? Perhaps she had been planted in the bar specially to talk to Rufus after the show and knew as little about *Showtime Madness!* as Posie did herself.

She slipped inside the Stage Door unobserved, heading down the rickety stairs to the dark depths of the basement, on into the tunnels of the dressing rooms and offices. Dressers and dancers were running to and fro along the warren of gloomy, chalky-smelling passageways, lit up here and there with bright white bulbs of light. Posie hugged the wall and shouldered her way along slowly, part of the chaos.

Ahead of her, an extraordinary-looking small girl with unnaturally bright blonde hair and a tape-measure looped around her neck was ironing out an enormous fluffy feather boa, blocking the corridor with her ironing board.

'I'm the Wardrobe Mistress. Can I help yer, lovey?' asked the girl in a strong London twang, her eyes roaming up and down Posie as if assessing her costume for defects, for last-minute repairs. The girl took a drag on a long black cigarette, sending a perfect 'O' of smoke spiralling expertly up into the air. Posie noticed the end of the cigarette was ringed in a bright silver circle of theatrical lipstick. She dragged her eyes away from the strange colour combination, which reminded her of a crescent moon on a chilly night.

'The Theatre Manager? Is his office along here? He's expecting me – I sent a telegram this afternoon.'

The girl looked at Posie strangely for a minute, then pulled her ironing board aside grandly as if she were removing a much larger obstacle, a boulder perhaps. She motioned further down the corridor.

'Second on yer right, Miss. You can't miss it, the smell of drink will hit you before you get through the door. Fair knock you out, it will. Like a distillery.'

Posie nodded and smiled. 'Thank you. What's his name please? The Theatre Manager? Mister...?'

The girl licked her silver lips. 'Blake,' she said disparagingly, 'Samuel Blake. No "Mister" about him, though. He's a buffoon. Knows nothin' about runnin' this place.'

Up ahead of her the corridor seemed to get smaller and lower. Here, there was no-one about. Posie found the office with Mr Blake's name written grandly in large capital letters above the door. She knocked on the flimsy wooden door, which was a little ajar.

'Anyone in? Hello! Mr Blake?' she called cheerily, and

then when no-one responded, she slipped deftly inside. She needed a lucky break, and her spirits lifted at the sight of the obviously empty room.

The office was a strange, smallish room, with a low curving roof which reminded Posie of being in a cave, or being trapped inside a tunnel underground. It was very dark, and even though she wasn't overly tall, Posie had to duck her head in order to move along. Blake's desk was on the left-hand side, and was illuminated by one reading lamp. The top of the desk, and the chair, and the floor-space all around were covered in stacks of paper. The only other furniture in the room was a hatstand near the door, and one grey metal filing cabinet, also piled high with papers.

A steady drip-drip could be heard. In the dim glow from the lamp Posie noticed that the office walls were completely damp, with horrible sweating beads of moisture forming on every surface. *How on earth can he work in here?* thought Posie, heading for the desk, and longing suddenly for her cream-painted office with its sash window letting in lots of light, despite the crowded office roofs it looked over. Never again would she complain she had no real view: a window was a window, after all.

Posie moved the papers from the chair and sat herself at the desk. She started to move her nimble fingers through the papers, opening the drawers quickly. Nothing. She carried on.

All at once Posie jumped. A strange booming sound was shaking the desk in front of her, papers spilling to the floor. The whole room was vibrating.

BOOM. BOOM.

The desk-lamp started to flicker and the empty bottles of whisky which Posie had found in every drawer of the desk started jangling together furiously.

BOOM.

Her heart was beating madly, the sound was enormous.

It was like nothing she had ever heard before, and she had heard some terrible things when she had been an ambulance driver on the Front at the end of the Great War in France: the shells, the screaming. She had tried to forget it mostly, otherwise she couldn't sleep at night.

For a horrible moment Posie thought the cave-like roof was about to collapse, and she remembered her old training in France and got down on her knees and started to nudge herself over to the door, elbow by elbow, making herself as small as possible.

'You're okay, Miss. You can get up. Don't be scared.'

Posie looked up and saw the tiny girl who had been ironing in the corridor. She was looking at Posie with some concern. Posie got to her feet, heart still hammering.

'It takes some gettin' used to, this place. We're right under the Orchestra Pit here. They're just startin'. Gettin' tuned up. Drums first, then the double basses. That's why it's so loud just now.'

Posie gulped in relief. 'Thank you. And thank you for not laughing at me. I must have looked quite a sight.'

The girl shrugged. 'No problem. I recognise a former war girl. I was in France too, nursin' on the Western Front. I had to crawl out several times when we took a hit from a shell, just like that. Dolly Price, by the way,' she said, extending silver-tipped fingers. Posie took her hand and shook it warmly.

'Posie Parker.'

'By all accounts they've got a fine mess on their hands up there tonight,' said the girl, indicating upstairs with a raised eyebrow.

'The First Violin's gone missin'. He never turned up for rehearsal this afternoon and he's still not turned up tonight. It's never happened before. Still, it'll give Mr Blake somethin' to think about for once. You'll find him in the Circle Bar, by the way. Drinkin' himself to oblivion.'

'So you knew he wouldn't be here? But you let me come in anyway?'

'That's right. I don't owe him no favours. You had a look about you, like you were on the hunt for somethin'. Did you find it?'

Posie shook her head. 'It's such a mess in here.'

'Whotcha lookin' for?' asked Dolly quickly.

'A list of names. Chorus girls. Chorus girls who've been employed here recently.'

'I see.' Dolly, quick as a flash, had gone over to the metal filing cabinet and was rifling through the third drawer down. She quickly brought out a thick manila file, stuffed full of bits of paper, receipts and photos.

'I can probably do better than just a list, a photo maybe... who you lookin' for exactly?'

Posie thought for a split-second. Could she really trust this girl? She decided on the spur of the moment that she could.

'I think her stage-name was Georgie le Pomme. But she may be known as Lucy, too. Or anything else for that matter. To make things worse I don't even know *if* she ever worked here. I can't describe her to you, either, as I've never seen her before. But she was stunningly beautiful, apparently. I'm sorry if I'm wasting your time.'

Dolly eyed her keenly. 'No, no. You're not.'

Dolly was down on her knees, tipping the contents of the manila file over the floor. There were perhaps twenty stage photos of girls posing for the camera. Posie thought they all looked the same. Dolly grouped them together, and running her hands through her cropped bleached hair she stared at them all for a minute.

'This one!' she declared triumphantly, and flipped the photo over on its reverse, as if performing a clever magic trick, finding the right card in the pack. She looked up at Posie, grinning.

'Knew the one you meant straightaway. I get to know all the girls here, bein' the Wardrobe Mistress. She was a tiny girl, like me. Slippery as a fish, but a rare beauty all right. Called herself Georgie. Gone now.'

Posie studied the photo quickly, and nodded. Dolly was right, the girl in the snap had a wide-eyed childish beauty about her and perhaps the loveliest face Posie had ever seen. No wonder poor old Rufus had been taken in. She tucked the photo inside her bag.

'Anything else in that folder you think will help me? An address, a reference, even?'

Dolly was searching frantically again, but with no luck this time. A loud bang in the corridor outside reminded them they shouldn't be snooping around in someone else's office. Dolly thrust the file back in the cabinet and they slipped out. The noise of the orchestra was less out there. Dolly lit up another black cigarette.

'Some sort of trouble she's in, is she? Georgie?'

Posie shook her head apologetically. 'I'm sorry. I can't tell you anymore just yet.' She checked her wristwatch. 'I've got to catch the Manager just now, and then I'm off elsewhere. I'm on quite a tight schedule.'

'Of course you are.'

Posie caught a flash of disappointment in the girl's face as she nodded her understanding.

'But tell you what,' Posie said earnestly, 'meet me tomorrow. How about eleven at Lyons Cornerhouse on the Strand? I'll tell you more then.'

Dolly nodded eagerly. 'Okay. Thanks. Now take these stairs to the bar upstairs. Up two floors. Don't expect to get any sense out of him though.'

* * * *

A nervous-looking barman was wiping glasses busily at one end of the bar, keeping himself well out of the way. At the other end a squat, angry-looking man in his early thirties in a velvet smoking jacket was keeping a bottle of bourbon company.

Posie observed the man picking at his teeth with a small wooden tooth-pick, and then replacing it, dirty, into the communal cut-glass holder on the bar. She suppressed a shudder and walked forwards.

'Mr Blake, I presume?' Posie advanced at a confident, brisk pace. Uninvited, she sat down quickly at the bar stool next to the Theatre Manager. Experience told her there was no point in dragging out niceties with men such as these.

'Who the hell are you?' Mr Blake asked rudely, looking at Posie from small piggy eyes in a greasy, tired face. 'You're too old to audition as a show-girl, I don't take anyone over twenty-five. You're too plain too.' The fumes of drink came off him strongly. Posie held her breath and waited.

'And you're too fancily dressed to be looking for any other work. So wad-daya want?'

Posie felt the stolen photograph burning a hole in her bag.

'Well, that was certainly a memorable introduction, thank you. But no, I'm not after work in your lovely establishment. I'm looking for someone. Someone who's disappeared.'

'Lionel? Lionel Le Merle?' asked Mr Blake suddenly, eagerly, thrusting his face further forwards. 'Related, are you? You missing him too?'

'Sorry? I don't know who you…' But in a blink Posie remembered the missing First Violin Dolly had spoken of. '…Ah, no. No. I can't help you there, I'm afraid.'

She looked at Mr Blake earnestly. 'I'm looking for a friend. She used to work here. Georgie le Pomme. She was a chorus girl, but I think she's left your employment. Do you have any idea where I might reach her? A forwarding address, maybe? A contact?'

Was it Posie's imagination or had a look of fear and barely disguised panic entered the eyes of Mr Blake at the mention of Georgie's name? A thin sheen of sweat glistened on his oily brow and Mr Blake looked slightly green beneath the bar lights. He downed what remained in his glass and poured another.

'Please, Mr Blake. I'm desperate. I'm worried for her safety.'

'I know nothing about it. One of my best dancers, Georgie was. No idea what happened to her. Here one day, gone the next. Shame.'

He was hiding something.

'How long had she been here exactly? I forget…'

He shrugged carelessly. 'Not even a year. Came at the same time as Le Merle.'

Posie nodded sweetly, innocently. Mr Blake avoided her eye.

'And that forwarding address for Georgie…do you happen to have it?'

'No, I do not,' Mr Blake snapped at Posie angrily. 'And even if I did, why should I give it to you? Who are you, anyway? What's your name? You still haven't told me.'

Posie got down from her stool primly. There was nothing more to be gained here.

'Rosemary,' she said, telling the real truth now. Her full name. 'Rosemary Parker. I sent you a telegram earlier, saying I would come and see you tonight. Perhaps you have mislaid it in all your, er, *busyness* this evening?'

The barman sniggered. Unwisely.

'You,' shouted Mr Blake at the barman, 'you watch your manners. Otherwise you'll find yourself out of a job. And you, Miss *Rosemary*. No. I did not receive your telegram. As God is my witness I did not.'

* * * *

Posie headed off down the stairs. She was puzzled. *He's just a hopeless drunk*, she thought to herself. But Mr Blake was a bad liar, too. He knew more about the missing dancer Georgie le Pomme than he was giving away.

And strangely, he had also seemed utterly convinced he had never received her telegram…and somehow Posie believed him.

The Foyer was very busy as the theatre staff made ready for the waiting audience to come in. Cigarette-girls and programme-sellers were hastily fixing their trays, the ticket staff standing ready, their arms loaded with dusty-looking red roses.

'Remember!' shouted a thin young man with a shock of very dark spiky hair, 'It's Valentine's Day! People will be in the mood for BUYING! Press the red roses on the gentlemen. Make them feel guilty if they don't buy one for their lady-friends. Work the whole theatre!'

Posie felt slightly sick at the calculated cynicism on parade. She peered outside through the gold gilded door-way. It was just starting to snow again. Suddenly she heard a newly-familiar voice behind her. It was Dolly:

'You forgot your coat, Miss!' Dolly called out convincingly. Posie looked at Dolly in bewilderment, but Dolly was already shrugging onto Posie's shoulders a magnificent black fur coat, luxuriously warm and cut in a very modern swing style.

'It's a fake, but it's a good one,' Dolly whispered, close up. 'I noticed you didn't have one with you. Give it back to me tomorrow. I've borrowed it from the theatre wardrobe. It won't be missed. Otherwise you'll freeze to death out there.'

Posie smiled a thank you, and turned the collar up against the night.

The queue outside was long, and people were bunching up under the awning of the theatre to keep warm. Posie was just trotting down the steps, already searching the street for a cab, when she heard a peal of high-pitched laughter she recognised.

Turning to her left, she saw the black shingled head of Babe, her laughter carrying across the crowd. With a pang Posie realised how very beautiful the girl was: she was getting all sorts of attention from most of the men in the crowd, much to the obvious annoyance of their wives and girlfriends. Babe was dressed up to the nines. Posie gaped a little as she saw the many fine strands of creamy pearls around Babe's neck and the snow-fox fur cape around her shoulders. It was, unlike hers, obviously *not* a fake. But how on earth could her secretary afford such things on the meagre salary they paid her?

Posie noticed that Babe was also holding a huge bouquet of red roses. Well, that was to be expected, wasn't it? Posie muffled herself up as much as she could under the fake fur, anxious not to catch Babe's attention and be placed in an embarrassing situation. A taxi was just coming past – if she was lucky she could catch it. It slowed, and Posie ran over and gave her next destination to the driver. A prickling feeling told her that someone was watching her from the queue.

In fact, she felt eyes boring into her back.

She turned and met the gaze of Len, standing next to Babe, a pair of brightly coloured tickets clutched in his hand. Posie stared back, her heart racing. So then, they had come together, for Valentine's Day.

She continued to hold Len's gaze. What was it she read there in his handsome face? He was looking at her imploringly, *willing* her to understand something. But what was there to understand?

She saw Babe take Len's arm, lead him up the steps,

tottering unsteadily to and fro on her sky-high heels. Len tore his gaze away from Posie reluctantly.

Posie clambered into the cab.

'Please, driver. Fast as you can!' she called through the glass divide, blinking back a flood of hot, useless tears.

* * * *

Four

As the taxi rolled through the iron gates of New Scotland Yard, Posie caught sight of a familiar trench-coated figure bowling his way out, scarf wrapped up over his face. He was lit up by the car lights against the driving snow, heading in the direction of the Victoria Embankment, beside the frozen river Thames.

'Stop! Wait!' she called to the driver. Pressing a handful of change into his hand, she jumped out of the cab and pursued the man through the snow.

'Inspector Lovelace!'

The Inspector halted under a lamp-post, and turned in surprise. His posture was of one poised for flight. Posie came panting up to him.

'I'm sorry I'm late, I was delayed. I don't blame you for leaving, you'd probably given up on me.'

'Posie?' asked the Inspector in surprise, raising his black felt homburg briefly and peering very uncertainly at her. Posie realised he could only see her eyes, and even those not very well. She brushed the snowflakes from her eyelashes.

'Yes. It's me! I said in my telegram I'd be here at seven-thirty but I'm late.'

'Let's go back to my office. Better get a brew on,' he said, turning on his heel. Inspector Lovelace sighed wearily. He had been heading home to his wife for a Valentine's dinner in their smart new house in the Clapham suburbs. Not anymore, though.

The Inspector strode over the snow-covered courtyard to the imposing buildings of Scotland Yard. A few lights were still on here and there in the office windows, blinking through the darkness. Rufus was here too, somewhere. Mouldering away in a tiny jail cell, like a real criminal. Posie shivered despite herself. Inspector Lovelace gave her a quick sideways glance:

'Just so you know. I wasn't expecting you. You seem to think I received a telegram from you? Well, I didn't.'

The Inspector was a good-natured man in the very early forties, a large man, nice-looking in a rugged-sort-of-way, with pale freckly skin and red coppery hair. He laughed, taking the curved stone steps at a fair old pace, like a young lad, two at a time. 'I'd say whoever sent that telegram of yours deserves a good beating.'

Posie laughed lightly alongside him but it was a hollow sound.

'Only joking, mind!'

Wretched Babe. What was she playing at exactly? Was this deliberate sabotage on her part or mere uselessness? However you looked at it, either way was bad.

* * * *

'So, what's this all about then?'

Inspector Richard Lovelace sank heavily down in his creaky leather chair and passed a beaten-up tin of biscuits across to Posie. She was clutching a steaming mug of tea he had just made. She couldn't remember when she had last eaten a proper meal, and she dived on the biscuits ravenously.

Inspector Lovelace eyed her with a look of half-amuse-ment, half-concern. Posie reminded him very much of a nurse he had taken a fancy to in the Field Hospital at Passchendale when he had spent some months there in 1917, lying injured, and he knew this fond remembrance made him not entirely impartial to Posie and her some-times unorthodox methods.

'You should take more care of yourself, my girl. Eat properly. Otherwise you're no help to anyone. Who *are* you helping, anyway? I take it that there is something important behind your scurrying here after office hours? And more importantly, what's it got to do with me?'

Posie explained between mouthfuls of biscuit about her day so far. Inspector Lovelace nodded grimly: he had heard all about the murder at the Ritz, it had been the talk of the whole station.

She opened her bag and pulled out the photo of 'Geor-gie'. She pushed it across the desk and told the Inspector where she had just got it from.

'Turns out Lucky Lucy *was* working as a chorus girl after all, at the Athenaeum Theatre. I know Inspector Oats had his doubts. So she didn't lie to Rufus about everything.'

Inspector Lovelace picked the photo up and studied it carefully under his green-glassed reading lamp. He whis-tled softly.

'You're right – that's Lucky Lucy Gibson, for sure. I'd recognise that face anywhere, even though she's cut all her hair off and dyed it white, and done something different to her eyes.'

He passed the photo back. 'She's on the most-wanted list of every police station across London, and every British border control has an order to seize her. One of the most dangerous, difficult creatures you're ever likely to encounter: like a ghost, never leaves traces, never incriminates others. But wherever she goes, she leaves a path of destruction behind her. And you say she's been here, in London, this whole past year? Right under our noses?'

'That's right. On the stage almost every night.'

'No wonder poor old Oats was in a bad mood! Letting her slip away like that at the Ritz must have been galling. So near and yet so far. She's a clever girl.'

'But what about Rufus? He's been wrongfully imprisoned for a murder! And what about the Maharajah diamond? We need to search for it!'

Inspector Lovelace smiled kindly.

'We can't do anything about the missing gem until its owner files a stolen report. And as for Rufus himself, wait here a minute.'

Two minutes later the Inspector was back, a big black file in his hands.

A white sticker read 'OATS – CONFIDENTIAL' down one side.

'I just "borrowed" this from Oats' office along the corridor,' he said tapping his nose comically. He flipped through the file for a few minutes, and then closed it. He folded his arms. He looked grim.

'Oats isn't a bad policeman, you know. Just unimaginative. And he hates toffs – that's a known fact. But he's got your pal in the cells here as an accessory to this murder because he has no other leads. He's hoping your pal will blab something useful.'

'But Rufus was duped!' Posie wailed. 'He knows nothing about the murder. He knows nothing about his fiancée, either, as it turns out. *I* know more than Rufus right now about pretty much everything – and that's not saying much!'

'They will hold a preliminary hearing tomorrow morning, here. Oats has made notes recommending that your pal should be set free if his father stumps up some bail money. But are you *sure* Rufus isn't caught up in this malarkey?'

'What *possible* motive could he have?'

The Inspector shrugged. 'Loyalty to the girl, perhaps? Perhaps he's covering up for her? Someone like Lucy would be pretty persuasive, let me tell you. Rufus could have helped arrange her getaway plan, onto a boat or a plane to South America, perhaps? He has plenty of money to arrange things…it wouldn't be too difficult.'

'You're forgetting she's robbed him of a priceless jewel,' Posie snapped. 'So just where in the getaway plan was that?'

'An elaborate cover-story on the side? A nice little earner? He can just claim the insurance money, anyhow.'

Posie shook her head resolutely and gritted her teeth. She snapped the catch of her bag and pulled out the telegram from Brigg & Brooks. As the Inspector read it his eyes widened, just for a second.

'Fine. I agree my theory was far-fetched. But from the file here your pal is in a bad way. He's blind drunk most of the time; there are hotel bar-bills here which make my eyes water just reading them. He's in and out of seedy pubs all day long, too. Tell me, just *why* exactly are you bothering with him?'

A sudden wave of anger flared up hotly, spreading out over Posie's head and neck in a vivid red flush. She counted to five and swallowed the anger down. When she spoke it was quietly and with absolute conviction:

'Don't ever ask me that again, please. What your dear colleague Inspector Oats seems to have overlooked is the fact that Rufus Cardigeon is one of the bravest men this country has ever known. He's a national hero! Does it say in that file that he was awarded the Victoria Cross not once but *twice* for his services in the Great War? The highest honour for bravery a man can get! I bet that's not in the file notes! And as for the drinking – I know he's a wretched soul just now, but he wouldn't be the first or the last man to hit the bottle as a way of forgetting some of the dreadful things he's seen, would he?'

Posie stared at Inspector Lovelace who held her gaze

calmly. Eventually he nodded, as if in agreement.

'How much do they want for bail?'

'Let me see,' Inspector Lovelace placed a finger on a page and jabbed at a paragraph. The figure he quoted made Posie's eyes water. Her heart sank. She knew Rufus' father was rich, but he was notoriously tight. He would *not* be pleased. With any of this.

'It says here that they still don't know *who* the murder victim was. Poor sausage.'

Some horrible photos slipped out of the pocket of the file onto the desk.

'What ho! Some good old blood-and-guts here. Poor fella.'

The Inspector had picked the photos up and studied them under his lamp, passing them to Posie casually as if they might be a theatre programme. She had seen the real body only hours earlier, and she had been so preoccupied with Rufus at that point that she hadn't felt time to feel shocked or sick at the grisly murder. Now, strangely, presented with the image of the body in graphic black and white frames, Posie felt the full horror of the murder sink in.

'Poor man,' she sighed, flipping through, feeling distinctly queasy at some of the close-ups. She looked up, and saw a look of puzzlement spreading over Inspector Lovelace's large, kind face. He had a photo in his hand and scrabbled in his desk for a magnifying glass.

'Thought so!' he said triumphantly. He passed the photo and eye-glass to Posie.

'Tell me what you see.'

Posie sat and stared. She could see nothing of any note. The photo was of the murder victim's torso and his blood-spattered white dress-shirt. As she had noted to herself earlier, the clothes were old but of a very good quality. The man had died with his hands outstretched uselessly, as if to defend himself from his attacker.

'Nope. Nothing. Sorry.'

Inspector Lovelace nodded. 'It's very unusual, I'll give you that. No wonder you missed it. It's the *hands*. See how carefully manicured they are? How the nails are cut right down to the quick?'

She nodded. 'Yes, but I don't see…'

'And the thick, crusty callouses on the fingers? He was a *musician*. Only years of being a musician can do that to hands. I'd say this chappie had been a musician of some sort for getting on for more than forty years. Mnnn, I wonder. Strings, definitely…perhaps the guitar, or perhaps…'

'…the VIOLIN!!' Posie shouted, interrupting.

'Yes! Exactly. Good thinking at last. So our victim is a musician. Shouldn't be too difficult to find out who he was. We'll put out a notice to all the orchestras in town, all the bands and nightclubs too.'

'There's no need,' Posie said, sitting bolt upright. 'I'd swear sure as bread is bread that this man is Lionel Le Merle, First Violin at the Athenaeum Theatre! He didn't show up at work today. Apparently that was very unusual.'

The Inspector was looking at Posie seriously.

'So he knew Lucky Lucy, you mean, at work?'

Posie nodded, bright as a button. 'But this was no bust-up between workmates. There's more to it than that, I'm certain. The whole thing stinks.'

Inspector Lovelace nodded.

'I'm inclined to agree.' He looked at his wristwatch and cursed, reaching for his hand-knitted woollen scarf and wrapping it around his neck.

'I've got to get going; my wife Molly will kill me otherwise. I'll tidy up here and leave a note for Oats with this man Lionel's name on it. I'll tell him you'll be along in the morning for the bail hearing, shall I? I can't imagine you'll be missing that?'

Posie nodded, gathering up her fur coat. Time to make tracks: she wasn't yet done for the night.

'You want me to get you a cab?' Inspector Lovelace asked. Posie thought of the cold snowy evening outside, and jangled her last few coins together in her pocket. She shook her head – she had already depleted the contents of the office strong-box enough for one night.

'No. But thank you. It's only a ten-minute walk.'

'Very well. But keep warm. And Posie?' Inspector Lovelace looked up from scribbling his note on top of the black file, 'Take care. Keep your powder dry. If you find anything out, let us know. Anything at all. Don't go this alone. It could be very dangerous. Promise me?'

Posie nodded dutifully, but she had secretly crossed her fingers behind her back.

****

She was heading off to visit Rufus' father at his club: No 11, St James. On Pall Mall.

But she had lied to the Inspector. It wasn't a ten-minute walk at all. It *might* have been in the summer, when the parks which were useful as shortcuts stayed open late; when she could have run through St James's Park, past the artificial island which was home to a hundred pelicans and over the hump-backed bridge. In the harsh reality of the snowy February evening, however, it was half an hour's brisk walk.

Posie turned sharply onto Whitehall and walked along as fast as she could without losing her footing. London was covered in its thick, white, fuggy blanket and still yet more snow was falling. As so often happens with fresh snow, the world suddenly seemed ridiculously quiet. Even the chimes from the tower of Big Ben, so close, announcing to the world that it was eight-thirty, seemed very small and far away; a tiny, tinny little sound which belonged to a doll's house clock.

It was as if everybody had left town in a hurry.

The government offices which ran down both sides of the broad street looked shut-up and deserted, and even the Prime Minister's house on Downing Street was in total darkness. All the way along Whitehall, normally so busy, Posie was passed by just one other person, a bent-against-the-wind government worker in a flapping black coat, wielding a useless umbrella. One cab passed by in a tearing hurry, but otherwise there was silence. There was something uncanny about it.

And in the strange muffled world of snow-covered London, Posie started to imagine things.

For all the quietness surrounding her, she fancied she could hear footsteps close by, clicking at her heels. It sounded like a man's brogues; totally unsuitable for the heavy snow. At one point she stopped underneath a street lamp and turned around quickly to face her assailant.

'Who's there?' she called loudly, trying not to let the fear show in her words. 'Who is it?'

There was no-one. At least no-one she could fathom, anyhow.

Trafalgar Square was up ahead, normally so welcoming with its bright lights and its familiar stone lions. She hurried to reach it.

But even here the world had changed. The newspaper sellers who normally thronged the place had packed up and gone, and the crowds of party-goers who flocked to the square at night to drink champagne had gone somewhere warmer.

Only a few poor wretches, soldiers who had survived the Great War but with limbs or their wits missing, sat underneath damp cardboard sheets, begging passers-by for money. Life had not been kind to them, and it was a cruel shame.

Posie remembered the famous newspaper photographs of Armistice Day in Trafalgar Square three years before, when the ghastly war had been stopped forever. She hadn't been there herself; she was still out in action in the boggy fields of Amiens with the Ambulance Brigade, picking up the debris and the bodies from the last few battles. But she knew that unimaginable crowds had packed the place out. Men in their thousands had climbed on the lions by the fountain and scaled Nelson's Column, angrily ripping down the placards inviting men to enlist.

Posie distributed the last of her coins among as many of the men as she could and continued up the road until she hit Pall Mall.

It was strange. She still couldn't shake off the feeling that someone was following her and she found herself turning around several times, heart thumping.

But there was never anyone there.

Ahead of her, up at Piccadilly, she saw the bright blue-and-white electric lights of the Circus glittering like cat's eyes through the snow, and beyond it again, the bright lights of the Theatre District in the distance. She tried not to think of Len and Babe, together...

And so she braced herself for her most thankless task yet of the evening.

The Tenth Earl, Rufus' father, was famously a man of few manners. He reminded people of an unexploded volcano at the best of times. Posie knew that he would be seething from Rufus' exploits earlier today, and in addition he would be tired from his long train journey down from his ancestral home, Rebburn Abbey. On the whole it was not a great time to turn up and expect his undivided attention. And if her telegram to the club had gone the same way as Babe's other two, Posie's visit would be unexpected too. But visit him she must: Rufus had asked her to.

The impossibly grand pale-yellow stone facades of the London clubs stretched ahead down Pall Mall, one after another, lining the street as far as the eye could see. Oil torches flickered at the entrance of each one. They were the exclusive preserve of men, and only men of the better sort; you were *born* a member, you could not *become* a member. These places always reminded Posie of the Italian Palaces of the Renaissance; so serene outside and yet so full of fearsome secrets inside.

Pall Mall this evening was indeed serene, with only a few chauffeured cars and taxis waiting politely in the snowy shadows for their aristocratic owners to emerge at any given hour. There was no sign now of the hoards of women who had famously chained themselves to the iron railings here, demanding the vote for women in 1914, before the Great War had come and changed everything.

Posie found No 11 and turned in quickly.

And there it was again – that tap of brogues close behind her, the soft cat-like stepping on snow, coming to a sudden halt a second too late. Like an echo.

So, she hadn't been mistaken. Someone *was* following her.

She looked out into the street. The burning torchlights at the club entrance blinded her, and beyond, on the street, all was pitch darkness.

'Who is it?' she called out sharply, uselessly; her heart hammering up into her throat.

No-one replied of course, but a sliver of shadow, just the merest flicker of black, slipped past the entrance of No 11 and slithered into the darkness beyond. Even now Posie knew that a pair of unknown eyes were watching her, boring into her.

But why?

Posie stared numbly into the space where the shadow had hidden, and just as she had decided that whoever it was had passed on into the night, or on to trail more exciting quarry, a blinding flash of light pierced the darkness, illuminating her in a white split-second on the stone steps.

A photographer's lamp whirred in the background and she could smell the chalky residue from the used flashbulb. Who on earth was trailing her and taking pictures of her too?

Posie was more scared than she could remember. She ran up the yellow stone steps and was begrudgingly whisked through the glass door by a miserable-looking doorman in a top hat.

'You can only go into the lobby, Miss,' said the doorman with a degree of smug satisfaction. 'Women aren't allowed beyond.'

'I *do* know that,' she snapped back, more tetchily than she might have done in other circumstances.

Inside, the dimly lit entrance hall was empty, and closer inspection revealed tall wood-panelled walls, bearing shelves full to bursting of highly polished silver trophies and sporting cups. Brown-faded photographs from the turn of the century were stuffed on every available surface. Posie went over to the shelves and saw that most showed teams of cricketers posing on the village greens of Kent and Surrey. The whole place reminded her of the games room at her brother's prep school when she had visited him there once. He had proudly pointed himself out to her in just such a photograph: poor dead Richard.

'Can I help you, madam?' asked an ancient-looking Butler, shuffling in, disapproval and admiration flashing in equal measures across his face. Disapproval won. She asked for the Earl of Cardigeon and watched as the Butler moved off, looking nervous.

Posie realised suddenly that she was not entirely alone in the lobby: a telephone booth at the very back on the left was occupied, and she could just see the bottom half of a man's black tuxedo-clad legs and shiny black brogues below a green baize curtain. She listened hard but couldn't make out any actual conversation going on.

And to the right, behind a discreet wooden-topped

counter, a club servant had suddenly appeared, frantically making notes and sorting telegrams into a hive of small pigeon-holes behind him.

A hidden door on the left swung open.

'What's this all about? And who the hell are you, anyway? Damned interfering womenfolk! I thought I was free of you all in this place, at least.'

Rufus' father was clutching a glass of dark malt whisky and he gave Posie a brutal, insolent stare. Short and toady-looking, he was still wearing his country tweeds and had obviously been at the bottle for a good part of the afternoon and evening. He was redder in the face, rougher and altogether more rotund than when Posie had last met him as a child. She was relieved to find that there was something slightly comical about him now though, rather than scary. Probably to do with the fact that now she towered over him, rather than the other way around.

Posie quickly explained who she was, and was rewarded by a very slight thawing of the frostiness. The Earl nodded a pinch of recognition: he had always approved of Posie's brother Richard as being a steadying influence on Rufus in the past, and now that Richard was dead he was, of course, beyond reproach. Not like poor old Rufey.

'I'm here to talk about Rufus. He's in a great deal of trouble,' she whispered down into the Earl's hairy ear. 'Is there anywhere we can talk here, sir, privately?'

'No, of course not!' the Earl bellowed. 'You're not allowed anywhere past the entrance hall, anyway. Out of bounds. Say what you need to here, girl.'

Posie sighed and indicated towards the man's legs behind them in the cubicle, and at the club servant bustling away with his papers in the corner.

The Earl swatted the air dismissively as if attacking a fly.

'No problem with those folk. Make it snappy.'

Posie talked hurriedly in as low a voice as possible.

She took the fateful telegram from Brigg & Brooks out of her bag, and passed it to the Earl. She bit her lip as he read it. His face went first white, then red and then redder. Posie thought he might be about to explode. Or faint.

'I thought you ought to know it was uninsured. I don't think Rufus got around to telling you.'

The Earl was rocking on his feet and Posie quickly clutched a dark wicker ornamental chair. She hoped it was up to bearing his weight. He slumped down into its delicate frame. He started to fan himself with the crumpled telegram. Posie squatted down next to him.

'There's something else sir.'

The Earl groaned.

'There's a hearing tomorrow morning, at Scotland Yard. Rufus needs you.'

The toady eyes looked at Posie for the first time with something approaching hope, or at least indicating a smidgen of gratitude.

'What does he need? A lawyer? I'll get the best in town to get my boy out of jail. Clear his name.'

Posie shook her head grimly: 'I think they are happy for him to leave jail, as long as he doesn't leave London, sir. He's still not officially off the list of suspects for murder. It's a bail hearing. They want a bond.'

The Earl rubbed his eyes in tired, whisky-soaked disbelief.

'How much?'

'Five thousand pounds, sir.'

Posie stood up as the Earl started to rock to and fro on the chair, judging it best to give him a little room for whatever reaction he might spring. He reminded her a little of a nightmarish Rumpelstiltskin, about to go up in a puff of smoke. Eventually, he got up and stared at Posie for a long, hard moment as if this were all her fault.

She gulped, but fished in her bag again and brought out her business card. It was small and neat with clipped square corners, and unlike Mr Irving's, she had made sure that the print was of a quality such that it would never come off over your hands.

'Take this, my Lord. You can find me at the address there. I promised to help Rufus, and help him I will. I never break my promises. I will clear his name, and try my best to get the missing item back for you, sir. I already have a few leads in this case.'

(The extravagant truth.)

The Earl stuffed her card into one of his tweedy jacket pockets without giving it a second glance.

'What the hell can *you* do, girl?' he barked at her rudely. The Earl turned on his heel and made for the hidden door he had come through. Just as it seemed he was about to disappear without even saying goodbye, he turned and half-laughed over his shoulder:

'You take my advice and stay well out of this mess. You know that the wretched thing has a curse on it? Blights everyone it touches.'

Posie stood still for a moment after the door had slammed shut in her face, thinking hard. She was just about to leave and brave the night (and her possible stalker) when she heard an unfamiliar voice calling her name softly across the lobby floor.

Mystified, she turned around. No-one else could possibly know she was here.

The most handsome man she had seen in her life (after Len, of course), was standing leaning by the telephone cubicle, one hand casually holding the baize curtain aside. She recognised the smart tuxedo trousers, the shoes. It was the man who had been on the telephone the whole time. Or at least, *pretending* to be.

She raised an eyebrow.

The man walked across to her. He was lithe on his feet, and he moved like a ballet dancer. He was about thirty, with a leonine head of slicked-back black hair, worn slightly long about the neck.

'Caspian della Rosa,' he smiled, extending a white-gloved hand, and Posie detected a slight foreign accent underneath his casually assured tones. Behind him the club servant was fluttering very closely, arranging papers on a tray: he didn't look up once.

Poise took his hand gingerly. 'Can I help you? You seem to know my name.'

'Yes,' he murmured, not letting go of her hand.

'Have a drink with me. It is still Valentine's Day, after all, and a beautiful girl like you should be out on the town. Funny how we should meet here like this, is it not? Sometimes, you know, the most beautiful, the rarest treasures in the world are to be found right under our very noses. They need no guarding, no protection: they exist, fabulously, alone. You, *bella*, are just such a creature.'

Caspian della Rosa did not take his eyes from her face once, and Posie realised there was something slightly wolfish about him, dangerous almost. When he smiled, his canine teeth, slightly too long for conventional beauty, were revealed. His black eyes flashed fire, promising adventure. Posie felt her heart skip a little faster for a second, and she allowed him a rare smile, a flutter of her unpainted eyelashes.

'Come with me, *bella*. You should not be chasing after disgusting old men in clubs such as these, or searching for horrid old diamonds. Let me take you to a little place I know.'

Posie froze. He had mentioned diamonds, but she knew very well that in all of the whispered conversation with the Earl neither of them had mentioned the word once. She had been careful not to do so. And anyway, how on earth did this man know who she was? She had whispered her name under her breath to the Earl. No, there was something far more sinister at play here than just casual eavesdropping.

Her gut feeling told her the man was truly dangerous. She must get away.

She was conscious of her hand still clasped in what now felt like his iron grip, and of the dark eyes boring into her, demanding her full attention.

'Thank you, Mr della Rosa,' she smiled gratefully, pulling her hand away gently but firmly and pretending to adjust her headband a little, patting the fake fur on her coat down. Casual movements.

'I am afraid I am otherwise engaged this evening. This was not my only stop tonight. I am meeting a *friend* in town.' She put special emphasis on the word 'friend'. All the while thinking of Len, damn him.

The man smiled his wolfish grin again:

'So, you are a very busy lady. I should have guessed as much. Some other time? Could I perhaps have one of the business cards you gave to your friend the fat Earl just now? So I can contact you?'

She shook her head. 'I am afraid that was my only one.' Posie almost flushed at the lie. Her bag had a good few tucked inside a silk inner pocket.

'No matter. I will find you anyway,' he said, shrugging a half-smile. Posie breathed hard at the implied threat.

'Good night, then, Miss Parker,' and Caspian della Rosa bowed low to her before disappearing fast through the same hidden door the Earl had used earlier.

Posie stared after him, feeling relieved and shaken all at the same time. Then she saw something shiny on the floor which had not been there a minute before, something which must have fallen from a pocket in the flurry that Caspian della Rosa had departed in. She was sure it was his. She bent to pick it up, and saw a small black fold of matches. A crescent moon was embossed in rich silver foil on the cover, with a distinctive '*LL*' written underneath. It was a favour or a souvenir from some fancy nightclub somewhere, she supposed.

Posie looked around for the aged Butler who had greeted her on arrival, or for the club servant to hand the matches to, but both had disappeared.

She headed over to the pigeon-holes behind the wooden counter, stuffed full with notes and brown-paper parcels. She scoured the many names of the club members. But Caspian della Rosa, even allowing for other variations of that name, was not listed there. Instead, and suddenly feeling very tired, she dropped the matches into the big pocket of her fake fur coat.

* * * *

With no money left for a taxi, and the thought of her possible stalker still lurking around outside, Posie did the only thing she could – she wrapped herself up against the chill and ran for it. She ran back to the bright electric lights of Piccadilly Circus as fast as her high-heeled shoes could carry her, and jumped on the back of a Number Ten bus which happened to be passing. She sat close to the driver the whole way home, scanning the other passengers continually for anyone who might be being paid to follow her, or showing a modicum too much interest.

'You all right, love? You seem awful jumpy,' said the conductor in his friendly cockney voice when he punched her travel coupon. She nodded a smile at him but continued to be on her guard.

She got off at South Kensington and walked the two minutes to the house she lodged at in Nightingale Mews.

It was only when she was inside and had bolted the door behind her that she found she could breathe easily again. The sound of her landlady, Mrs Rapier, singing along loudly with her radio programme, normally so annoying, and the smell of fried fish wafting up from underneath the tiny kitchen door downstairs were strangely comforting in that very moment.

Just before getting into bed, Posie checked the street outside, peering through her thin blue-and-white checked curtains nervously, as if expecting to see a shadowy stranger lurking for her under the street lamp directly opposite.

But all she could see was thick snow coming down, and yet more snow.

* * * *

Tuesday 15th February, 1921

Five

The bail hearing early the next morning in the small Court at Scotland Yard was a subdued, dismal affair, with Rufus looking so wretched in his handcuffs and greasy dinner suit that the Tenth Earl seemed almost eager to stump up the five thousand pounds required for his release.

Posie sat at the back, in the small empty public gallery, and watched both father and son leave through a door on the left when it was all over. She had no wish to intrude on their privacy, and she was just getting ready to leave when she realised that Inspector Oats was standing in front of her, clutching a piece of paper. She recognised his black 'OATS – CONFIDENTIAL' file from the night before. It had looked less sinister then.

He cleared his throat pompously:

'It seems I have *you* to thank for the name of the murder victim at the Ritz,' he said in what sounded less like a thank you and more like an accusation. He shook the note at her:

'And Lovelace says that you've found out that Lucky Lucy was working in a theatre here for the past year?'

'Yes,' said Posie demurely, 'at the Athenaeum Theatre. So was Mr Le Merle, the victim. But Lucky Lucy left a few weeks ago. You might want to investigate the theatre itself – it seems a strange place. The Theatre Manager, Mr

59

Blake, is definitely a shady character: he knows more than he was willing to tell me, anyway.'

The Inspector snorted, placing the note into his file with a brisk snap.

'Listen to me, girlie. If I was to spend my days chasing after every shady character and every strange place in London I'd never get any real police work done. Now, you take it from me: there's no need to investigate the theatre. That particular bird has flown the coop, no point spending valuable time gallumphing around in an empty nest. I'll put my men on other active leads…we'll see if we can dig Lucky Lucy out. Like a fox from a hole.'

Posie was on the cusp of asking *what* other leads he might possibly have, having only just found out the identity of the victim, but she buttoned her lip. The Inspector wagged his finger at her.

'Lovelace seems to think you're quite the bees' knees. But don't go getting ideas about fooling around in *my* investigation. I always hate Private Dicks, but I've never yet met a female one, thank goodness. Take my advice, and stay away.'

Inspector Oats made to leave.

'But what about the Maharajah diamond?' Posie asked. 'Can't you look for that at the same time as Lucky Lucy, at least?'

The Inspector looked like he was chewing a wasp. Then he spoke to Posie slowly, as if she were a particularly dim-witted child:

'Don't you worry your pretty little head about *that*. Your pal has gone off with his father to file a missing item report. Once the paperwork goes through I'll add it to my list of things to do; maybe I'll notify my contacts in Hatton Garden where the diamond dealers hang out. But to tell you the truth I'm not going to get myself in a spin over it, and if I was you I wouldn't go getting your hopes up. It's probably left the country by now, on its way to be cut up into a million little pieces and resold in Antwerp or New York.'

The Inspector put on his homburg hat, that regulation Scotland Yard staple. He looked at Posie smugly.

'The beauty of a diamond is in its transportability, like drugs. Not as cumbersome as gold. Now, I can't be standing here all day, talking to you. Good-day to you, Miss Parker, and remember what I've told you.'

As she watched his trench-coated back retreating further down the grim Court room, Posie was struck by something the Inspector had said to her, but she couldn't think what exactly. It was as if the Inspector had given her a clue, ripe for the picking, but it was obscured by a particularly heavy cloud.

She sighed, hoping the fog would clear.

* * * *

Lyons Cornerhouse on the Strand was very busy. It was coffee-time and every table was taken, the smart but harassed waitresses bustling around the hungry customers, serving all manner of cakes and cream-topped fancies.

Posie located Dolly straight away. She was sitting over by the window, watching the world go by. She was eating her way steadily through her own purple tin of Peek Frean's Marie biscuits, defying Lyons' rules about not bringing in food from outside. They greeted each other warmly and Posie sat down and ordered tea for two and a plate of iced Chelsea buns.

'My treat,' she declared and tactfully moved the Marie biscuits onto the window ledge, out of direct view. In the harsh light of day and out of the dank theatre cellar Dolly looked even more extraordinary than ever; her pale elfin face and bleached cropped hair made her look somehow other-worldly, vulnerable. The silver greasepaint and black clothes of yesterday were gone, and instead she was wearing crimson lipstick and a matching red-and-white polka-dot smock. She looked like a little rag-doll.

'Gasper?' she asked companionably, offering Posie a black cigarette from a very scratched silver case. Posie shook her head, and attacked her sticky cake instead.

In a few concise sentences she told Dolly what she was up to and why she had needed her help the day before. She even told Dolly about the murder of Lionel Le Merle, and the fact that Georgie the chorus girl was in fact a famous criminal known as Lucky Lucy.

Dolly looked at her, open-mouthed, cigarette unheeded, a mountain of ash steadily piling up on her plate.

Posie gave her one of her business cards, and unlike the Earl, Dolly looked very impressed. She studied it properly before tucking it carefully into her own red handbag.

'Is that what you always wanted to do, then?' she asked, in slight awe. 'Become a Detective? Is that what kept you goin', during the war? Was it your dream? Did you think to yourself in all the carnage – after all of *this*, I'll run my own Detective Agency?'

'No. Not really.' Posie laughed. She had never really considered it from that point of view before. 'I just always liked solving puzzles. I was left a small amount of money when my father died, and I thought, why not? I had no-one in the world and no place in the world. So I thought, let's try London. What about you? Did you always want to be a Wardrobe Mistress in a theatre?'

Dolly hooted with such a high shriek of laughter that virtually the whole café turned around.

'Jeepers, no. Not on your nelly,' she said, shaking her head and blowing a well-aimed smoke ring ceilingwards.

'I always wanted to be a nurse. Trained up for it too, but I couldn't get a job for love nor money before the war.

The only reason they took me on in the Field Hospital in Flanders was because they were desperate; not many would put up with the sights and smells and sounds we had to in the trenches. And I spoke French too, my mum was French, from Paris, and it came in handy. I'm proud of what I did there. And I'm equally as proud of what I did *before* the Great War, too.' Dolly sounded defiant, as if challenging Posie on something.

'Sorry?' Posie was bemused. '*What* did you do before the war?'

'I was a suffragette. Chained myself up with the best of them. I was in jail for more than six months. That's why no self-respecting hospital in London would have me; no doctor either. You can't get far with a criminal conviction on your CV.'

Posie nodded sympathetically. She had not joined the Women's Movement herself, but she had admired them from afar.

'After the Great War I came back to London to find myself in exactly the same situation as before: no job, no money, no family, same stinking bed-sit and the blight that will never go away; the spell in jail as a women's rights activist. They were dark days for me, I'm tellin' you.'

'But you got the job at the Athenaeum Theatre anyway?' Dolly chortled.

'That was a rum thing!' She took a drag on a newly lit cigarette.

'About a year ago everythin' changed at the theatre: a new owner, a whole new cast and show. Mr Blake too, he was new; came with his cousin Reggie, the programme-seller. He needed a Wardrobe Mistress quickly and he wasn't asking any questions. He was willin' to pay more than I could have hoped for, and after two years without a job it seemed like a god-send. I don't think he even looked at my CV once! No-one had a clue whether or not I could actually sew, even myself…but I convinced myself I was so good at stitchin' men and bandages together that a few sequins and feathers couldn't be too hard!'

Posie laughed. She felt brighter than before, cheered by Dolly's optimism. She waved at a passing waitress for the bill.

'You'll let me know if you hear anything, or *see* anything of Lucky Lucy, won't you? Or if you remember anything you think may be helpful. Even about Mr Blake; I'm sure he's hiding something. The police are worse than useless, they won't be questioning anyone at the theatre, so I'm on my own here. My friend Rufus is very badly in need of help.'

Dolly nodded, packing her things together. Posie noticed she handled her cigarette case very carefully.

'It was my young man's,' she whispered, following Posie's gaze. 'It was his "lucky" case. He was an old romantic: said it would protect him from stray bullets if he wore it by his heart, poor blighter. It couldn't protect him from drowning in a flooded trench, though, could it? I keep it out of fondness.' Dolly tucked it away, smiling sadly.

'You got a fella?'

Posie shook her head. It was all too much to explain.

She took the borrowed fake fur coat from a brown paper carrier bag and checked its pockets before handing it over to Dolly for returning to the theatre wardrobe. Posie pulled out a few hair-grips, her travel coupon and the strange packet of matches from the night before.

As the morning light caught the silver moon on the packet Posie had a vivid flashback of Caspian della Rosa from the night before, and she thought the nocturnal image was somehow appropriate for him: in her mind's eye he had become the stuff of nightmares, vampire-ish, deadly.

'Jeepers!' Dolly shrieked suddenly, grabbing the matches. Fear flooded her huge eyes. 'Do you know where this comes from?'

Posie shook her head, laughing. 'No idea. A nightclub? For bright young things? Somewhere fashionable, I'm guessing?'

Dolly spoke in hushed tones, entirely serious.

'Don't joke. It's a members club, it's called *La Luna*. I don't know much about it, but Lucky Lucy was definitely a member. She was proud of it too. I heard her talking about it once, indiscreetly, when she didn't know I could hear her. Only a select few know the exact location of the place. And it rarely opens, so it's not your regular club. Some of the orchestra members go, too. After a performance I've seen them bundle off in a taxi, secret-like. Very cloak-and-dagger.'

'But what do they *do* at this club?' asked Posie nervously, not sure she wanted to know the answer.

'No idea.' Dolly shook her head. 'Truly, I have no idea. Drink, smoke, take drugs, dance? Who knows? Whatever the case, I'm sure it spells trouble. Where did you get these from, anyway?'

Posie had told her everything so far. No point missing out key facts now.

'I picked them up off the floor when someone dropped them accidentally last night. The man who dropped them was called Caspian della Rosa.'

Dolly emitted a small high-pitched squeak and covered her mouth and nose with her hands, as if she had been physically struck.

'What? What is it, Dolly? You look like you've seen a ghost! Does that name mean anything to you?'

'I'll say,' she whispered unexpectedly, looking terrified.

'Jeepers. You mean *Count* Caspian della Rosa; the richest, most dangerous man in London. He's the owner of the Athenaeum Theatre. Scares us all stiff whenever he appears. He's a nasty piece of work, although harmless and likeable enough on the surface. Don't say he's mixed up in this somehow?'

Posie screwed up her nose, biting at her lip. 'It's beginning to look like it,' she said softly.

'Oh, lovey!' Dolly said, clutching at Posie's hand.

'Be careful. And you should know somethin' else. You said these matches were dropped accidentally. Well, as sure as bread is bread I can tell you that the Count is not a man to do *anythin'* accidentally. These matches were dropped on purpose. To lure you in. It's a trap, Posie. And it's got your name written all over it.'

* * * *

Six

For the first time in days a brilliant blue sky arched over London, with not a cloud to be seen. It was still bitterly cold though, and the snow packed along the pavement of the Strand showed no sign yet of melting.

The chestnut sellers and newspaper boys grouped outside the newly built Bush House plied their trade cheerfully enough, although close up they were shivering. Posie noticed that some of the younger lads had wrapped layers of newspaper underneath their thin coats for added warmth, and the extra padding made them walk in a curious crab-like manner. They made a strange contrast to the elegance of the black-suited men in bowler hats who moved in a constant stream through the shiny gold and burnished glass doors of the offices.

It was now almost lunchtime, and as she turned onto the Kingsway, Posie was relieved to see that the break in the weather had made the office workers brave the cold; they were out in force, heading for cafés and cake shops. Posie walked along steadfastly, ducking the crowds of cheerful girls walking four abreast down the grand boulevard. She was unworried now by the fact that someone could be following her. If there *was* someone on her tail he'd have a hard job keeping track of her here on these busy pavements.

This was how Posie liked London best: busy, frantic, people from all walks of life thronging the roads; a far cry from the ghost-town she had walked through last night. The bitter cold of the air and the brightness of the day brought a rosy glow to her cheeks and filled her with a zest for living.

She skipped around a resourceful female street artist, who, unable to sketch on the frozen pavements due to the snow, had resorted to creating caricatures for a penny a piece. A large crowd had gathered around.

Posie needed to send an urgent telegram. She had decided that she could not and *would not* trust Babe Sinclair to do anything for her anymore at work, so she walked into the big Post Office on the corner of High Holborn opposite the Tube.

It was busy, and as she waited in the queue she had time to think about Babe. For the moment Posie decided she would do nothing. She would just carry on as normal and quietly observe, and wait until the time was right to confront her. Posie tried not to think about what she had seen last night, and of how much her dislike of the girl came from pure downright jealousy. There *was* an element of that, for certain, but there was something more worrying: a niggling feeling which had been there from the off, which just wouldn't go away, that Babe was simply a rotten apple in their midst. But was she just a lone troublemaker, or, as Posie feared, had she been placed somehow by skilful hands puppeteering her from higher up the food-chain? And if so, by who?

Posie shivered in the damp cold of the Post Office hall and snuggled into her thick brown tweed coat.

She forced herself to think of more cheerful things as she waited her turn.

* * * *

Posie was in a world of her own when she opened the glass front door of the Grape Street Bureau and entered the waiting room. She was determined to get to her office without seeing either Len or Babe, and she was halfway across the room when she realised with a start that a man was sitting waiting by the flaming fire, reading a newspaper. A real client!

'Can I help you?' she asked, removing her hat and gloves. Mr Minks shimmied into the room and leapt onto the man's lap, purring contentedly. Sometimes he could be an incorrigible flirt of a cat.

'Oh! I'm sorry about that! Mr Minks! Come here, now!'

The man looked at her over the top of his *Times*. He patted the cat and set him down again on the floor casually, brushing down his trousers. He was short and stocky, with wild dark hair, about forty years old and generally unremarkable-looking, but he looked a little familiar all the same.

When he smiled his eyes creased up in a friendly fashion. He was smartly dressed but his suit and shoes were rather cheap. By his feet was a large canvas sports bag, and a tennis racket handle poked out of the top. He smelt strongly of mints, and Posie's eyes were suddenly drawn to a bag of humbugs bulging prominently out of his jacket pocket. He was not police, of that she was sure. He was not obvious enough, somehow.

'I'm fine waiting here by the fire, Miss Parker. You take your time, get settled in. Bitterly cold outside, isn't it? That your office there?' The man nodded companionably at her own door directly opposite. She hesitated before nodding once.

'I'll knock in a couple of minutes, once you've had a chance to take your coat off and thaw out. Perhaps your secretary can make us a spot of tea?'

He spoke with the accent of the educated middle-class English gentleman, and he nodded in the direction of Babe's small office, from which the sound of ferocious angry typing came.

Thrown by this strange situation, Posie found herself nodding and walking to her office, wrong-footed somehow. She didn't know whether to be angry or pleased at the man's strange conduct, but then she hardly had any real-life clients to compare this man (she still didn't know his name) with. She stoked the fire in its hearth in her office and then settled herself at her clear, clean desk. She took out a notepad and pen and waited.

And waited.

When the knock came after what seemed like ages, she called out in a cheerful voice:

'Come in!'

Posie started in surprise as Len poked his head around the door. She saw he was backing in nervously, carrying a heavy tray with the silver office tea-pot and some mismatched cups.

'Peace offering?'

Thrown, Posie looked at Len in panic. He came into the room anyway.

'What about my client?' she said, rising from her chair and hurtling out to the waiting room. But there was no-one there. *The Times* lay neatly folded on the low coffee-table with a stack of other magazines and journals. Posie bolted out onto the landing, and scoured the dark winding stairs below. No-one. She hurried into Babe's office.

'Did a gentleman, about forty, come in here just now? With messy hair? Did you see him?'

Babe stared dumbly back, and shook her head.

'I sure ain't seen no-one, Miss, and that's the God-honest truth. Swear on it. No-one's been in all morning, except Mr Irving, of course.'

'Fine. Thank you,' Posie muttered. How very strange. But maybe this was what real-life clients did. Perhaps he had realised he needed to be somewhere else? Perhaps his lunch-break was coming to an end? Perhaps he was late for his tennis practice?

Back at her desk, Len had poured the tea. He was standing at her window looking out over the grey rooftops. A flock of pigeons were whirling around the offices in great droves.

'They think it's spring, poor beggars,' he indicated, sipping his tea. 'Look how lightly they fly.'

Posie glowered at him, and took her own cup. He came and sat down and faced her.

'I want to clear the air, Po. I know you saw me last night and it breaks my heart to think that you might be imagining something which didn't happen. Which *doesn't exist*.'

'I don't know what you're talking about,' she snapped at him, ignoring the desperate look of pleading; the troubled green eyes which sought out her own. Even now he was heart-flippingly lovely.

'I saw you with my own eyes. With *her*. Don't try and tell me that what I saw didn't happen, didn't exist. And anyway,' she added, meeting his eyes for a brief second, 'don't feel you have to explain it to me anyway. What you do in your spare time or who you spend it with is none of my business.'

Then Len did something he had never done before.

He reached out across the desk and took Posie's hand in his. An action which caused a shock-wave of energy to tingle down her spine. She bristled, still angry, but she let him hold onto her hand.

'Of course you saw me. With Babe. But it's not what it looked like, that's all. It wasn't planned, it wasn't what I *wanted*. She came to me in my office last night about six, all sad and doe-eyed, telling me she'd been let down by some fellow at the last minute. She had a pair of tickets to the theatre, and would I like to come with her? I felt sorry for her I suppose. She seemed on the verge of tears.'

'She looked pretty happy to me when I saw you both.' Posie said coldly.

'Yes, well. She seemed to recover pretty quickly when I told her I'd come along; I'd had my own plans cancelled earlier, anyway. She dashed off and smartened herself up with a lot of jewellery and then invited me to a pre-theatre supper on the Strand, at Simpson's.'

'*Simpson's!*' Posie practically shouted. Simpson's was a very good, very expensive restaurant much in favour with the bright young things, and by people who wanted to be seen around the place. 'On *her* salary?'

'That's what I thought, too,' said Len, frowning. 'I said thank you all the same, but maybe we could grab a quick cone of fish and chips just off Shaftesbury Avenue if she was feeling peckish. Quicker. Cheaper.'

'And?'

'So we did. It was a bit awkward really. Us standing there gobbling away on the street corner, with her in her posh fur coat. Everyone was staring at us. Babe kept drinking too. She'd brought a hip flask and every couple of minutes she was swigging away. Goodness knows what it was; strong stuff though by the state she managed to get herself into. And then, to make matters worse, this poor chap came up to us…you know the sort, an ex-soldier, half-blind and limping, carting a bucket of single cheap red roses for Valentine's Day. I really didn't want to buy one for her, but I felt sorry for the man. And then, what do you think happened?'

Posie shook her head, and stared into his eyes. She was almost convinced he was telling the truth now. She was also conscious of her hand, still in his. His strong touch. His desire to make everything right between them.

'She bought the whole bucket of roses herself! Bless the chap, he couldn't believe his luck! But everyone in the

72

queue at the fish and chip stall was staring and whispering, and giving me evil looks. One woman even shouted out "*What sort of fella makes a lady buy her own roses on Valentine's Day?*" Well, I swear I flushed as red as the roses. And then Babe carted them around all night long. Making a spectacle of herself. She was half-cut by the time we reached the theatre, so I took the tickets from her so as not to lose them. I was embarrassed. She was making eyes at all the other fellows in the queue by this time, and I was on the point of running off, getting away from her, when I suddenly saw you. I couldn't believe my eyes!'

He clasped her hand tighter. 'I swear to you Po, when I saw you there I almost died. I could only imagine what it looked like. With all my heart I wanted to come with you, to explain. I would have jumped in the cab with you like a shot.'

'Why didn't you, then?'

'I couldn't leave her there, in that state, alone. How could I? A minute later it was all over, anyway.'

'Oh?'

'She spewed up all over the red carpet, and some poor beggar in charge of the programmes had to come out and clean up the vomit. I put her in a taxi and then I headed home myself.'

'You didn't want to see the play?'

'Not on your life! Not after what you'd told me a few weeks ago.'

Len took her hand in both of his:

'Can you forgive me? Say you understand.'

Posie nodded. Her office was very still. There was just the clanging sound of the typewriter coming from the outside office.

'There's something funny about our Miss Sinclair,' she whispered softly. 'I think she may have been placed here, that she's watching us somehow. She's deliberately trying to cause trouble, sabotaging my work. I think she's a phoney.'

Len raised his eyebrow questioningly.

'I was beginning to think the same thing. But look, let's not talk about that now. She's just a silly girl. Actually, there's something I'd like to do more than anything…' and Posie almost jumped out of her skin as he kissed her hand, his eyes looking directly into hers.

He leant across the desk in one fluid movement and came very close, his mouth just a fraction away from hers. She closed her eyes.

His lips were suddenly on hers: a light fluttering feeling at first, like a wave of butterflies landing. Len leant further in, and there was an unrepentant yearning desire in the way he took her face in both his hands and started to kiss her passionately.

She pulled away, suddenly chastened:

'But what about your girlfriend…? We can't…'

'Shhh,' he murmured, soothingly.

It was not much of an answer but it was enough. Posie closed her eyes again and reached for him, as she had wanted to for almost two years.

Just then came a fearsome knocking noise at the door.

* * * *

Seven

Len and Posie jumped apart.

The fragile glass door was sent banging backwards on its hinges with the force of a hurricane and as Len and Posie turned around they saw the Earl of Cardigeon and a sheepish-looking Rufus trooping in.

'We didn't know where else to come, old thing,' said Rufus simply. There was a strain of desperation in his voice. 'So we came here.'

Posie smoothed her hair down and jumped up, offering the Earl her own seat. He took it without question, surveying the room with his beady eyes and saying nothing. He seemed tired. Rufus perched on the desk, an image of pure dejection. Len stayed where he was.

'Tea?' asked Posie, in as normal a tone as she could manage.

'Got anything stronger?' asked Rufus hopefully. She shook her head and went to get more cups. When she returned she found introductions had been made, and the Earl was busy smoking a fat cigar.

'There's something I've discovered, Nosy,' Rufus whispered. 'Something I need to tell you.'

He cast his eyes down for a second and flushed red. He gave a sideways, ashamed glance at his father. He opened his mouth to speak but no words came out. He was shaking and sweaty, presumably from not having had a drink since yesterday.

'Well?'

He seemed to change his mind and shook his head. 'No, it's probably nothing. Don't let's worry about it. I just couldn't stand hanging around in that awful club of my father's for a minute longer, and he's banned me from going back to the Ritz.'

'Too right!' puffed the Earl. 'It's too expensive by half! Our family has always had membership of No 11, St James and that's where we stay when we're in town, not at the Ritz Hotel. Especially now we're seven hundred thousand pounds down! The police are a bunch of useless nincompoops, so we've come here. My son seems to set a lot of score by your supposed abilities, Miss Parker. So I thought you could keep us up to date with your *progress.*'

The Earl spat out this last word sarcastically as a sort of challenge and he glared at Posie as if she should have come up with a solution by now.

'I say, hang on a minute! I'm not sure if that's entirely fair,' started Len, rushing to Posie's defence.

'It's fine, Len,' Posie smiled. 'No solutions yet, I'm afraid, sir,' she said to the Earl, 'but I do have several leads in the case.'

She noticed the Earl was using the business card she had given him the night before as an ashtray and she smiled to herself wryly. She explained as briefly as possible about her eventful night the evening before, leaving nothing out. Except being followed to Pall Mall: they all had quite enough to be worrying about, she decided.

Len let out a whistle at the end of her tale.

With a final flourish Posie brought out the photo of Lucky Lucy from the depths of her carpet bag. Rufus shrieked and grabbed the photo, before being battered around the head by his father who snatched it and stared at it for a long time, grimacing.

'So this is how I see it,' Posie said authoritatively, summing-up.

'First, we need to locate Lucky Lucy, *sorry* – Georgie. Then we can track the diamond, *if* she still has it, and also force her to admit to the police that Rufus had nothing to do with the shooting of Le Merle. Somehow, she's linked to this mysterious *La Luna* club, and she could well be found hiding out there, lying low; she won't be stupid enough to return to the theatre. So our next step is to find out *where* the nightclub is and *when* it's next open. So far, it's the only lead we have and we need to investigate it. I've already started asking around, but I draw the line at asking this Caspian della Rosa fellow for more information; he gave me the creeps, quite frankly. My betting is that he's mixed up in this whole affair too.'

The Earl let out something between a snort and a smoke-filled cough.

'They're not leads!' he bellowed. 'That's all just hot air! Why on earth are you focusing on tracking down some willo'-the-wisp nightclub? What a waste of time!'

Posie shook her head. 'It's interconnected, sir. I'm sure of it. If we find the nightclub, we find the girl.'

Len glared at the Earl across the room.

'Your Lordship,' he said, not entirely deferentially, 'one thing puzzles me in all of this mess. If the Maharajah diamond is worth so much, and forgive me, but you seem to need the money, why didn't you just sell it? It seems strange to me that you left it mouldering away in a bank vault somewhere...'

Rufus had covered his face in his hands.

Len carried on, regardless. 'There must be a market for such a stone, surely? There are rich foreigners crawling all over London right now, I'm sure one of them would be only too happy to snap it up. Or you could have sold it to a dealer, had it split up into smaller pieces? I don't understand.'

The Earl had gone redder than ever in the face. Rufus spoke up for the first time yet:

'It's tricky. It's part of the Cardigeon legend. It *cannot* be sold. It's part of a pact, a promise.'

The Earl seemed to have calmed down somewhat. He nodded slowly in agreement. 'Out of the question for it to be sold, but out of the question for it to be worn, too. My idiot son knew that. Safest place for it was in the bank.'

'And was it out of the question for it to be insured, too, your Lordship?' asked Len, innocently, provocatively. The Earl balled his fists up in fury but did not reply.

Posie and Len looked at each other with a look of shared incredulous understanding: it was obvious to both of them now that the Earl was either harder up than he would have them imagine, or simply very, very tight, and that he had shifted the responsibility for paying the hefty insurance premiums onto Rufus as a way of lightening his own outgoings.

The Earl got up and paced around. He stubbed out his cigar on Posie's blackened business card and stood with his back to them all, looking out of the window at the pigeons. He had tucked his thumbs into the belt-loops on his smart town waistcoat, as if about to address an important congress. He sighed deeply.

'I might as well tell you the whole ruddy story,' he said puffily, his back still to them. 'It's quite frankly an unbelievable tale.'

He was, much to their surprise, a very good storyteller...

* * * *

It was 1858, and the Viceroy of India had just been appointed. He decided he couldn't get around all of India on his own, so he organised for some of his pals to come out and help him.

My great-grandfather, the Seventh Earl of Cardigeon, had known the Viceroy at school, and he jollied off out to India and became a Captain living in the beautiful little city-state of Gwilim. Not that Gwilim needed any real ruling, you understand. It was run very nicely indeed by the local Maharajah, who lived in a lovely white palace in lush green gardens where peacocks danced about merrily. Happily for the Seventh Earl, the Maharajah gave the grandest of parties, and my great-grandfather was having a high old time of it out there...

Everyone was getting on awfully well together when the city was suddenly overrun by rebels, hungry for change and ready to overthrow anyone who stood in their way. My great-grandfather led his men, alongside those of the Maharajah, in attacking the rebel army and for a few days the whole place was a living nightmare.

Slowly, slowly, the rebels were defeated until there were just a few of them left, holed up in a great fortress on the hill overlooking the city.

After two more days of bloody fighting, my great-grandfather found himself standing face-to-face with the last of the rebel soldiers.

This last rebel was unarmed, and badly hurt, and offered to trade something precious with my great-grandfather in return for his life and his freedom. When the Seventh Earl asked what exactly he would trade, the rebel brought out a great glittering black-as-the-gates-of-hell diamond, the size of a quail's egg. He told my great-grandfather that the rebel forces had broken into the Maharajah's Treasury only days before and taken the prize piece.

He told my grandfather that the diamond was famous throughout India for its beauty, but that no-one would wear it on account of a centuries-old curse it carried.

"You may have it, sir," said the rebel, "but know that it comes steeped in the blood of very many men. It is a very strong power."

My great-grandfather was a greedy sort of cove, and he pocketed the stone. Then he killed the rebel anyway: he didn't believe the man and thought that he was probably being sold a dud; a desperate story told by a desperate man.

It was only days later, at a banquet at the white palace to celebrate the end of the fighting, that the Seventh Earl casually mentioned that he had been told a story by a rebel about a stolen gemstone. He did not mention that he had actually been given the stone. He was surprised to notice that the whole table suddenly went quiet, and turned to him in silent horror.

"Did you actually see this diamond, my Lord?" asked the Maharajah quietly. The Seventh Earl played dumb and said he had not.

"And did the rebel say where it had ended up?" asked the Maharani, the beautiful young wife of the Maharajah. She seemed very scared. The Seventh Earl shook his head, and the whole table sighed in a sound very like despair. Or was it relief?

"It is not so much its value, although it is priceless," whispered the Maharajah to the Seventh Earl, "as its power. It is a thing destined to bring sorrow and despair to everyone who possesses it. Even for a very short time. It is a thing best kept locked up. My family have spent the last five hundred years guarding it here."

The very next day my great-grandfather packed his things up in a frantic hurry. He organised a berth on the next ship homebound to Southampton; he couldn't get away fast enough from India or from the hospitable Maharajah.

The diamond burnt a hole in his pocket the whole way home, and the very first thing he did on landing was head to Brigg & Brooks in London for a valuation. When he found out it really was priceless, my great-grandfather became like a man possessed. He carried the stone with him wherever he went; slept with it under his pillow at night.

But he slowly went mad, poor beggar. He began thinking he was being followed – that the rebel he had shot in the fortress at Gwilim was haunting him around our great house at Rebburn

Abbey; that the beautiful Maharani was coming to him at night, sobbing and wailing for her stone to be returned to her. He shot himself in the head a year to the day after he had come into possession of the thing.

And then, unbelievably, it was the very same thing with my grandfather, the Eighth Earl.

The jewel had been locked away, a good thing too, until the Eighth Earl had come of age: he was just twenty-four and was due to marry a lovely girl. He scoffed at the old story of the curse and decided to open the safe and to give the jewel to my grandmother as a wedding present. But when it actually came to it he couldn't bring himself to give it away, not even to his wife. He wanted it all for himself. After the wedding the thing started to get at him. He found he couldn't sleep anymore; he just sat in his study all night long, exhausted, fascinated by the thing, turning it over and over in his hands like a simpleton. Then he took to carrying it around with him in the daytime too, on a leather cord around his neck.

At twenty-five he quite lost his head over it and hung himself from his study ceiling, still wearing the wretched thing on the cord around his neck. My pregnant grandmother found him. She decided enough was enough and locked it away again.

Fortunately the pattern changed. My own father was a sensible sort of fellow, and capable of sorting out such messes. He decided to write to the then-Maharajah and tell him the whole story. It was 1899. He said he was willing to post the thing back to Gwilim, and he apologised profusely for what had happened.

The Maharajah wrote back and said they had known all along that the stone had been stolen by the Seventh Earl, and that they had been relieved it was no longer under their watch.

Together, the Maharajah and my father made a solemn pact that the stone should be kept locked up in a secure vault in London, and insured, unused and unworn; away from those who might be tempted by its powers...and it's a pact I've been very happy to keep to. I myself have never touched the thing, *never wanted to. I always instilled the importance of keeping it locked up in Rufus too.*

But it seems it may have been working its spell again lately...'

* * * *

'Pah!' scoffed Len incredulously. 'I don't believe it! A physical object can't have that much power! It's unbelievable! It's just a good old yarn.'

Posie shook her head at him seriously. 'No, Len. *I* believe it. Maybe not that the gem itself has power, but the fact that people are willing to believe in its story. Then they act accordingly. It's like the Emperor's New Clothes – people believe what they think they are supposed to.'

'Anyway,' said Len briskly, 'what are you going to do with it *if* you get it back, sir?'

The Earl shrugged. 'Either lock it up again or insist we send it back to Gwilim. It is theirs *rightfully*, after all.'

'Huh!' laughed Len. 'Although when you thought it had been stolen and there was a whole heap of insurance money about to fall into your lap, then it was yours to claim, *rightfully*, sir?'

The Earl bristled and for a moment it seemed as if he was on the verge of punching Len, when a sharp knock on the door fortunately halted proceedings.

'Come in,' Posie shouted, expecting Babe to make herself useful for once. But she was wrong. It was Dolly, big-eyed and looking like some kind of exotic bird. She was clutching a blue letter and a telegram in her tiny hand. Posie smiled a vexed greeting.

'Postman!' Dolly trilled cheerfully, coming into the now very overcrowded office. Everyone stared at her.

'These letters were downstairs, on the mat. I thought I should bring them up.'

'Bad time, is it?' She passed the letters to Posie and lit up a cigarette. 'You seem very busy in here. Lovely office, by the way.'

Posie started to rip open the telegram, but she was conscious of Rufus, who had now moved from his place propping up the desk and had sidled around to Dolly's side. He moved as if he was in a dream or under a spell, and he took the battered cigarette case unconsciously from Dolly's hands, much to her surprise. He held it to his lips, all the while looking at Dolly as if in shock.

'Dash it all, I had one of these once,' he whispered. 'Almost the very same thing in fact. I wore it in my breast pocket at the battle of Ypres and do you know what? The ruddy thing saved me! It stopped a bullet going right through my heart. Took the full force. I always said it was my lucky charm after that.'

'What happened to it?' whispered back Dolly, as if in a trance.

'I lost it my first week back in London.' He laughed sadly. 'Had it stolen from me when I was half-cut one night, over at the Dog and Duck in Holborn. My luck's never been the same since.'

'Really?' she breathed back, captivated.

For once, the Earl and Len seemed to agree on something and both let out a great derisive snort.

Rufus and Dolly stood only inches apart, as if a magnetic force were holding them together. Len started muttering about how gullible people were, believing in the power of possessions.

'Who the devil *are* you anyway, girl?' the Earl asked Dolly rudely.

Dolly snapped out of the trance quickly and stammered out her name and her position at the theatre as if she was being interviewed for a new job.

At the mention of the Athenaeum Theatre the Earl emitted a low groan and gave Dolly a venomous stare before turning to Rufus:

'Wretched boy! Step away now! You seem to have a thing about bottle-blondes, and if there's some unsavoury connection to the theatre, so much the better. You've had your fingers burnt once, my boy. Dash it all – can't you learn from your mistakes?'

Meanwhile, Posie had read the telegram and passed it to Len.

He read it aloud:

NOT BEST PLEASED TO GET YOUR TELEGRAM THIS MORNING. WHY YOUR SUDDEN INTEREST IN **LA LUNA**?

OF COURSE I KNOW ABOUT IT. IT'S THE HOTTEST CLUB RIGHT NOW IN LONDON.

THE LOCATION IS A SECRET. HALF MY UNDERCOVER BOYS ARE READY TO CASE THE JOINT AS SOON AS WE GET A TIP-OFF. STAY OUT OF IT POSIE. PLEASE.

BEST, R. LOVELACE

P.S. I HAVE NEVER HEARD OF THIS COUNT DELLA ROSA CHAP YOU ASKED ABOUT. NOT A DICKY-BIRD.

Dolly beamed.

'But that's exactly what I've come about! I hurried over as fast as I could. When I got back to the theatre I happened to be passin' the Green Room. The wind section of the orchestra were all in there. I thought I heard the words "*La*

Luna" muttered, so I took it upon myself to hang around outside the door. And I was right,' she nodded proudly.

'One of the men told another that "it" was on tonight, that they would go after the performance was finished. And not to forget the oboes.'

'The oboes?' Len repeated, gobsmacked. 'What does *that* mean? Is it a code? You sure you heard right?'

'Mnn-hmnn,' said Dolly, nodding, blowing smoke rings. Rufus was still looking at her adoringly. Posie shook her head in disbelief, trying to sort out facts from what seemed like chaos.

'Hang on a minute, Dolly,' she said calmly, 'did you happen to get an address? An indication of where the club might be? Any clue?'

'All I heard him say was "the usual". And then "four sharp raps".'

Posie let out a defeated sigh. 'What a shame! So near and yet so far! I'm sure the nightclub is at the heart of this mystery. Too bad we can't locate it.'

'Well, never mind. Let's just follow them,' Len said simply. 'Easiest thing in the world. I spend my life shadowing people. We'll follow on in a taxi behind these orchestra chappies when they leave the theatre and see where they go.'

Dolly was nodding enthusiastically. 'I'll come with you. Give you a sign when they leave,' she announced and looked hopefully over at Rufus, egging him on in the action. He started to beam back but the Earl positioned himself between Rufus and Dolly like a small round boulder:

'You've enough on your plate, young fellow, without getting even further mixed up in bad goings-on. Don't forget, you're still out on bail! Tonight you are staying with me at No 11, St James. No drinks, no action. An early night is in order.'

For once, Posie was inclined to agree with the Earl.

'Fine, let's do it,' Posie said, hearing resolve in her voice.

'But I need to telephone Inspector Lovelace. This is the tip-off he's been waiting for. I owe him this favour. He can follow on from the Athenaeum Theatre in an unmarked car. I'll tell him to be subtle.'

'If you must,' sulked Len half-heartedly, for he and the police were on no great terms. He liked to go things alone.

'You know, Posie lovey, you'll need a disguise tonight,' said Dolly as Posie was buttoning up her tweed coat again, ready to run downstairs to an office on the corner where they let her use their recently installed telephone equipment.

Posie turned and smiled. 'You know, I was just thinking the same thing. Caspian della Rosa has never seen Len, but he's clearly marked my card. If he's mixed up in this, as I think he is, then he'll probably be there tonight, so I should either sit this one out or change how I look if I'm serious about searching for Lucky Lucy.'

'I could dye your hair blonde, like mine? It's all the rage,' Dolly offered eagerly. Posie shook her head and laughed:

'You're not a Wardrobe Mistress for nothing – I'm sure you'll find something convincing for me.'

Just as she was about to leave, secretly hoping that everyone else would take her cue and leave too, she heard Rufus explode behind her in an almost wild scream.

'What is it, deary?' Dolly was asking.

'By jove, it's from HER!' he was stammering. 'The blue letter! It's her handwriting! I'd know it anywhere. It's from my fiancée. It's news!'

Posie stepped back into the room: she had totally forgotten about the blue letter.

* * * *

Eight

They crowded around the desk. The letter in its pale blue envelope was addressed to Posie, so she opened it with her father's old college letter-opener. They all peered to read:

Dear Miss Parker,
Stop sticking your nose into matters which don't concern you.
Take this as a warning. Get off my case. IF NOT, YOU WILL BE SORRY.
Someone you love will be badly hurt, or worse.
Yours,
LL

'Nice tone she has,' Len said, arms crossed. 'Talk about theatrical!'

Posie turned the envelope over. 'Look! It was sent by this morning's post. It has a London postmark on it too. So she hasn't gone far then. Unless of course…'

'Unless WHAT?' shouted the Earl. Rufus had gone white, and silent.

'Unless Lucky Lucy wrote it, and someone else posted

it,' Posie said thoughtfully, 'or, perhaps she was *made* to write it.'

Posie sniffed at the paper. It was cheap, thin notepaper; the sort you could buy at any Post Office counter, as delicate as tissue. There was something familiar about the smell, too: a chalky, sulphurous smell which reminded her of something recent.

'What's that smell?' she asked Len, shoving the letter under his nose.

'It's zirconium! The element used to make the flash for taking photos! I'd know it anywhere. When I have to use it in my line of work I can't get the smell off my hands for days – even scrubbing with carbolic soap is no use.'

'So? What does that prove?' asked Rufus, confused.

Posie remembered the bright white light on the steps of No 11, St James yesterday, the smoky tang in the air afterwards.

'I think it proves that Lucy, or her accomplices, have been following me. Staying abreast of whatever I've been up to.' Posie briefly and rather reluctantly told them about the footsteps she had heard the night before, the photographer outside the club.

Len groaned. 'You should have told me this earlier. The whole thing looks much more sinister now we know she's got you directly in her sights. I was hoping this might be an empty threat.'

'That's why the police need to be involved,' Posie said reassuringly, patting his arm. The letter didn't really worry her in the slightest.

Len merely rolled his eyes.

Posie frowned at Rufus. Something was niggling at her brain:

'You sure you don't want to tell me whatever it was from earlier? Something you had discovered?'

He hung his head and grimaced. 'It's nothing. It can keep.'

'Fine, then. If you're sure. I'll keep you up to date with developments at the nightclub tonight. Who knows? Maybe we'll even find Lucky Lucy for you?'

Rufus smiled but there was no hope in his eyes.

'I wish you'd ruddy well stop calling her Lucy,' he said, miserably. 'I even saw her official documents once. I think it was a passport, but not one I'd ever seen before: it said *Georgie* on it. Georgie le Pomme.'

* * * *

It was ten-thirty at night and Len and Posie sat together in the back of a parked cab. The road alongside the Stage Door outside the Athenaeum Theatre was very dark. It was quiet enough for them to hear the sound of the audience spilling out of the theatre around the front.

'Almost time,' said Len, squinting at the luminous dials of his wristwatch in the dark.

Behind them sat another parked cab, but this one was driven by a police-driver, and filled with Inspector Lovelace and two of his underlings from Scotland Yard, all dressed in black dinner suits.

Posie had her eyes fixed on the Stage Door, which so far hadn't opened once. She felt strange, and she knew she looked strange: the proof had been when she had got into the taxi twenty minutes earlier and Len had fixed her with an incredulous, wide-eyed look before turning quickly away without commenting. She wore a long black wig fixed at the nape of the neck in an exotic bun, and her skin had been wiped twice all over with dark walnut tanning- oil, banishing her pale English-Rose complexion immediately. Dolly had tut-tutted when Posie had protested that it was all hideously over the top:

'No, no, lovey! Who cares if you look like a flamenco dancer? The thing with theatrical people, you can never be too over the top. The key is to blend in among them – it's a whole other level. If you're dressed *down* you'll stand out.'

So Posie found herself armed with dark sunglasses, a very garish red lipstick and a low-cut crimson gown in a clingy mousseline fabric, all courtesy of Dolly. Strings of glittering fake red pearls covered her modesty a little up top, but she found herself wishing for a sensible pair of shoes and a skirt she could actually move her legs in.

Len had come as himself tonight, but he looked more than usually gorgeous: he wore a dinner suit and sported a red rose in his buttonhole. Posie had never seen him look so lovely. Just now he reminded her of a nervous blood-hound, ears and eyes and all senses visibly alert for any sign of action, his whole body tensed in anticipation of the next move; she felt his desire to pound the pavements, pace the streets, get close to the action. *He must be like this when he works as a shadower*, she thought to herself briefly with a stab of wonder, and she felt relieved that she only ever had to see him in his more cheerful, relaxed, off-duty hours. He was starting to make her feel nervous.

Suddenly, the Stage Door was flung open and four men came out quickly, their dark silhouettes picked out against the bright light of the inside. Then they were hugging the wall and melting into the shadows of the night. Out of nowhere a dark cab with no headlamps bumped against the kerb where they were lurking and the four men bundled in, in a frantic hurry. They seemed weighed down with musical instruments.

'Start up the engine!' hissed Len to the driver. 'Follow that cab! Remember, no headlights. Go!'

'What about Dolly?' asked Posie fearfully, chewing one end of her sunglasses. Len just shrugged, and as the engine shook itself into life and they started to move off, the Stage Door flew open again and a tiny figure shot out, hurling itself towards them. Posie opened the door wide and a breathless Pierrot Doll jumped in. Behind them the second taxi full of policemen had started moving, and as they turned they saw it was following closely behind, bumper to bumper.

'I can't believe you were gonna go without me!' Dolly squeaked, adjusting her black skull hat which had come askew.

'Shhh! Keep your voice low,' Len whispered at her, crossly.

'What's wrong with him?' whispered Dolly to Posie, the painted black eyebrows on her white grease-painted face rising comically. Posie sniggered, 'I think he's in work mode. He can't see the funny side of anything right now.'

Len ignored them both and a nervous silence settled in their cab. The snow meant less than the usual amount of people were out and about in town, but the roads were still fairly busy with groups coming out of theatres and restaurants. The cab ahead of them swung out of the Theatre District and passed through Trafalgar Square before turning onto the Strand. It started to pick up speed and drove along at a fair old pace.

'Keep your distance! Keep your distance! We can't have them know we're following them!' said Len to the driver as the cab up ahead passed by the Law Courts and the entrance to Fleet Street. St Paul's, the greatest cathedral on earth, glowed like a beacon in the distance at the top of Ludgate Hill.

All the newspaper buildings and printing presses in London were crammed together here on Fleet Street and Posie noticed how the lights in most of the buildings were still on, casting long blue shadows out over the snowy street. Vans were parked waiting and lads with carts and horses were standing ready outside most of the buildings. There was a frantic, festive Christmassy atmosphere.

'Late-night copy,' said Len knowledgably, glancing up

quickly at the huge art-deco black and white clock which dominated the entrance to the *London Evening Press* building they were passing. It was almost eleven o'clock. 'Tomorrow's morning editions are coming hot off the press right now. Now, hang about…where's he heading now? This is very roundabout!'

The cab up ahead had turned quickly left and was racing up Chancery Lane, taking its bends and corners at speed. At the top it hurtled onto High Holborn and then turned another sharp left before the Holborn Viaduct. This part of town was much quieter as it mainly consisted of office buildings and residential flats.

The cab in front was now noticeably slowing down, and ambling along next to a deserted snowy square. In the darkness ahead it came to a sudden halt. There was a flurry of movement as the four men got out and the cab skittered off again into the night.

'Wait!' ordered Len. 'We'll count to ten before we get out. Understand? We can't just jump on them. We need to *follow* them, not ambush them.'

Their own taxi moved in stately darkness to the same kerb, and they got out. The police cab behind them did the same, and deposited Inspector Lovelace and his two tuxedoed Sergeants on the pavement before sailing off again to wait in the shadows. There was no sign anywhere now of the four men from the theatre.

Posie kept off her dark glasses; she needed all of her keen eyesight right now to try and squint at the place they had come to. It didn't seem much, to be honest: a small quiet cobbled square surrounded on two sides by snow-clad skeletal trees, a few empty iron benches scattered around the place, and a shuttered wooden cabin at the back on the left, with a large painted sign saying 'TEAS AND SANDWICHES SOLD HERE'. It was a typical workers' lunchtime spot.

The square was illuminated weakly by one street lamp

which cast a fragile amber glow over the frozen snow. There were no people anywhere. It was very dark and there was no moon above them.

Inspector Lovelace came up behind them, his Sergeants hanging back. When he had first learnt of the outing that afternoon he had spent almost half an hour trying to dissuade Posie from having anything to do with it, and when he realised she wouldn't be shaken off lightly he had finally given in with a begrudging acceptance. He didn't look too happy at the total lack of any sign of the nightclub, but to his credit he didn't try and apportion any blame.

'Looks like we lost them, eh?' he said flatly, blowing on his hands for warmth.

'Never mind. It was always a longshot. I guess they realised they were being followed; so they jumped ship and scarpered. Thought they'd lead us a merry chase across town first. There's nothing here. We're way off the mark. Let's be heading homewards.'

'No,' whispered Len, shaking his head, and holding back his ear as if he was listening for birdsong.

'Listen carefully. Can you hear that? What's that noise?'

They all looked at Len as if he were slightly mad, but then, in the quiet of the snowy silent square, they heard a distinct but muffled BOOM.

Then again, at regular slow intervals: BOOM, BOOM, BOOM.

'It's a bass!' whispered Dolly excitedly. 'Or maybe a drum. It's music, anyhow. Nightclub music! But from where? This place is dead as a dodo.'

They all started frantically looking around the dark square.

'Rainbird! Binny! Off you go!' instructed Inspector Lovelace.

The two men headed over to the sandwich hut, reminding Posie of a couple of flat-footed black crows trying not to skid across the ice. They came back bemused when they found nothing.

Then Posie and Dolly walked around the whole square, leaning on each other so as not to go flying on their heels on the puddles of black ice. And then Posie saw it, ahead.

'That *must* be it,' she muttered to herself, and headed over to the very back of the square, at the far left, next to the sandwich hut.

A black wrought-iron staircase led downwards, with an old-fashioned gothic Victorian sign welded into an arch above:

GENTLEMEN

'It's just a toilet!' hissed Dolly, following her friend's gaze, peering down uncertainly. At the bottom of the dark, damp concrete steps was an old wooden trapdoor covering a space no bigger than two foot square. The trapdoor looked damp and rusty around the edges. The toilet had obviously been boarded up years ago. At the top of the steps, near their feet, was a length of metal chain and a broken padlock, kicked to one side in a slushy pile of old sandwich wrappers and cigarette ends.

'No. It's a *closed-up* toilet,' Posie said, 'there's a huge difference.'

Just then there was another BOOM, this time very close. They felt the ground tremble just a little underneath their feet. Posie rushed across and herded the group back towards the old toilet in a state of some excitement:

'It's here! I'm certain of it.'

Inspector Lovelace looked uncertain. 'There's no light though, is there? I'd expect to see light coming up from the cracks…' He was studying the trapdoor from the top of the steps. Just then there was another BOOM.

'Yep. It's here all right,' nodded Len, looking pleased as punch. Inspector Lovelace nodded too and snapped into action:

'Rainbird, go and get back-up, urgently. Find a telephone and call the Yard: we need armed men here in plainclothes. We also need lads from the drugs squad, the liquor squad and our specialist in late-night licences. I'm sure this lot are breaking every rule in the book. Everything about this place is illegal, and I'm going to pin them for it.'

'Are you calling for Inspector Oats to come too?' asked Posie, fearfully.

'Nope,' he shook his head. 'This hasn't got anything to do with him. Not yet.'

'Just one thing, Inspector,' cut in a nervous-sounding Rainbird, '*Where* are we exactly, sir?'

The Inspector looked uncertain too for a moment. 'Radnor Square,' he said quickly to his Sergeant, his eyes alighting with relief on the black and white enamelled plaque behind them.

'I'd say we're at the back of Hatton Garden,' said Len, trying to be helpful. Rainbird nodded and ran off into the darkness.

'Hatton Garden, eh?' muttered the Inspector. Posie caught a gleam of interest flash across his face. But before she could ask him more, out of the corner of her eye she saw cars drawing up, over on the far side of the square.

'We'd better hurry. More people are coming now. We'll draw attention to ourselves if we just stand here lurking around. Like we don't know the score.'

'Well, they'd be right about that!' said Len crossly.

'Come on. I know what to do,' Posie was bluffing, but she knew they had to move fast. 'Follow me, all of you.'

The sound of the car doors slamming in the distance had spurred her into action. She linked arms with Len and dragged him down the steps. Before he could say anything she rapped sharply on the trapdoor four times. She put her sunglasses on quickly.

For a horribly long second nothing happened. She was aware of Dolly pressed in close behind her, her face sweating with fear under her thick greasepaint, despite the cold; Inspector Lovelace and Sergeant Binny were pressed tightly on either side.

Then the door moved.

There was no creaking, no swing of rusted hinges. Instead, it curved upwards and to the left smoothly. Posie saw at once that the old wooden trapdoor was a mere decoration: thick shining metal casing and a rubber seal ran around the underside. From the exposed square in the ground a smoky greenish light emanated upwards. It looked like the entrance to a submarine.

'What on earth?' whistled Len beside her, and just then the head of a big burly man popped up.

'Password?' he snapped impatiently. He appeared to be balancing at the top of a staircase or a ladder. He was holding a list of names and was brandishing a stubby pencil in his hand.

Jeepers, thought Posie. *No idea*. She felt Len tensing beside her.

'Darling!' she said, laughing light-heartedly, bluffing for her life. 'I've no idea! Caspian just told me to come here tonight and knock four times on this funny little door! There was no mention of passwords. He gave me these, though.' She brandished the matches she had fortunately remembered to bring.

'What's yer name, then?' the man asked gruffly.

Oh, hell's bells. They hadn't thought of this. Stupidly. Posie suddenly remembered her exotic Spanish disguise.

'I am a Countess,' she said haughtily, and raised her sunglasses a smidgen to give the man what she hoped was her best withering glance. 'Countess Faustina,' she added in a clear autocratic voice, supplying the only Countess' name she could think of on the spur of the moment; the aristocratic victim of the Carino Affair. She surprised herself with the fluency of her performance. Beside her she heard Len stifle a laugh.

'No,' the man said, scanning his guestlist. 'No Faustina here. Sorry, love. You and your mates 'ad better scarper, quick-like.'

Posie felt for a horrible fluttering second that she had lost the battle. Behind their little group a crush of fabulously dressed people were gathering, spilling down the steps in a drunken riot.

'Hurry up, you oaf!' shouted a man with a very plummy voice from the back of the group. Posie pressed on:

'Look, mister. You go and find Caspian now. Tell him who I am, and that you locked me out of here. He'll be mad as hell, I promise you. I didn't like to mention it before, but he's my first cousin.'

Posie heard Dolly's sharp intake of breath behind her. At the same time a slight glimmer of fear crossed the man's face.

'You just tell him his cousin the Countess is here. You'll lose your job in a second, believe me.'

The man looked quickly back at the gathering crowd, and then nodded at Posie:

'All right, yer grace. I'm sorry. I didn't know. Please come on in.'

The man disappeared from view and Posie looked down into the green misty light. She saw a burnished metal staircase, wide and modern, twisting away to one side.

She gathered up her tight red skirts and stepped down into the hole. She felt a cool smooth bannister under her hand. She continued walking about twenty steps down into the smoky green light, thankfully aware of Len close behind her. At the bottom the ground hollowed out.

And what she saw there made her gasp in surprise.

* * * *

Nine

'Great Scott!' Len was standing beside her. 'It's enormous!'

A long, low, cavernous space stretched out before them. The room was the size of a full-scale theatre, with a bar running the length of the right-hand side, and a glittering spangled-curtained stage at the far end. It was very crowded: there were probably over seventy people gathered at the bar alone and another two hundred or so sitting in clusters at the round tables which were scattered tightly across the space.

The guests were dressed fabulously, theatrically – an angel here, a devil there. There was even a girl in a mermaid's outfit, replete with a complicated hinged tail. Dolly had been right: to have been underdressed here would have been a mortal, noticeable crime.

The walls and floor were entirely lined in a silvery thick metal casing. Posie looked upwards; the ceiling too was covered in it, punctured every now and then with a tiny crescent moon-shaped hole.

'Miniscule airvents,' Inspector Lovelace muttered in wonder. 'My God, they're clever! I'll give them that. This is all lead casing: the place is almost totally soundproofed! It's as if it didn't exist. Must have cost a fortune...'

'There's a free table here, sir,' said a pretty waitress,

coming up to Len, and directing him to the very middle of the room. The girl was dressed in a teeny-tiny dress of black and silver crepe which did very little to contain her ample curves – it was little more than a bathing costume really – and Posie was glad of her dark walnut oil to hide the flush she could feel spreading hotly across her face.

'What can I get you all?' the girl asked when they were sitting down.

'We'd just like the usual, please, Miss,' said Posie, holding her nerve and nodding with conviction. She didn't usually smoke but she took a gasper quickly from Dolly's silver case which was lying on the table. Sergeant Binny offered her a light: she hoped no-one noticed her hands were trembling, and that the smoke caught in her throat.

'Very well,' nodded the girl, purring in approval. 'Back in a tick.'

'I say, *you* should've been on the stage as well,' said Len grudgingly. 'Countess Faustina, my hat! You've got some nerve.'

In their own ways, all of them were busy checking out the nightclub, while trying to act normally. The Jazz band up on the front stage were coming to the end of their set, playing their final crescendo. The nightclub was dark, lit by a single green revolving Pier Light placed at the end of the stage; its beam, normally used to guide ships home, was powerful enough to penetrate to the back of the place, cutting through the heavy smoke-filled air.

Their drinks arrived. Five thick, syrupy sour-apple Martinis – the drink of choice for all of London just now, it seemed. Len slapped a pound note down on the table casually as if he had reels of them to spare. The waitress smiled and flung some change down. Posie took a sip of her drink and almost choked.

'Look!' whispered Dolly, excitedly. 'Look who's in the front row!'

They craned their necks and saw a crowd of fawning

women surrounding a table right up against the stage. A man had just arrived. He was shrugging off a big black fur coat, the green light illuminating his face for a second: a beautiful face, framed by black hair curling back in waves like a Greek God. It was a face currently printed on the cover of every magazine in town, on billboards outside all the cinemas and on nearly every London bus.

'Ivor Novello!' said Sergeant Binny excitedly. 'Jeepers! Wait 'til I tell the missus! We just saw him at the cinema in *Carnival* – a real film star!'

'Calm down Binny, for goodness' sake!' said Inspector Lovelace gruffly, trying not to show his own excitement. 'Act naturally. As if you see film stars every day of the week.'

The Inspector nodded around in admiration, surprised.

'It's quite the respectable gaff, this place, isn't it? Stars at every turn. Quite frankly, I'm impressed. I was expecting something distinctly second-rate.'

As they watched, Novello ran lightly up the little stairs at the side of the stage. The Jazz band had now finished, and Novello clicked on a microphone, adjusted the piano stool and sat down. A spotlight from nowhere swivelled onto his face. He turned to the audience, cracked a beautiful smile and then started playing some of his well-known numbers from the time of the Great War. The whole club erupted in applause and cheering. In all the excitement Posie and Len took the opportunity to scan the crowd for Lucky Lucy, a girl they had never seen in the flesh before, which made matters difficult. After a couple of minutes of hard searching, Posie felt sure Lucy was not among the many young beauties gathered around.

'That's Mr Blake, the Theatre Manager, over there at the bar,' she said to Inspector Lovelace discreetly. 'And that lad with the shock of spiky black hair, I recognise him too from the theatre. He's Reggie. He organises the sales of the programmes.'

On closer inspection it seemed that many of the people

milling around, even the barman behind the bar, were actually staff from the Athenaeum Theatre, transplanted into this dim, green subterranean world as if by magic. A cluster of well-known bright young things were led with much bowing and scraping by Reggie the programme-seller towards a table at the very front of the club.

'Everybody who is *anybody* in London is in this place tonight,' Len whispered.

Posie nodded. 'If Lucky Lucy is still in London, this is where she'll be,' she said, 'otherwise, she's long gone and that letter sent to me today was planted.'

Novello was standing now, bowing and laughing as the applause rippled over him in waves. He was joined on stage by a tiny, breathtakingly lovely blonde girl. The whole club seemed to take a collective intake of breath. A spotlight hovered over her.

'Is that *her*?' Len hissed at Dolly, his jaw practically on the floor. 'Is that Lucky Lucy Gibson?'

Dolly shook her head, frowning. 'No. Although she's very similar.'

'Please give a big welcome to Miss Kitty La Roar. With one of my new songs!' Novello announced into the microphone. The crowd cheered as he sat back down at the piano.

Miss La Roar was dressed in a silver-sequinned dance-dress, and her every move across the stage made it seem as if an army of fireflies were following her. She grabbed a microphone and jumped on top of Novello's grand piano and reclined luxuriously. At Novello's first chord, she started to sing upside-down: the sultry tones carried easily through the strange green-filtered air. It was an old-fashioned dance song, and couples had started to move towards a clearing near the stage.

'Don't look now,' said Inspector Lovelace easily, his eyes glued to Kitty La Roar at the front, 'but we're being watched. Several men on the serving side of the bar have had their eyes fixed on our table for the last couple of minutes. My guess is that any minute now someone will come across and ask you some specific questions about your *exact* relationship with this chap you mentioned, Count Caspian della Rosa. You might want to make yourself scarce, Posie. Or else, find the ladies' room…'

'Or dance,' said Len decisively, hauling Posie to her feet so quickly she thought her flamenco wig might fall off. 'Countess Faustina, we are going to dance. They can't interrupt us out there in front of everybody.'

As Posie followed him she heard Dolly start in surprise behind her:

'Why! The men watching us are *all* members of the Athenaeum Theatre! Orchestra members! I know them all!'

Posie caught a brief glimpse of a length of plate-glass mirror running behind the bar, and a shadowy line of perhaps ten men pressed up against it, their heads swivelling in her direction, following her every move. Her heart started to beat faster.

'Relax,' Len ordered, leading her onto the dance floor. In one fluid movement he had positioned himself around her with the obvious ease of an expert. He pressed his hand into the small of her back, forcing her body very close to his. He led her around in time to the music, smiling calmly, his movements liquid, only an occasional flicker of his eyes over Posie's shoulder betraying his nerves.

Posie hated dancing – she feared she looked a fool – but her fear of being found out and her sheer relief at having Len with her forced her to smile, to try and look like she was loving every minute of it. She was so close to Len that she could feel the steady beating of his heart, and at the small of her back, where he held her very tight she could feel…*what on earth?*

'*What* have you got crammed into your cuff?' she hissed crossly. 'It's hurting me. Move your hand up a bit. Oh my goodness…'

She almost came to a standstill, knocking into another couple as she realised with a jolt that Len was carrying a revolver.

'A gun?' she whispered crossly. 'When did you start toting weaponry around with you? This isn't the Wild West, you know!'

'No,' Len said, turning her quickly in an expert spin, 'it could be a whole lot more dangerous. Besides, I always carry it with me. It was my service revolver. I never gave it back.'

Posie gasped at this revelation, but at the very moment Len twirled her again to face the audience, she saw that all hell was breaking loose.

'It's a raid!' someone shouted.

A stream of what seemed like hundreds of policemen were rushing down the metal stairs at the back of the club and guests were running in all directions, screaming. The long plate-glass mirror behind the bar suddenly pivoted inwards, and the men behind the bar disappeared inside the secret space it revealed before it swung firmly shut again.

'Move, boys, move!' Inspector Lovelace was shouting at his men as they hurtled over to the bar in a great mass. For a brief moment Posie saw the leonine head of Caspian della Rosa silhouetted against the bar, his hands resting on the burnished metal worktop, surveying everything around him with the air of a Captain on a sinking ship. In that moment she knew for certain that the club was his. It was his baby, his masterpiece; the mysterious, magnificent jewel in his crown.

Then there was sudden and absolute darkness. People were screaming.

'Get down!' whispered Len urgently, and he and Posie lay on the dance floor. She heard the 'click' of his revolver as Len loaded the barrel next to her.

Girls were still screaming when the lights went on

again, but this time it was not the green Pier Light which was used; instead, a stark unforgiving white light flooded the club, giving it the air of a bright hospital ward, or a vast refrigeration unit, with the cold metal walls shining horribly. Upturned tables and smashed drinks covered the floor. But thankfully no-one appeared to be hurt. Up on the stage, Ivor Novello and Kitty La Roar were still sitting as they had been before Scotland Yard stormed in, both sipping champagne at the piano.

Over at the bar, Inspector Lovelace had handcuffed Mr Blake and Reggie, and both were looking murderous. Several burly policemen were throwing themselves against the plate-glass mirror, trying to break it down or force it open, but it looked like a thankless task.

'Nobody leave! Stay where you are!' shouted Sergeant Binny uselessly, as people scrammed in every direction. A cigarette-girl who had been squatting down next to them on the floor obviously judged this as a good time to go, but Len grabbed her by the arm:

'We need to leave too, Miss. Any idea if there's another exit, apart from the main stairs to Radnor Square up there?'

The girl nodded and beckoned. 'There's an emergency exit, down this corridor, past the cloakroom. Quick. But follow me, this place is enormous and has hundreds of tunnels everywhere: you could easily get lost.'

Len and Posie followed, elbowing their way through the crush of people who had started to file down a long, dark corridor. On their left a series of identical small doors were cut into the metal walls, each with a tiny crescent-moon window in the top. They lost the cigarette-girl in the scrum. Len looked pleased:

'We may as well try and have a nosy around while everyone is tied up in that ruckus back there, don't you reckon, Po? We won't get the chance again. This place will be closed down as a crime scene.'

'What about Caspian della Rosa?' Posie asked fearfully.

She had no wish to run into him after Inspector Lovelace's spectacular rumble, which she was indirectly responsible for.

'Pah! Him and his cronies will be long gone! They won't hang around here waiting to get arrested. You heard that girl; there are loads of secret ways out of here.'

'Hang on a minute,' Posie said, feeling uneasy suddenly. 'I can't believe I forgot! What about Dolly? We should go back for her. I don't know if she's safe.'

'*No*,' Len said in such a forceful way that Posie gasped. 'Why ever not?'

'I don't like her, I don't trust her. And frankly, I'm surprised you do so easily. You don't know the girl at all! She's too innocent-seeming by half. Naïve. Likely it's an act. Who's to say she's not in with this mysterious Caspian della Rosa after all? *She* told us about tonight. Got us to come here. It could all be a trap. Take my advice and stay away from her.'

'What? Don't be so ridiculous,' Posie exploded at him. 'I've never heard you talk such rot before. Why on earth would Caspian della Rosa want to bring his fabulous house of cards crashing down on him with a raid from Scotland Yard? *Of course I trust Dolly*. She's one hundred per cent loyal. I always follow my gut instinct and it's never let me down so far. Unlike yours…'

By now Posie was really worried about Dolly. She was halfway to turning back towards the main clubroom when the lights went off again. She froze in the total blackout, as did Len ahead of her.

A sharp volley of gunfire close by punctured the darkness. People dived for cover. Silence followed. Then a further stream of bullets came frighteningly close, whizzing down the corridor and ricocheting off the metal walls in a dangerous flurry, as if whoever was shooting was purposefully clearing the tunnel up ahead of them.

'Quick, get inside.'

Posie felt an arm pushing her urgently and a slamming sound. Len had shoved her through one of the small metal doors with the moon-shaped windows, and they waited hunched up together in what was a very small space indeed. A store cupboard really. Outside the window everything was dark and silent. They peered out and held their breath.

'Someone's coming,' Len whispered.

Two men were whispering to each other as they walked along, guided by the light of a burning match, and as they passed the store cupboard Posie recognised the honeyed foreign burr of Caspian della Rosa's melodious voice, even if she couldn't see his face. Her stomach lurched. Were they looking for her? Were they going to hunt her down? Did they know she was here?

'Everything is out, thank God,' an unidentified second man muttered, also in a slightly foreign accent.

'Yes, it is. And those fools Blake and Reggie won't talk. The police can clear this mess up – it's no great loss anyhow. We needed a new location anyway: this one was getting stale. We'll open up somewhere else next time. We've got the prize anyway.'

'You stored it out of harm's way?'

'Of course I did! I'm a professional! Not like that fool of a girl.'

'Shh. Be careful what you say,' hissed the other voice petulantly.

'Why should I be? At least we got a little extra prize into the bargain too. Shall we keep it up our sleeves for now, save it as a reserve?'

And then their voices tailed away. After a few minutes people could be heard picking themselves up off the floor and running for the exit.

Len exhaled loudly. They both felt nervous, sick and claustrophobic. They had had enough of feeling like they were trapped in a closed, pitch-black submarine. Len struck a match.

'Come on. Let's go,' Posie insisted. 'I'm sure Inspector Lovelace has sorted things out by now. He'll be wondering where we are.'

'That's what *I'm* doing,' said Len softly, moving his light around carefully. 'I'm wondering where on earth we are...'

His voice took on a panicked note:

'I just reached out and touched a stone-cold leg, complete with a high-heeled shoe stuffed on the end of it. I thought at first it must be my imagination so I felt again. Then I thought it must be a mannequin, or some sort of prop for the stage. But now I'm not so sure.'

By the light of the match, he illuminated the tiny cupboard space and they both gasped in horror as the body of a girl was revealed to them, a girl they were familiar with from only one photograph.

It was unmistakeably Lucy Gibson: shot through at the temple, vacant eyes staring, a gun clasped loosely in her right hand, a pale blue colour spread patchily over her face and lips.

As beautiful in death as in life, perhaps. But certainly not as lucky.

* * * *

Ten

'Come on. Really *look*. It's the size of a quail's egg. You can't miss it. Whoever finds it will get a reward.'

Posie was trying her best to encourage Inspector Lovelace's men to search the whole club for the Maharajah diamond, but they were tired and wanting to go home. The Inspector had given her ten minutes of their precious time. It was now up.

'It's a mare's nest, Posie,' he said, running his hands through his gingery hair. 'Lucky Lucy has been killed in cold blood, probably *for* that diamond. The last place the killer would have left it would be here. Accept that.'

Len, who never agreed with the police on principle, nodded wholeheartedly.

'Fine,' she said in defeat, knowing in her heart of hearts that both spoke the truth.

The nightclub was flooded with the bright electric light again, and there was a sense of disappointment and failure hanging palpably in the air. The raid had not gone well: despite having finally prised the plate-glass mirror behind the bar open and found a series of empty rooms and a warren of many twisting corridors, the police had recovered little other than a few empty instrument cases, oboe cases mainly, hastily abandoned by their fleeing owners. And the body of Lucy Gibson, of course.

Posie stared down at the body of the girl, which had been moved out of the cupboard into the garish light of the corridor, and she felt a giddying rush of tiredness and sadness. Poor creature: whatever her faults, of which she supposed there were many, Lucky Lucy hadn't deserved to die like that – shot and dumped in a store cupboard. All for the sake of this one wretched diamond. Or was there more to this than met the eye? Who had wanted to kill such a lovely creature?

Inspector Lovelace looked tired, and was giving muttered instructions to Sergeant Rainbird who wrote frantically in a notepad. Sergeant Binny was directing a team of police photographers who were dancing around the body, jumping in and out for a better picture. The pale blue-flushed face of Lucy Gibson, a faint touch of grey greasy glitter still visible on her eyelids, was brought into sharp focus again and again by their flashbulbs, and the smell of what Posie now knew to be zirconium, sulphury-sweet, hung in the air.

Len was interested in the photographer's methods, and he leant in carefully to observe, paying little interest in the team of forensic scene-of-crime officers who had also appeared. They were scraping inside the cupboard for clues, spraying a fine inky powder on Lucy's hands and pressing her poor dead fingers up against carbon paper to retrieve prints. A police pathologist was staring through a magnifying glass at the gunshot wound.

'Here, photographer! This is odd, but important.'

'How close do you want the picture, doc?'

All of that technical blarney was very good, but Posie needed *real clues*. She needed the body to tell her a story: the dead could only speak through the clues they left behind. Posie scanned Lucy, taking in the details. Posie sank down on her high heels, squatting next to the body.

She observed the strange blue flush across the face.

Hadn't she heard somewhere that that was usually caused by poison, but *which one* exactly? She studied the vivid purple bruising on the ring-finger of Lucy's left hand, and the badly scratched crimson nail-polish on the fingers.

She noted too the expensive but surprisingly demure black woollen dress paired with smart leather day shoes. So then, she could be pretty sure that Lucy hadn't been dressed for a night out dancing at the club; the other girls at *La Luna* had all been wearing a uniform of short spangled dancing-dresses, and heaps of jewellery. Instead, Lucy was dressed respectably for an afternoon in smart London society; primly really, considering she was an actress and a glamorous gangster's moll.

Posie was just struggling to her feet when she thought she heard it again: the second voice which had accompanied Caspian della Rosa earlier along the dark corridor, when she and Len had been hiding out in the metal cupboard. She reeled, momentarily dizzy, searching all around her for the speaker's face, but the bright lights flashed in and out of focus and the world seemed to tilt. A darkness threatened to engulf her. Was she going crazy? Hearing imaginary voices? She decided she *must* be: those men would be long gone by now.

'Posie? You all right?' she heard Inspector Lovelace saying, as if from a distance of two hundred miles away. She felt two sets of strong arms hauling her up.

'Maybe she's not so great with dead bodies, guv?' said Sergeant Binny, helping her to her feet, together with a photographer.

'No. That's not it. I bet she hasn't eaten anything all day, have you Posie? You can't live your life on just biscuits, you know. You need to eat dinner now and then. Len!'

Len darted through the crowd.

'Take Posie for a good square meal somewhere. I'm sure you'll know a place open at one-thirty in the morning. I'd love to join you, I'm starving actually, but I've got to sign off on all of this. Oh, hello! Here comes trouble. I *had* to call him in. Technically, it is *his* body, after all.'

Through the corridor swung the familiar, unwelcome figure of Inspector Oats. He looked at the body of Lucky Lucy Gibson for a brief second, before sniffing disdainfully and indicating it could be covered up and carried off. He looked around with a distinctly scornful expression:

'Quite a mess on your hands here, Lovelace,' he muttered towards the Inspector. 'What's all this? A failed raid?'

'And who's this?' he nodded at Posie with a deeply suspicious air. She suddenly remembered her disguise and whipped off her black wig, shaking her own shingled bob out carefully.

'Oh, no. Not *you* again,' Oats growled. 'The proverbial bad penny. And where's your pal, Lord Hoity-Toity? Is he here as well?'

'Rufus?' Posie exclaimed in surprise. 'No, of course he's not here. He's at his father's club in St James.'

'Aha! Well, that's where I'm heading to now then,' Oats snapped angrily, making to turn on his heel. 'Now your pal's got *two* unexplained deaths on his hands, and bail or no bail I'll have him back in for questioning before the hour's up.'

'Hang on a minute…' cut in Len as Posie gasped in horror at the sheer stupidity of Oat's reasoning.

'I say!' shouted Inspector Lovelace at Inspector Oats' retreating back. 'You've got this all wrong, old fellow. Don't make a blundering fool of yourself. The person who murdered Lucky Lucy has probably got something to do with this wretched underground nightclub we're all standing in. The answer lies here, not with Rufus Cardigeon!'

But Oats had disappeared out into the dark night, trudging along with a clear, if misguided, purpose.

* * * *

Posie ate two fried eggs, several rashers of bacon, a sausage and a side portion of potato cakes. When the waitress came around to refill her mug from the big metal tea-pot, she ordered the same again.

She ate in silence, and Len watched her quietly. He smoked a Turkish cigarette and leant back against the grease-smeared red plastic banquette, discreetly seeing if he knew anyone in the place.

It was a dive of a caff really, he supposed. It was nestled between Fleet Street and the Inner Temple, tucked into a side alley which the law clerks used as a lazy shortcut. Open twenty-four hours a day, it was frequented by nervy journalists, late-night printers, and a whole raft of people who didn't seem to fit in anywhere else, but needed to kill time for one reason or another. There was no sign or advert outside the caff, just a white-painted scrawl on the sooty window, which had been there forever, announcing *NO KIPPERS TODAY – SORRY.*

Sal ran the place. And Len had spent many hours there over the last few years, waiting for a punter to emerge so he could begin tailing him, or waiting for a tip-off from one of his lawyer clients. But there was no-one he knew in tonight: just a couple of poor souls who looked like they had served in the trenches, and in the far corner a young journalist, his half-moon spectacles pushed down low on his nose, hurriedly writing copy for his newspaper. As Len watched, the journalist rubbed his ink-stained hands over his forehead in worry, smearing his pimply face. He looked new to the job.

Sal appeared beside their table, huge and resplendent in an oil-cloth overall.

'Thought yer might enjoy this, Mister Irving,' she announced grandly, and placed a steaming spotted dick pudding in front of Len, who smiled gratefully. It looked magnificent and Sal dolloped a ladle of custard over the plate, giving Posie just a flicker of interest before stomping off.

'Don't eat it,' hissed Posie suddenly, as Len moved to pick up his fork.

'Why ever not?'

'I need it.'

Quick as a flash she had grabbed the pudding and moved to the table in the corner where the young journalist was fretting with his copy. She put the pudding down carefully next to him.

'Hello!' she said cheerfully, and placed one of her business cards next to the pudding. She looked at him expectantly. He squinted up at her, as if surprised to see another living breathing soul awake at this time of night.

'Hmm?' he said, nervously, inky fingers ruining her card.

'Which paper do you work for?'

'*Associated Press*. Why do you want to know? Miss, er… Parker?'

'Spotted dick? Here, have it. It's all yours. What's your name?'

'Sam Stubbs, junior journalist. Here's my press badge.'

Sam Stubbs eyed the cake eagerly, as if just remembering his hunger. He took up a fork and ate greedily. Posie watched in satisfaction: she was always secretly amused at how easy it was to win over some men, particularly with old-fashioned puddings which reminded them of their childhoods.

'I've a scoop for you, Mr Stubbs. And no, I don't want money. I'm certain this will blow whatever you're writing there right out of the water. It might just make your career. But it *must* go to press tomorrow. It should make the lunchtime edition. And you *must* name me as your source.'

Sam Stubbs gasped, and pushed his spectacles back up onto his nose.

'Go on,' he nodded, chewing the end of his pen.

Posie outlined the details of the evening's events: the discovery of the infamous *La Luna* club; the police raid;

the discovery of the body of Lucky Lucy. She spelled out Caspian della Rosa's name carefully. Sam Stubbs wrote everything down in a nervous shorthand which looked nothing like Babe Sinclair's.

'Are we done here?' she asked after a few minutes. Sam scanned his notepad, checking the detail. He nodded and looked up:

'One thing I'm not clear on, Miss Parker,' he asked, frowning, as he gathered up a cheap-looking tweed over-coat and hat. 'What's in this for *you*, if not money?'

Posie smiled sweetly.

'Let's just say I'm hoping for a particular outcome. And also, I'm hoping that you may be able to help me out in the next couple of days. The *Associated Press* is one of the best papers in town: it must have a very good archive of clippings. I think I'm going to need access to them. And I think *you* are just the man to help me.'

* * * *

'What did you go and do *that* for?' said Len angrily, kicking the snow. They were walking along the Strand together, taking care to avoid a man and his little boy leading a horse and trap, liberally sprinkling the road with salt from a bucket at the back of the cart.

'Inspector Lovelace will be mad at you, you idiot! The raid was supposed to be hush-hush. It didn't exactly go very well, either. Now all of London will know about it! And why choose that spotty nincompoop, just out of school? I have loads of contacts at newspapers if you wanted to blow the thing right up in our faces. Good grief, Po! I almost wonder if you haven't lost your wits!'

Posie smiled, taking his arm and crossing over to the

Aldwych. The bell of St Clement Danes Church was just tolling three a.m.

'I know you have contacts, Len. But none of them happened to be *right there*, tonight. So much in life comes down to timing, doesn't it? Sam Stubbs was the right man for the job, at just the right time. I need this news to break tomorrow, in the lunchtime edition, latest.'

'*Why*, might I ask?' Len said, his tone heavy with sarcasm.

'We need to flush out Caspian della Rosa. Expose him. So far he's managed to remain under the radar. No-one even knows about him. Not even the police! But all that will change. He needs to know we've got him cornered.'

'Jeepers. I know he might be up to his neck in all manner of dodgy goings-on, but so far you have no *direct* evidence linking him to anything, let alone two murders or stealing that wretched diamond. What do you hope to achieve?'

'We'll just have to wait and see,' Posie said with conviction. 'But sure as bread is bread I'm not going to let Rufus hang for this. I'm going to solve this.'

Len looked at her and decided he had said enough.

A cold wind was blowing along the dark street. He groaned inwardly to think of the long and expensive cab ride back to Leytonstone. As if she could read his mind Posie turned to him and smiled:

'I thought we could sleep over at the office tonight. It's so close by. Besides, it's only five hours until we need to start work again. No point trekking home, is there? I can't think why I haven't done it more often!'

Len gasped. 'What will people say? We can't *both* stay over!'

'*What* people?' scoffed Posie. 'Mr Minks?'

Len muttered into his coat collar and flushed a dark red, but continued walking.

They walked back to Grape Street with no real further conversation, still awkwardly arm-in-arm, but with Posie feeling she had crossed some invisible boundary between them, and Len feeling he had been made to look a prude. When they reached the Detective Agency they were both glad to take to their own offices, light their own small fires, and close their own doors on what had been a very long and complicated day.

As Posie was settling down to sleep on the small cream rug in front of her fireplace, with her brown tweed coat over her as a blanket, she couldn't help but think that in among all the strange, wonderful and terrible things she had experienced that day, something closer to home wasn't quite right.

She was so tired…so very, very tired.

She blinked in an effort to keep her eyes open. Something was missing.

But as she struggled to remember what it might be, she drifted off on a wave of blissful, welcome, long-overdue sleep.

* * * *

Wednesday 16th February, 1921

Eleven

Grey morning light filtered into the office, and Posie woke blearily, stiff as a board in front of the cold, extinguished fire. A flurry of snowy hail smattered against the window.

The office clock showed it was eight a.m., and Posie rustled to her feet, still wearing the red mousseline dress from the night before. She picked up her work clothes from the back of her chair and headed off to the little bathroom to change. She felt grimy and tired, and she was longing for a hot bath, but she made do with splashing her face with ice-cold water and Pears' soap in the tiny cracked basin.

Len was singing in the kitchen, and passing by, Posie saw him making tea. He grinned at her and passed her a mug, leaning back companionably against the green melamine counter-top.

'Good morning!'

'So you've forgiven me then, have you, for selling the story last night to the nincompoop? You ought to watch it, you know; you're turning into Dr Jekyll and Mr Hyde.'

Len shrugged. 'I'm sorry. I guess I was tired. And I figure you must have your reasons. You've never been wrong yet.'

The strength of the sweet tea seemed to revive them both, and Posie was just turning to leave when she remembered:

'Where's Mr Minks? It's not like him to miss remind-ing me it's breakfast time.' She strode over to the tattered velvet curtains he liked climbing in and shook them, as if he might have hidden himself in their folds.

'I thought he was in with you last night,' said Len, frowning anxiously. He cared more about the cat than he would admit to anyone.

That was what had been wrong last night, Posie realised with horror. The office just wasn't the same without Mr Minks. And he had been missing, even then.

They looked at each other in slow-dawning panic, before running in opposite directions. They searched all over, which didn't take long – the three little offices, the waiting room, the kitchen, the landing and its tiny bath-room. Len ran up and down the stairs several times, Posie hammered on the door of the office downstairs and she searched the ground-floor entrance hall to the building. But no-one had seen the cat.

Back upstairs they started all over again. Cupboards and drawers and even the fireplaces were searched frantically.

'What if he got out on the window-ledge looking for a piece of chicken and fell off?' Posie voiced quietly, trying to disguise the tremor in her voice that was breaking through.

'Impossible,' said Len, hauling up the sash window and gulping at the huge drop. 'We're always careful never to leave any windows open. It's the rule here. Two years and we've never had a problem. Mr Minks would never stray anywhere, he knows he has it too good here. What changed?'

Just then a terrible thought entered both their minds. *Babe*.

As if on cue, Babe could be heard fumbling at the office front door, jangling her key in the lock. They darted out into the waiting room and stared at her accusingly. She turned and looked at them with a big-eyed stare, then smiled uncertainly.

'I picked up these for you downstairs, off the mat, just now. One's a hand-delivery. Say, is something kinda wrong with you all? Gee, I'm not late, am I?'

Posie grabbed the two envelopes without really looking, never taking her eyes off the girl's face:

'Mr Minks is missing,' she said levelly. 'Do you know anything about it, Babe? And you'd better tell me the truth. You locked up yesterday. Did you leave any windows open when you left? Have you anything unusual to report?'

Babe stared at both of them, and shook her head, but for a brief second a high pink colour flushed her face. Then she burst into tears, sobbing uncontrollably. Posie sighed, and Len uncrossed his arms and went across to pat the secretary on the shoulder.

Either this girl is a very good actress, Posie thought wearily, or else she *really* doesn't know what's happened to the cat. *What was it with actresses and the theatre at the moment?* They seemed to be surrounding her.

Posie ripped open the first envelope. It was a telegram from Inspector Lovelace informing her there would be a formal Inquest into Lucy Gibson's death at eleven o'clock at Victoria, and their attendance was required, as they had been the first people to find the body. He went on to say that Inspector Oats had re-arrested Rufus and that he was being held in the cells again at Scotland Yard, on very tenuous grounds. Posie was so wrapped up in thinking about this terrible latest piece of news that she was halfway through automatically ripping open the second, hand-delivered letter when Len stopped her with a panicked shout:

'Wait! Stop! What do you notice?'

Posie looked down at the envelope. It was blue, cheap, like tissue paper. It was addressed to her in exactly the same hand as yesterday's letter.

'Oh my goodness. It's from Lucky Lucy!'

She pulled out a single folded sheet of blue paper, but before she could open it a wad of pale and silky cream-

and-brown Siamese cat hair slipped out, falling to the floor in shimmering strands. Babe yelped, and Posie felt a fist of fear grabbing at her throat, tears pricking her eyes.

'Oh Mr Minks! Oh no!'

Len was on the floor gathering up the cat hair, his mouth set in a grim line.

'Read the letter,' he said quietly. Posie read aloud:

Dear Miss Parker,

I warned you someone would get hurt if you didn't butt out. I have the cat, as you can see. It's safe for now, if a little bald in places.

Drop the whole case and the cat will be returned to you unharmed. To indicate acceptance, wear a yellow rose in your buttonhole today where I can clearly see it. If not, accept the consequences. This is only the first bad thing to happen to you: it will get worse, I promise you.

Yours,

LL

Posie sunk down on the visitors' couch. She put her head in her hands. When she looked up she saw Len was opposite her, looking worried. He was more shaken than he was letting on. Babe was nervously pulling at a large and shiny amber choker around her neck, twisting it over and over. Posie ignored her.

'Something doesn't add up,' she said at last, irritably. 'Dead girls don't write letters about missing cats.'

'She wrote it before she died, obviously,' Len snapped. 'Thing is, where did she hide Mr Minks? There was no sign of a cat, dead or alive, in that wretched nightclub yesterday. Maybe whoever killed her killed the cat too?'

'No, no, that's not the problem. Lucy was dead as a

doornail late last night. Remember? But this letter was hand-delivered *just now*. Both you and I went up and down the stairs earlier this morning, and there were no letters on the mat downstairs in the hall at all. So the letter has only just arrived.'

Len nodded. Posie went on, insistently:

'Either there was a hitch in delivering this note from Lucy, and it got delayed, or else, it wasn't written by Lucy Gibson at all, but by someone else masquerading as her; perhaps someone who doesn't realise she is dead, or who does know, but thinks *we* don't yet know that...'

'They do a pretty ruddy good job of imitating her writing then – Rufus believed it was the real deal when he saw the letter yesterday. But what I don't understand is *why* take Mr Minks at all? *Why?*'

Posie crossed to her office, frowning uncertainly.

'Either to frighten me, as the letter says, or more likely, to show they are in control. They must have realised how much the cat meant to me.'

'I don't like this,' Len said angrily. 'If it wasn't Lucky Lucy who took the cat it could have been *anyone*.' His eyes rested momentarily on Babe, before coming back to Posie. 'Where do we start? I think we need to cast the net widely for suspects. Think of some of your *new friends*...perhaps?'

He gathered up his camera.

'I'm sorry, but I have to go out and take photos of a naughty Lord a-leaping in someone else's bed. Want me to buy you a yellow rose while I'm out in Covent Garden market?'

Posie turned and gave him a watery smile.

'Of course I don't, you idiot! We'll get Mr Minks back somehow or other. Alive. See you at the Inquest.'

* * * *

At her desk Posie sat thinking, making a steeple of her hands.

The priority, of course, was clearing Rufus of both of these murders, but she couldn't stop thinking about poor old Mr Minks...

She frowned and picked up the cheap blue letter again. *Should* she have more of a suspicious mind?

Should she, like Len, distrust people she felt in her heart were good people and cast the net wider than Babe Sinclair for potential suspects? What if – could it be possible – could *Dolly* perhaps have written that note, and stolen the cat, for that was who Len suspected, wasn't it? Her *new friend*...

An image of Dolly rose up before her as she had first encountered her; her black and silver crescent-moon-tipped cigarette dangling from her silver-painted finger-tips. A nocturnal, strange creature, whose natural habitat would surely be somewhere like the *La Luna* club...

Len had indicated that he didn't trust the Wardrobe Mistress one jot, and it was true that Dolly hadn't been seen since last night; since before the shoot-out at the nightclub, giving her ample time to steal the cat and organise delivery of the note. And Dolly wouldn't necessarily know they had found Lucky Lucy's body last night, either, leaving her wide open to misguidedly deliver the note to Grape Street this morning.

But for what reason? Simply for money?

Posie found her thoughts were running away in crazy suspicious directions, tumbling over each other in a hurry. Was Dolly acting alone in this? Or perhaps, as Len had suggested last night, Dolly was in the pay of Caspian della Rosa after all...part of some bigger plan. It was true that Dolly was a tough cookie; a born survivor. And she had seemed short enough of money to do anything. She worked at the Athenaeum Theatre too, and Posie only had Dolly's word for it that she had never been to the *La Luna* club before, and that she was scared of Count Caspian: perhaps she too was just a very good actress?

But would Dolly really stoop to such methods of intimidation, even for a nice pay-check? Posie shivered and felt goose-bumps break out over her skin.

Get a hold of yourself, she told herself briskly. When the only thing you had in this world was your conviction about someone's character, your trust in them, you had to hold onto that. She remembered Dolly's kindness with the fake fur coat. Of course Dolly was who she said she was.

Posie vowed she would make contact with Dolly later in the day. She felt rather guilty that in all the fiasco of finding Lucky Lucy's body they had not even managed to put Dolly safely home-bound in a taxi. She would arrange another tea with the girl, and invite Len too, so he could put any remaining doubts he might have about her to rest. Something told her Dolly was set to become a good friend of hers, for a long time…

Seeing the time, Posie hurriedly smartened herself up for the Coroner's Court. The weather outside was changing; cloud was shredded all across the sky, ragged fragments of purple-grey, promising a storm.

She grabbed her black umbrella and charged out of the door.

* * * *

Twelve

The Coroner's Court was near Victoria Station, housed in an old, dark, forbidding stone building behind black-painted wrought-iron fencing.

Two uniformed policemen stood outside the door and ticked Posie off a shortlist of names. The overpowering smell of disinfectant and a horrible undertone of rank sweat hit her as she stepped inside, and Posie was pleased she had never had occasion to visit the place before.

She spritzed herself liberally with her sweet violet perfume and entered the Court.

* * * *

'First, I call Miss Rosemary Parker, Private Investigator.'

Posie got to her feet and stood solemnly in the dark wooden witness stand at the front of the tiny white-tiled Coroner's Court. She faced the Coroner, a beady-eyed little man who reminded her of a sleek black raven, trained to miss nothing. The Court Official continued pompously:

'Miss Parker is a key witness and was first to find the body of the woman known as Lucky Lucy Gibson. Now, give me your right hand and swear on the Bible that what you tell this Inquest will be the truth, and nothing but the truth. Do you understand?'

Posie gave her account of the night before, and was followed by Len, who gave a similar account. Neither of them were asked any questions, and she saw the Coroner taking notes, nodding grimly.

Sitting down again she took some time to survey the other people attending the Inquest. It was a 'closed Court', which meant all of the people there had been invited specially, and there was no public gallery, which meant no nuisance from journalists. There were fewer than twenty people in all, including herself and Len. She caught sight of Inspector Lovelace and Inspector Oats sitting together on a wooden bench opposite, both of them looking like they wished they were not in the other's company.

Behind them sat a senior-looking black-uniformed man in his late fifties, taking notes, and Posie guessed he must be their Scotland Yard superior – a Commissioner or an Assistant Commissioner, perhaps? She spied Sergeants Binny and Rainbird sitting further back, and a couple of other policemen whose faces she recognised from the *La Luna* raid. The Police Pathologist and the Forensics Specialist, both of whom she had seen at the crime scene the night before, sat on the third wooden bench which made up the connecting arm of the horseshoe-shaped gallery. Along from where Posie and Len were sitting, and almost totally obscured from view, sat Rufus, head bent low, handcuffed miserably between two uniformed policemen. The Tenth Earl was nowhere to be seen: he had probably not been allowed in, which was probably for the best.

Next to Posie sat a fat little priest wearing a black cassock and an old-fashioned black Biretta hat, ceaselessly click-clacking an enamelled string of rosary beads through his fingers. A Catholic then; Posie found herself surprised at his presence. Why was he here? Was he a witness?

Was he going to tell the Inquest something interesting about Lucky Lucy? The large hat almost obscured his face but from the side, Posie caught a glimmer of gold round-framed spectacles and a pudgy, slack profile. The heavy scent of church incense wafted up from the folds of his black clothes, strangely reassuring in the unfamiliar surroundings. The occasional sucking sound which came from underneath the Biretta, which she had taken at first to indicate the wearing of badly fitting false teeth, turned out to be a fondness for pear drops, a crumpled pink bag of which the priest brought out at regular intervals, as if in a cinema.

The Inquest was running along nicely – the Coroner was an efficient man who wanted to be out in time for his lunch. The Police Pathologist, Dr Poots, was called to the stand, bearing a heavy-looking file which the Coroner looked at with distaste. He came straight to the point:

'So, was it suicide or murder? Don't bore me with the contents of that whole file. Cut to the chase, man.'

'It was murder, your Honour. Superficially it looked like a shooting, but I can confirm that in fact it was murder by potassium cyanide, which accounts for the very pale flushed blue colour in the face. I think she was forced to drink something, and she put up a fight. Evidenced by the state of the fingernails. A horrible, painful death – poor kid. But quick.'

There was a collective intake of breath.

The Pathologist continued:

'The shot-gun wound to the head was incurred *after* death – it was purely cosmetic. A clumsy attempt to make it appear as if it were a suicide; placing the revolver in the right hand, closing the fingers around it. But our murderer made an obvious mistake. Perhaps a rushed job?'

'He made a mistake?'

'Yes, your Honour. The gunshot wound was on the right side of the head, but there's no way Lucy could have shot herself in that manner. She was left-handed.'

'You have proof?'

'Yes. Everything indicates she was left-handed, your Honour. Her left-hand middle finger bore the typical pronounced calluses associated with writing, or some kind of artistic employment requiring use of the hands. Actually, I was quite surprised – you'd normally only see that on a writer, a journalist, a printer, or an academic person perhaps… And she smoked with her left hand too; there were singe marks from cigarettes on the middle and index fingers of her left hand.'

The Coroner took careful notes, ticking his way down a green piece of paper.

'So what time did she die exactly, Dr Poots? And spare me the medical mumbo-jumbo, man.'

The Pathologist nodded, unperturbed.

'Earlier than we first thought, your Honour. Although she was found last night, tests indicate she had been dead at that point for over twenty-four hours. In fact, I can be more accurate. She died of poisoning by cyanide on Monday 14th, somewhere between around two o'clock and five o'clock in the afternoon.'

'*WHAT?*' bellowed Inspector Oats, standing up and propping himself up on the wooden barrier. 'That cannot be right!'

'Silence in the Court!' thundered the Coroner, his pen jabbing the air violently, and Posie strained to hear the black-uniformed Commissioner whispering angrily:

'Get a grip of yourself, Oats. An utter disgrace…'

Inspector Oats had turned puce but sat down again, defeated. His prime suspect had just been given the all-clear. Indeed, Rufus had been locked up inside the tiny jail cell at Scotland Yard during the whole afternoon of Monday the 14th, and you couldn't ask for a better, more cast-iron alibi than that. In fact, Inspector Oats *was* the alibi for Rufus, and Posie smiled in satisfaction at the bitter irony of it. She watched with pleasure as Sergeant Binny looped around the back of the wooden benches to quietly inform the uniformed policemen that they could set their prisoner free and unshackle him. She heard a sound somewhere between a sob and a hiccup from Rufus' direction, but there would be time for comforting him later.

So then, Posie thought, Lucky Lucy had gone fresh from her engagement lunch with Rufus at the Ritz to meet her own death only a couple of hours later. Which would account for her conservative clothing – but not for *why* Lucy was at the *La Luna* club when she died: *if* she had indeed died there. The early time of death was interesting for other reasons too: the two letters which had arrived at the Grape Street Bureau supposedly written by Lucky Lucy could now definitely be classed as forgeries. Someone had been deliberately impersonating the girl. But who? And why?

Still puzzling, Posie watched the Forensics Officer, Mr Maguire, take the stand.

Without any warning he brandished a shining revolver from a white silk cloth cover. The Court took a collective intake of breath. The priest bit hard on his sweet, almost choking himself. There came another hiccup from Rufus' direction.

'Less of your amateur dramatics, Mr Maguire,' ordered the Coroner, looking at his pocket-watch. 'What do you have to tell me about that gun? Something useful, I hope.'

'Yes, your Honour. I do.' The Forensics Officer beamed.

'This is the actual gun recovered from the scene of crime last night, it was in Lucy Gibson's hand when she was found. It's a standard issue Webley Mark IV revolver, a 1915 model; a beauty, in fact. They were issued to nearly all officers who served in the Great War. In fact, the British government kept careful records of *who* the exact guns were issued to. Each has a special serial number.'

'And?' demanded the Coroner, eyebrows raised.

'I traced the number. This particular revolver was issued to Lord Rufus Cardigeon before he left for the French Front in August 1915.'

The Court took another sharp intake of breath and all eyes swivelled around to face Rufus, who had turned red and was shrinking down against the bench. Posie felt herself growing hot in the face with anger.

Why on earth hadn't he told her? And suddenly, with a horrible stinging sensation she realised he may have been trying to, yesterday in her office, but he had been overtaken by shame or sheer uselessness under the scrutiny of his formidable father, unable to admit to yet another failure.

So: Lucy had stolen Rufus' gun as well as his diamond and his heart, it seemed.

'*SEE?*' shouted Inspector Oats, jumping up again. 'I *told* you he was in on it! Up to his soft-coddled neck in it!' Inspector Lovelace pulled him down.

Rufus stood up. He looked terrible. 'She stole it from me, I swear. I only discovered it missing yesterday morning. Honestly, by jove, I had no idea she had taken it.'

'Silence,' ordered the Coroner, almost growling. 'It is not the job of this Court to apportion blame or convict suspects. It is merely to confirm the details of the death, and gather the facts. Continue, Mr Maguire, I take it you are not finished?'

The policemen sitting next to Rufus looked around uncertainly, unsure if they should handcuff him again. They made do with moving in very tightly against Rufus, to make sure he couldn't go anywhere if he tried anything rash.

'Yes, there is more. By matching up the bullets found at the scene of the, er, *connected* murder of Lionel Le Merle at the Ritz Hotel on Monday, I can confirm that this Webley was the gun used to shoot Mr Le Merle.'

Inspector Oats was nodding savagely, sending dark looks across the room at Rufus.

'However,' the Forensics Officer continued, 'that is a mere detail, a red herring. I can also confirm that while the murderer placed this Webley in Lucy Gibson's hand, perhaps to frame Lord Cardigeon, or simply to make it look like a suicide, *it was not this gun she was shot with after death.*'

All eyes were on Mr Maguire.

'The post-death bullet-wound on her right temple was made by an altogether different gun. Unusual. I'd say the killer messed up by using it, as it's so rare. I've never handled one before. It was a US Browning revolver, the 9mm Model.'

'American, you say?'

'Yes, your Honour. Although it was made specially for the Belgian army. It's a smart little gun. It was issued to Belgian officers in the trenches. I should mention that while we don't have the actual gun, special bullets from this Belgian gun were also found in one of the corridors at the *La Luna* club last night, and bullet-holes in the metal walls are entirely consistent with its being freshly fired. So the same gun used to shoot Lucy Gibson in the head was being brandished around the club again late last night. I'd say your killer was in that club last night.'

Len whistled next to Posie. 'Coo-ee! That means it might have been your Count Caspian who killed Lucy, don't you think? We practically saw him waving a gun around the corridor before he made his escape last night!'

The Coroner was nearly at the end of his green paper. 'But without the actual gun, can you trace the bullets to find the owner of the gun, Maguire?'

Maguire shrugged. 'I'm trying, your Honour. I've put telegrams through to Brussels and Antwerp, where the army records were kept at the main recruiting stations. I expect it will be a mare's nest, though. Not everybody has kept their guns or bullets from the Great War. In fact, not many have. It's not really safe to keep guns on civvy street.

Leads to accidents. Deaths.'

All eyes were again on Rufus, as if judging him for his sheer stupidity. But Posie was scowling intently at Len who was sitting calmly at her right-hand side, pointedly avoiding her gaze and looking straight ahead.

'One last thing. Have you determined if the victim was killed in the same place as she was found?'

The Forensics Officer shook his head. 'It's impossible to say one way or the other. Sorry not to help more, your Honour.'

'Thank you, Mr Maguire. That was most useful.'

Pulling together his papers, and putting his sheet of green paper on top, the Coroner pursed his lips together and rapped his gavel on the desk.

'I will now conclude. Lucy Gibson's death was murder or manslaughter by person or persons unknown, at a place unknown. Cause of death was cyanide poisoning, followed by a post-mortem shot to the head using a Belgian-issued revolver. Time of death was the afternoon of Monday 14th February. Now, I will just sign off. I say! Hang on a minute…'

The Coroner rustled through his papers, and then again, more urgently this time. He called over to the Court Official and whispered at him insistently. The Court Official shook his head dismally.

'Gentlemen, we have a problem.' The Coroner turned to the Scotland Yard Inspectors.

'It seems that the lady whose death we have been investigating here today has absolutely *no* official records whatsoever, save for some old payslips you have provided me with which are no use to me at all, and the death certificate which I am supposed to sign. Have you no proper official information about her? I thought she was famous?'

'She is!' barked Inspector Oats. 'She's Lucky Lucy Gibson! We've been after her for years.'

'Well, Inspector. It seems you have been after a shadow,

or a ghost, or something that doesn't exist. There is no birth certificate, no passport, no identity papers; *nothing* for a Lucy Gibson. I've checked and my Court Officials have been frantically calling everyone they can – the Registry Office, the Passport Agency. No stone has been left unturned. No-one has *ever* been registered with the name Lucy Gibson who matches the corpse in our Mortuary here. It seems we have been doing your work for you, Inspectors, and I'm not best pleased.'

Next to Posie the priest was scrunching up his bag of sweets and gathering up his umbrella, ready to leave. The Commissioner looked ready to explode, and Inspectors Oats and Lovelace were looking at the Coroner, incredulous.

'So, I will leave the name blank on my report,' he concluded, patting his papers. 'When you find out her real name, let me know. Now, this Inquest is adjourned and I am off for my lunch. I sincerely hope for you, Inspectors, that you have some other leads in this case?'

And both Inspectors looked at Posie, and Posie looked at Rufus and he rolled his eyes to heaven.

'I *told* you that Lucy Gibson wasn't her real name,' he muttered crossly. 'I *told* you.'

* * * *

Outside on the pavement, they stood together in an awkward little group: the two Inspectors, plus Posie and Len and Rufus. Overhead, storm clouds scudded across the sky. There was already the tang of brine in the air. The heavens opened suddenly and they huddled under umbrellas.

'Ah, rain!' said Inspector Oats, taking a drag on his pipe. He felt uncomfortable standing next to a freed Rufus;

unsure of what the next steps would be. The Commissioner had just spent the last ten minutes bellowing loudly and for all to hear at Inspectors Oats and Lovelace: they were now instructed to work together on the investigation, with Inspector Lovelace taking the lead. They were instructed to take whatever advice and leads were forthcoming, including to 'use that girl who calls herself a private detective *if you have to.*' Which meant co-operating with this annoying girl and her pals, for now.

Inspector Lovelace was downhearted too.

'All I can say is thank goodness the press weren't allowed in. We got a mauling enough without it being front-page news. We need to get this case back on track, Oats. Pronto.'

Posie coloured a little at his mention of the press; if her plan was going as it should, the story of the *La Luna* bust would be all over news-stands just about now, on the cover of the *Associated Press*. And then there would be a mauling, she thought uncomfortably, and *she* would be the one getting mauled.

'You should have told me she stole your gun,' she hissed at Rufus. 'It would have been good to know.'

'I'm sorry,' he muttered at the pavement. 'I wanted to tell you, then I just clammed up. I knew it didn't make it any better for me.'

'Cyanide poisoning, eh?' said Len, cocking his head inquisitively and lighting a cigarette against the wind.

'Mnnn,' nodded Inspector Lovelace. 'Took me down a peg or two, that. I'm ashamed to say I didn't spot it. The blue was a very light shade, just a fraction darker than normal rigor mortis…'

'It doesn't help much anyway,' growled Inspector Oats. 'The world and his wife can get their hands on cyanide at a moment's notice in any chemist! Why, I even put it down in our shed in Isleworth to deal with rats…and gardeners use it all the time for snails.'

'Mnn, I wonder…' said Len, half under his breath. He

stubbed the cigarette out on the kerb. Posie saw a gleam of interest in his eye.

'What?'

'It's maybe nothing. But cyanide is used by photographers. On a daily basis. We have to use it in the darkroom.'

Posie nodded, interested.

'And we know one of the gang following you is a photographer…even the paper these people use is impregnated with the smell of zirconium, so…'

'Go on.'

'I can't. It takes us no closer to finding the killer, or your stalker for that matter…and no closer to the Maharajah diamond, either.'

'Come on, folks. I think we should all go back to the Yard, have a hot lunch and then work out a plan of action,' said Inspector Lovelace, gesturing forwards, trying to take charge. Posie nodded, but Len and Rufus shook their heads in unison.

'I have a lunch date,' Rufus muttered, and turned on his heel. He made a pitiful figure dashing through the rain in his creased clothes, without a coat or hat, a mere sketch of a man. But Posie understood: he had spent more than enough of his time lately at Scotland Yard.

Len shrugged and waved over his shoulder:

'Maybe later? I've got to follow up on something else just now.'

So it was only Posie who walked the ten minutes to Scotland Yard with both Inspectors. They walked in silence and rather awkwardly, negotiating their umbrellas carefully among the crowds on the pavement, where the sudden rain was washing away the ice and snow into soggy grey rivers of unattractive slush. Victoria was busy. It was lunchtime, but even so, and even with the sound of the rain slapping down on the wet pavements, she thought she heard footsteps trailing behind her, just on her tail. Again.

Turning abruptly, she saw a black mass of umbrellas

and dark rain-jackets, and close by she saw the top of a priest's black Biretta hat, sailing hurriedly off to the left somewhere in the crowd. Her heart jumped into her mouth. Was it just a coincidence?

'I say,' she hissed to the Inspectors, 'why was that Catholic priest at the Inquest? Did you invite him specially? I thought he might be a character witness, but he was never called.'

'What priest?' asked Inspector Lovelace, surprised. Oats shook his head.

Posie laughed. 'You couldn't have missed him! He was crunching sweets so loudly I thought the Coroner was going to order him to be quiet.'

'Nope, no idea,' said Inspector Lovelace, ushering her in through the big iron gates, and signalling left towards the staff canteen.

Posie felt a stab of fear. *What exactly was going on?*

Who were all these people who, quite simply, didn't really exist?

* * * *

Thirteen

'The thing I don't like about this whole case is that nothing and no-one is quite what it seems,' said Inspector Lovelace anxiously, frowning and crossing his arms behind his desk.

Posie nodded: it was exactly what she thought. She sat more primly than she might have done otherwise, aware of Inspector Oats, equally uncomfortable beside her, holding onto his weighty black file.

'The victim is not who we thought she was, and we have no real suspects for her murder. Apart from your pal, Rufus. And the entire of the London underworld, that is...'

Rain slashed in angry fingers against the window pane, and although it was only early afternoon the sky was dark purple outside. The office seemed grimmer than usual, and less welcoming. No biscuits were offered today.

'So, then. Any thoughts, either of you? And we'd better come up with something pretty special. I've been informed our jobs are on the line.'

Posie's mind was a blank. She wanted desperately to help Inspector Lovelace but the puzzle wasn't coming together how it was supposed to just yet.

Oats was very quiet, stroking his moustache. Posie glanced at him for a second – she noticed now how his pinstriped suit looked like it needed a good pressing, and there was a spot of what looked like egg yolk on his tie. He looked a mess, and tired too. And now his job was under threat. Surprisingly, Posie felt a stab of pity for him, but then she remembered the way he had treated Rufus so abominably over the last few days, and the way he had loomed up in front of her after Rufus' bail hearing yesterday, when he had told her to keep away from the case, although all she had done was try and help. He really was a useless oaf!

'Could I take a look at your file, please. Inspector?'

Oats darted Posie an incredulous look, before glancing at Inspector Lovelace, who simply nodded. Oats surrendered the file with an ill grace. She ran through it briskly, head bent in the light thrown up by the reading lamp.

It was mainly a well-assembled series of press cuttings and police reports involving the antics of Lucky Lucy Gibson, covering a criminal career reaching back over the last ten years, mainly involving stolen jewels. Inspector Oats had been thorough, Posie had to admit. Every few pages Posie turned, she came face to face with a different photo of the girl; the same coltish eyes staring out at her from a number of different hairstyles, various different disguises. Posie scanned reports of various Mayfair hotel jewel robberies, a spectacular theft of some magnificent yellow diamonds from a royal princess, and lastly, over a year ago now, a stint as a sales girl in a well-known jewellery shop on Bond Street which had culminated in a theft of gemstones on an enormous scale. In each of these crimes the girl had been working under the name the police had come to know her by – Lucy Gibson – and there were even inky copies of official payslips from the Bond Street shop addressed to her in that name. These must have been the payslips the Coroner had been supplied with.

It was evident that Lucy had never been caught, never brought to trial. Pages of initial witness statements were bunched together in one fat envelope from various crimes, but each was ruled through with thick red pen with the words INADMISSIBLE.

'When it came to the crunch, no-one would ever stand up in Court and testify against her,' explained Inspector Oats, reading over Posie's shoulder. 'We think Lucy or the gangsters she worked with intimidated or bribed these witnesses. So we could never get her. We never had an address for her either, to track her down; she just seemed to disappear into thin air.'

'She was a clever girl,' Posie whistled. 'What went wrong this time, I wonder?'

Posie flicked back through the file. 'It looks like she started her life of crime in 1911. She was busy for five years, then she went quiet through the Great War, and she started up again two years ago. Then a year ago it all went quiet again, which is when we now know she started to work at the theatre. Interesting, about her going missing during the war...'

'Why?'

'It's nothing really. I wonder where she went to then, that's all... I would have thought London in the war years was rich pickings for gangsters. Fewer policemen. Less security. Countless aristocrats hiding out here, waiting for peace, carrying their treasures with them. Easy pickings, surely, for a girl like Lucy?'

There was a very short report made on the search at Lionel Le Merle's lodgings the previous day. He had lived in a room in a run-down house in Soho, which he had apparently shared with almost the whole orchestra from the Athenaeum Theatre. The search had yielded no real results: no papers, nothing of value or interest.

'There's no background information on Mr Le Merle?' Posie asked, surprised. 'No history of previous employment? Reports of previous crimes?'

'No,' snapped Inspector Oats, clicking his tongue angrily against the roof of his mouth. 'We haven't found any official records for him. None whatsoever. It's as if he didn't exist either. That's why there was no formal Inquest into his death before now.'

'Perhaps he was just in the wrong place at the wrong time?' ventured Inspector Lovelace.

'Absolutely not,' Posie shook her head insistently. 'They were in on something together. Mr Blake said they joined the theatre at the same time. And why is there no mention in this file of Caspian della Rosa, owner of the theatre?' said Posie in exasperation.

'He's key to this whole case, I'm sure of it. You heard the Forensics Officer at the Inquest. The murderer of Lucky Lucy was in the club last night, shooting around carelessly with the same gun! And we as good as saw Caspian della Rosa; we *heard* him anyway, coming down a corridor following a series of gunshots.'

'That's not evidence!' scoffed Inspector Oats. 'Besides, Count della Rosa was a name I had never heard of until today. He's not known to us here at the Yard; never has been.'

Inspector Oats glowered at Posie, thinking what an annoying little troublemaker she was, and how he would have liked to have given her and her toffee-nosed pals a good hiding.

'Tell me just what kind of unknown criminal can come out of the blue and cause this level of mayhem?'

Posie slammed the file shut, ignoring the pages and pages of carefully typed up evidence against Rufus which made up the last part of the folder.

'I take it that Rufus Cardigeon is no longer a suspect in these investigations?' she asked sweetly.

'Rufus Cardigeon is a suspect for as long as *I* say he is. He's still out on bail, remember? I still have no proof he wasn't up to his neck in the Le Merle murder. Damned unreliable fool. All that twaddle about his stolen gun. What kind of idiot doesn't realise his gun has been nicked?'

Posie stared back at Inspector Oats. He looked cross, and smug too, just like he had after the bail hearing on Tuesday. But what was it he had said to her then, which hadn't made sense at the time but which she had stored up for future reference?

It suddenly became clear to her. Thoughts jumbled together in her mind, a few pieces of the puzzle making sense at last. Blindingly obvious.

'YES!' Posie exclaimed, excitedly. 'I think I may be able to help.' Both Inspectors stared at her, a mixture of hope and wary expectation on their faces.

'It was something *you* told me, Inspector Oats, on Tuesday.'

'What did I tell you?' Oats said gruffly, flustered. He couldn't remember imparting any pearls of wisdom to this stuck-up little madam, especially not about the case.

'You said that "*the beauty of a diamond is in its transport-ability, like drugs*". Do you remember?'

'Um, I may have said that. I don't recall. But, yes, the statement itself is true enough.'

'What's your point, Posie?' insisted Inspector Lovelace gently. 'The *whole* case is important: we can't just focus on that one wretched missing Maharajah diamond, I'm afraid.'

'I'm not talking about one diamond, although it would be lovely to find that particular one, of course,' she shook her head. 'No, I'm talking about *diamonds*. In the plural. Hundreds of the things; thousands of pounds' worth of them. I'm talking about smuggling diamonds! Lucy was an out-and-out jewel thief; she knew her stuff, that much is clear from the file. I think that what we may have blundered into is a wholescale operation of smuggling diamonds in and out of the country! Which is why the *La Luna* club, despite being a hotspot for celebrities, was a useful venue for the gang, as it burrows right under...'

'HATTON GARDEN! Diamond centre of the City of London!' exclaimed Inspector Lovelace, banging his fist down on his desk in glee. 'I wondered if there was some possible link-up.'

He frowned. 'But let's not get ahead of ourselves,' he said, more reservedly now. 'We scoured the main club itself within an inch of its life and we found nothing. And there are hundreds of tunnels and passageways which will take our boys weeks to investigate properly. But so far not so much as a diamond chipping! We've found nothing!'

'No,' said Posie firmly. 'That's not quite true, Inspector; you recovered musical instrument cases. I'll bet you sure as bread is bread that if you give them to Mr Maguire in your forensics team he'll be able to find some miniscule carbon particles which will turn out to be tiny diamond fragments. That's how they're doing this! They smuggle diamonds inside music cases.'

'Who?' said Inspector Oats, sluggishly.

'Members of the Athenaeum Theatre's orchestra, of course!' said Inspector Lovelace, nodding. 'And Posie's right: if this mysterious Count is the owner of the theatre, what's the betting he's ringleader of the gang too? We need to speak to this man. Ask him questions.'

'But the theatre's nothing to do with any of this,' insisted Inspector Oats stubbornly.

'I disagree,' said Posie, shaking her head, 'I think this case has everything to do with the theatre. But it's what happens *offstage* which counts. It's a slick operation. Both of the dead victims were part of it.'

Inspector Lovelace had a fiery glint in his eye, and he nodded excitedly. 'I think you might be right, Posie. We need to move.'

'But *why* were they killed? And by *who*?' asked Inspector Oats, flabbergasted.

'I'm not sure yet. But we'll do our best to find out,' said Inspector Lovelace reassuringly, taking charge.

'Oats, you go and make enquiries among the diamond merchants; find out if anyone will talk about their dealings with Lucky Lucy, or Lionel Le Merle, or even this Caspian della Rosa fellow – perhaps we'll get a lead that way? And also try the theatre, as we should have done already. Search the place. Try and find some incriminating evidence. Search Le Merle's house in Soho again too. I'll interview that fool of a Theatre Manager, Blake, and his right-hand man, the programme-seller, Reggie. They're sitting in the cells downstairs.'

'What shall *I* do?' asked Posie eagerly. 'We need information on Count Caspian and you don't seem to have anything here at Scotland Yard. Can I call the club in St James where I ran into him first? I simply assumed he was living there, but thinking about it now I expect it was a clever mirage to simply give me that impression. But he *must* leave traces somewhere – he's not a ghost.'

Inspector Lovelace shook his head feebly. 'Only authorised police personnel can investigate, I'm afraid, Posie. Sorry. I'll get a couple of my lads on it now though. You can watch my interview with Mr Blake if you like? Through the mirrored-glass screen?'

It was annoying, certainly, and belittling somehow, to be excluded like this, but Posie secretly doubted that the police would be able to find anything on Count Caspian anyway. She suspected he was too clever by half for that. She nodded in resignation:

'Fine. But also make sure your men check the title deeds to the Athenaeum Theatre carefully at the Land Registry, too. Is the Count's name actually on them? Perhaps the deeds will give us some more useful information about him: an address, a bank account, a business partner... something concrete you can follow up on?'

Posie was just about to open her mouth and mention the breaking story in the lunchtime newspaper, her hopes of flushing the Count out in that way when Inspector Lovelace got in first, clapping his hands together and effectively dismissing them both:

'Let's meet again this evening. Reconvene here at six-thirty sharp with our reports.'

Posie picked up her coat from the hatstand, behind which she now saw a faded green-and-brown wall-map of the world. Inspector Oats opened the office door for her, as politely as he could manage, his black file safely stashed under his arm again. He was like a terrier straining at the leash, anxious to be out of the confined space, happy to have some new purpose. But something made Posie stop still.

She reached up to the old map, wiping the dust away from central Europe. She stared at it until it went blurry before her eyes, and then a light went on in her head.

'OF COURSE!' she exclaimed certainly. 'THE KEY IS BELGIUM!'

'What now?' snapped Oats.

'*Belgium*! Isn't Antwerp the diamond capital of the world?'

Both Inspectors nodded, surprised.

'The bullet which was meant to look like it had killed Lucky Lucy came from a Belgian pistol, didn't it? So what if we've been looking at this the wrong way around?'

'What *are* you on about now?' Inspector Oats said, fists clenched in frustration.

'What if the gang are actually all Belgian? Or mostly Belgian?' Posie nodded in excitement, more sure of herself now.

'We know that the theatre players were swapped last year, and almost a whole new orchestra and cast were brought in overnight, including Lucky Lucy. I reckon Count della Rosa took over the theatre as a cover for his smuggling activities, but he was very clever. He only brought in people who were *unconvicted* smugglers, with no complicated records or criminal pasts; "clean" people who would never really be questioned by HM Customs or the Belgian Customs when they were making trips in and out of Belgium concealing diamonds in their music cases!'

'*Why* would they never be questioned? What do you mean by "clean" people?' asked Inspector Lovelace, bemused.

'Because I bet all of the theatre workers are Belgian themselves, carrying totally genuine Belgian paperwork. The reason you can't find anything in the official records *here* about Lionel Le Merle or "Lucy Gibson" is that they were both Belgians! I bet the Belgian police can help you out though. Telephone them! Ask them for anything they have on a violinist who matches Le Merle's description, give them his name too. And send them Lucy's photograph. Maybe they'll be able to tell you her real name?'

A flash of realisation suddenly hit her: perhaps Lucy had been lying to Rufus about almost everything else but Posie was suddenly certain he had known her by her real, Belgian name. She felt stupidly, ridiculously relieved for him. As if it mattered now, anyhow.

'No, even better! Give them the name Georgie le Pomme. That was her real-life name! When she got involved in Count Caspian's high-octane smuggling ring it became important that she had a "clean" record for travelling about the place, so she stopped being famous Lucy Gibson and re-invented herself, reverting to her roots. Rufus said he even saw some official paperwork with that name on it. He didn't recognise it though: perhaps it was a Belgian passport?'

'No,' said Inspector Oats obstinately, shaking his head, 'I don't accept your theory. There's no way Lucky Lucy was ever anything other than full-blown English. In all the years I've been after her, no-one has *ever* reported her as having a froggy-sounding accent. She was the real, British deal.'

'But that's where Count Caspian really scored a hat-trick!' said Posie, her eyes ablaze. 'For in Lucky Lucy Gibson he got a Belgian national who was not only a five-star jewel thief but a first-rate actress as well! It would have been as easy as anything for her to put on a British accent for all these years. Bet my life on it!'

Inspector Lovelace gasped, but his hand was already on the telephone. He covered the mouthpiece, looking up:

'Anything else I should ask the Belgian police?'

'It's a longshot, but you could ask them if they have ever heard of Count della Rosa? It's a shame we don't have a photograph of him to send them, but never mind.'

Inspector Oats fled, shaking his head in disbelief. Inspector Lovelace started to bark instructions at the International Operator in surprisingly immaculate French.

FRENCH! Of course! Posie realised suddenly that most of her tit-bits of information so far had come from good old Dolly, who had been handily listening in to whispers at doors and corners, hearing things people had said indiscreetly in front of her at the theatre. And all because they hadn't realised she understood their common language. But she *did* understand: Dolly had said she spoke fluent French; her mother was French. She would have understood the language of the cast and orchestra without even thinking twice about it, as naturally as breathing. So naturally in fact that she wouldn't have thought to mention it…

Just then there was the tinkle of the tea trolley, a welcome sound. Posie was just wondering what sort of biscuits were regulation fare at Scotland Yard when her heart flipped a beat; she suddenly saw that the tea-lady was also responsible for delivering the afternoon's newspapers.

A fat wad of the lunchtime editions were slapped down roughly on the Inspector's desk. First up on the pile was the *Associated Press*, with its glaring headline, penned by Sam Stubbs:

'LUCKY LUCY DEAD –
KEY SUSPECT IS COUNT DELLA ROSA!'

Inspector Lovelace was just finishing up his conversation with the Belgian police when his eyes caught sight of the upturned newspaper. His face froze, and Posie swore that under his freckles he had turned a pastier than normal white. He flicked his eyes up for a moment at Posie and she read disappointment and confusion there:

'*Oui, oui, merci. J'attends.* I look forward to hearing from you. *Au revoir.*'

She waited, steadfastly, heart thumping – *Would he understand why she had done it?* – when there was an urgent banging at the Inspector's office door.

A bobby put his head around the door and Inspector Lovelace slammed his telephone back in its receiver.

'What?' he snapped at the man with an unaccustomed sharpness.

'You'd better come quick, sir. Two lads are beating each other to a pulp in Reception. One of them's well known to us, guv'nor. It's that young Lord Cardigeon wot spent the last two nights here in our cells! The way he's heading just now he's about to spend another here tonight!'

Rufus?

Posie and Inspector Lovelace clattered to their feet, the newspaper unheeded.

What on earth was happening now?

* * * *

Fourteen

Rufus and Len were glaring at each other across the tiled Reception of Scotland Yard, each man pinned at the arms by a burly officer in uniform, held at opposite sides of the room.

Both had stopped struggling and were giving each other looks of pure hatred. A trickle of blood ran down from Len's nose.

'*LEN?*' snapped Posie in surprise. 'What on earth is going on?'

Her voice echoed around the room loudly and the Duty Sergeant looked up in surprise. A small cluster of people had been waiting patiently in turn on a long wooden bench, each holding a pale orange numbered ticket. They now swivelled around in unison to watch what could potentially be an exciting new development unfurl before them.

Inspector Lovelace sighed and gestured down the corridor to a large interview room, making a sharp zipping motion across his mouth at all of them. When they were settled on hard wooden chairs in a dark room with bars at the window he asked what was happening.

'DOLLY PRICE!' shouted out both Rufus and Len in unison, an edge of panic in their voices, shooting angry glances at each other.

'Hold on. Hold on fellas, one at a time. Rufus first, please.'

Rufus explained in a snivelling wheeze that the previous day he had invited Dolly Price for lunch at Lyons Cornerhouse. Today, at one p.m. sharp. She had seemed eager to come. More than eager, in fact. And then she hadn't turned up.

So he had waited and waited, and got more and more nervous. He hadn't got her home address, but he knew she worked at the theatre, of course. It was nearby.

'So I went there, hoping there was some explanation. But the place is all boarded up: there's a big sign outside for punters saying "SHOW CLOSED TONIGHT". Anyway, I found a way in, and walked around and around the dressing rooms and the Wardrobe Department, but everything was deserted.'

Rufus started coughing and wiped a phlegmy mouth with the back of his shirt sleeve. He had obviously got soaked in the rain several times so far that day, and Posie noticed that his shirt was still damp, sticking to his skin, and a fiery colour was burning in two spots on his otherwise pale cheeks. Posie was concerned: the combined effects of going cold turkey for the last three days with a possible case of bad flu could prove fatal for Rufus.

'So then I really panicked. It felt *wrong*. I knew Posie was here at Scotland Yard; that she might know Dolly's home address. So I headed here as fast as I could. That's when I ran into *him* in Reception, making his wild allegations…' He indicated sharply at Len in distaste. 'You see, I know something's wrong. By jove, it *must* be. Dolly would never have stood me up like that.'

Len hooted with laughter and rolled his eyes. 'How do you know, you fool? You only met her for the first time yesterday! I don't know why you care so much, she's a nasty double-crossing piece of work. You should have learnt your lesson with Lucky Lucy. Fingers burnt and all that. Idiot!

You're unbelievable!'

'Don't you dare make your horrible accusations again in here!' shouted Rufus.

'Is that all?' Inspector Lovelace interrupted. 'Go home, both of you. I've never heard anything so stupid. I've got plenty to do, chaps, so please…'

'You haven't heard me out!' snapped Len in disbelief. 'I didn't just turn up here to brawl with Cardigeon, you know. I've got something to show you. Something I showed Cardigeon in Reception, that's when he went and punched me. It's conclusive evidence!'

With this he brought out something silver and glittery from his trouser pocket. With a flourish he placed it on the interview table between them. Posie gasped and turned it over in her hands:

'It's Dolly's cigarette case! Where on earth did you get this, Len? She never goes anywhere without it!'

Posie snapped it open. It was still half-full of Dolly's thin, black cigarettes.

'She must be in trouble! She's addicted to these! She must have dropped it!' whispered Posie nervously. Len folded his arms:

'I found it at the *La Luna* club. After the Inquest this morning I decided I would go back there, have another nosy around and see what I could find.'

'That was strictly out-of-bounds,' said Inspector Lovelace, outraged. 'It's a police crime scene! My men are still searching it! It should be taped off, secured. There should be uniforms guarding it! How did you get past them?'

'I told the rozzer at the entrance that I was a police photographer. I just waved my camera in his direction and said I'd left my white coat down there; said I needed a couple of last-minute photos. That's the thing with photographers, you see, we can get into most places other people can't… We're almost invisible; almost anonymous.'

Inspector Lovelace waved him on wordlessly, his face set

in an angry line. 'What did you want to find there anyhow?'

It was Len's turn to colour a little. He blushed, and sighed:

'I was looking for something I thought might be down there, something stolen from the Grape Street Bureau, possibly by Lucky Lucy or her gang…or by Dolly Price…'

Inspector Lovelace's eyes had widened. '*What*, exactly? The whole truth, please, Irving.'

'A cat. If you must know. Posie's cat.'

For a long minute there was silence in the room. Len rubbed his eyes wearily. He briefly described the theft of Mr Minks, the arrival of the blue letter with the shaved cat hair that morning.

'Anyway, I didn't find him. I scoured the place back and forth, including the hidden rooms behind the bar. And it was in one of them, kicked under a table near the back, that I found this. Recognised it at once, of course. Wretched silly girl was only flashing it around yesterday under our noses…'

'So what do you think it proves, exactly?'

'Well, Inspector. I'd say it was pretty damning evidence against our girl Dolly. She's in on it with them. Part of the gang. I'd suspected it for a few hours, actually. I said so yesterday to Posie; I said Dolly was a bad hat. But Posie wouldn't believe it. I reckon Dolly works for this della Rosa chappie, stole the cat and also planned to lure us to the nightclub…but we foiled her plan, we got away…'

'But *why*, you noddle!' cried Posie. 'Why would she do that? It doesn't make sense.'

Len shrugged. 'Who knows? But it failed last night. She escaped with the rest of them behind that sliding mirror-thing when they realised they were outnumbered and the game was up. And she dropped this on the way. That's why we haven't seen her since…'

Inspector Lovelace was standing at the barred window, thinking.

'Posie's right, Len,' he said quietly. 'It doesn't make sense. Dolly Price doesn't fit the type of person the Count had working for him. We know more about that now. She wasn't Belgian, a criminal *or* a jewel expert…It makes more sense to me that somehow Dolly's been kidnapped and whisked away by these people. Maybe the cat is not all they're going to blackmail you with. Have they made threats about taking anyone else?'

Posie nodded, hanging her head. She brought out the flimsy blue letter from her handbag.

'There,' she said apologetically, sliding it across the table. 'I didn't realise how serious…'

While Inspector Lovelace read it she had another horrible thought. Something half-forgotten becoming clearer:

'Oh my days! I've just remembered. I heard them talking last night in the club,' she said in a small voice, avoiding Rufus' eye. 'I heard Caspian della Rosa telling his companion that he had the "prize". I think he meant the Maharajah diamond. He went on to say that he had "*an extra little prize*" and that he would "*save it as a reserve*". What if that extra prize was Dolly?'

Inspector Lovelace was nodding warily. 'I think you're right.'

Len was glowering silently but was starting to look panicked, too. Rufus was beyond words. Inspector Lovelace took control: 'Before we assume she's been kidnapped, or start wondering *why*, we'd better just check she's really not at home in bed with a cold or something.'

Everyone nodded, disbelief etched on every face. Inspector Lovelace shouted down the corridor for a policeman to come running.

'So, do you have her address then, Posie? Where does she live? In one of those women-only hostels?' Inspector Lovelace indicated that the ruddy-faced, fat policeman who had appeared should write it down in his black leather fob-book.

'No!' wailed Posie. 'I don't know her address! I only met her for the first time on Monday night!'

She looked up at the barred window in despair, wanting air and light. She hated feeling like she was in a prison.

Then she turned and smiled in relief.

'But YOU have it, Inspector. On police file. Dolly was a suffragette. She told me she had been in prison somewhere in London before the Great War because of it. I know she lives in the same flat now as she did back then. Please hurry. I feel dreadful that I didn't realise she was in danger before.'

* * * *

Fifteen

The waiting seemed to last forever, but it could have been no more than forty minutes in all.

Rufus sat huddled in a blanket, shivering, while Len sat reading the Sam Stubbs piece in the *Associated Press*, over and over again, studiously avoiding looking at anyone. His handsome face was flushed darkly with anger and nerves. You could have cut the atmosphere in the interview room with a knife.

Inspector Lovelace had gone off to interview Mr Blake, and Posie sat watching a cup of grey, insipid tea growing cold on the table before her. She poured another from the thermos flask which had been provided, but it was not much better.

'Good piece this, after all,' Len said begrudgingly, putting the newspaper down at last. He smiled in grim satisfaction. 'The police don't come out of it too well though; it makes it sound like you busted the joint single-handed. Your name, everywhere. Even a big photograph of you, you're not looking too shabby, either… It should have the desired effect, anyway. Should make della Rosa furious, especially if he's innocent. He's definitely going to make contact with you or the police now. Practically names him as the murderer!'

Len drummed his fingers on the table in boredom, echoing the heavy rain outside. Posie wondered how Inspector Lovelace was getting on with Mr Blake and his side-kick Reggie. She remembered Caspian della Rosa saying that they would never talk. She sighed in exasperation.

The clock on the grey-painted wall ticked loudly on. An annoying grating sound.

'Come with me,' she grabbed Len suddenly by the shoulder, jolting him upright. She needed to do *something*. She opened the thick metal door and frogmarched Len along the dark corridor back towards Reception. It was deserted now save for the Duty Sergeant scribbling in his jotter at the counter.

They stood on the porch steps together. It was almost totally dark now outside, pin-points of lights from cars and horse-drawn carriages on the main road behind the wrought-iron fences glittering strangely through the slanting rain.

'What have I done now?' asked Len waspishly, lighting a cigarette under cover of his coat collar and taking a deep drag. His face was half in shadow.

'Nothing. I need you to do something for me. Now. All that waiting around in there is driving me crazy.' She pulled out some change.

'I need you to go and buy two large bottles of Scotch. Nothing fancy, no single malts. Just make sure it's very strong stuff. And bring it back in a brown paper bag. Hidden.'

Len frowned at her, before taking the money and nodding knowingly:

'I understand. For Cardigeon, is it? I thought he'd be better off with a spot of drink inside him too, but I never thought *you'd* be the one to get it for him. That's the trouble with the toffs – they can't do anything without a drop of the old grog. Addicted. Saw it in the trenches time and again.'

Posie said nothing, too tired to argue or explain. Some-times Len could be annoyingly narrow-minded, for all his gorgeousness.

'I'll be back in ten minutes. There's a place I know over at Victoria Station, Moonshine Harry's.' He squeezed her hand, then winked and left.

She watched from the doorframe as Len cut across the rain-swept yard, a jaunty figure disappearing into the darkness who, under normal circumstances, she would have longed to run alongside and accompany, keen not to be parted from.

But these were *not* normal circumstances and he was acting like an oaf, and she was pleased to be rid of him for a few minutes: she had forgotten how much Len hated the upper classes, so perhaps his conflict with Rufus was not so surprising, after all. He reminded her suddenly of Inspector Oats, and she suppressed a laugh: for surely that was one comparison she could never, ever make out loud.

* * * *

Ten minutes later they had the news that Dolly Price had *not* returned home to her bed-sit in Billingsgate market the night before, and had not been seen since.

The fat ruddy-faced policeman looked worried. He flicked through his fob-book for the details:

'Miss Dolly lives alone in a bed-sitter on the top floor. But there's an old woman wot lives in the flat below, above a fish and chip shop. She's a font of all knowledge. She seems to have made it her duty to keep an eye out for Miss Dolly; she said Dolly always came home late at night, on account of her work at the theatre, but in all the years she'd known her, she'd never known her *not* to come home at all. The old woman was on the verge of calling the police herself when I showed up. Most upset she was…'

Posie nodded, but she felt sick to the bottom of her stomach. It seemed certain now that Dolly had been kidnapped, and it was all her fault that Dolly had ended up in this position. An image of the dead, vacant face of Lucky Lucy floated up before her eyes: Posie had to get to Dolly before she ended up like that; discarded like so much rubbish.

But *how*? And where could she possibly be?

* * * *

Rufus was packed off in a taxi to his father's club, with strict instructions to have a hot bath.

Len looked on in surprise when Posie returned to the empty interview room and threw most of the contents of the thermos flask down a ceramic sink in a corner. She deftly unscrewed the two cheap, evil-smelling bottles of whisky which Len had managed to procure at Moonshine Harry's, and she tipped them neat into the empty thermos. She poured the last cold dregs of her cup of tea on top and shook the flask roughly after sealing it up.

Just at that minute Inspector Lovelace put his head around the door:

'I've just heard the news about Dolly. Rotten luck. I'm so sorry. We'll add it to the list of things to do. I'm busy now but I'll see you at six-thirty, as planned?'

His eyes caught the newspaper still lying on the table and he looked towards Posie impatiently:

'I take it you have your reasons for *that*,' he said coldly.

Posie nodded and tried to explain. At his stony silence Posie blundered on: 'Did you have any joy talking to Mr

Blake and the programme-seller?'

'No. Not a dicky-bird out of either of them. Both of them clammed up tight, won't say a word. Absolutely useless.' He ducked out of the doorway.

Posie and Len lingered at Reception.

'Where are the cells please?' Posie asked the Duty Sergeant, smiling. He looked at her suspiciously, before waving her back down the corridor they had come from, indicating to take a sharp left at the bottom and go down a spiral staircase.

The row of cells loomed ahead, ceramic-tiled walls arching above a concrete floor which was damp and sickly with fresh disinfectant. Ten little doors with barred windows stretched along the horrible corridor, all set behind a locked, iron-barred gate. Poor old Rufus had had to stay down here two nights in a row, and Posie felt tears pricking her eyes.

'Now what?' hissed Len anxiously. 'What on earth are you playing at, Po?'

Posie glanced around nervously but as luck would have it the ruddy-faced constable who had just been sent to Billingsgate to look for Dolly Price was coming out of one of the cells at the far end, jangling a big bunch of black keys.

'I say!' shouted Posie sweetly. 'Can you help me?'

The policeman frowned and then came towards them, unlocking the iron gate. He looked at Posie keenly.

'I know Mr Blake, the Theatre Manager. He's down here, isn't he?'

The policeman nodded and indicated to the cell nearest him with a backwards jerk of his thumb.

'Inspector Lovelace said he'd let me give him a flask of tea. It's just the stuff we didn't drink upstairs. Could you possibly…?'

She passed the police regulation thermos flask to the policeman and held her breath. She hoped against hope that he wouldn't open it, or come too close and smell it, but she was lucky: he flicked the small barred window of the nearest cell and shoved the flask through it with a rough warning to the man inside to 'be grateful for small mercies.'

Posie nodded her thanks and turned on her heels and walked as fast as she could out of the police station, Len just behind her. She breathed in big gulps of air outside, pleased to be out at last, more so because she had the feeling she had been skating on particularly thin ice all day long. She heard the chimes of Big Ben coming muffled through the heavy rain.

There were two free hours before she needed to be back again with the Inspectors. And she swore she would use the time well.

****

The offices of the *Associated Press* on Fleet Street were a stark contrast to Scotland Yard. Huge glass windows ran the length of the building from floor to ceiling; in the day-time the building was simply flooded with natural light. It was an art-deco landmark, a stopping-off point for visitors looking at the recent architectural splendours of London.

Inside, the offices were open-plan, all white lacquer and silver metal, and each of the seven floors was visible from the huge entrance hall, glass elevators speeding up and down connecting the floors at what seemed like a giddying speed. Everywhere there was movement; smart young journalists tearing to and fro, beautiful girls wearing thick make-up and high heels trotting endlessly backwards and forwards.

'It's just in here,' Sam Stubbs called out, cheerily. Gone was the nervous manner of the ink-smeared boy they had met last night at Sal's caff, and in his place was a confident, eager-to-please young journalist who felt, quite rightly, that he was at the very beginning of a promising new career. The scoop had obviously worked a treat, and now it was pay-back time.

The Archive Room was on the ground floor, just off Reception, and like the rest of the place it was ultra-modern and brightly lit.

'What are you after exactly?' he asked, head cocked to one side.

'Anything you have on a certain Count della Rosa,' Posie said. She needed to be doing something and having been excluded from the action at Scotland Yard, as she had known would be the case, she felt a relief at being able to get stuck in here.

'No go, I'm afraid, Miss Parker.'

'Sorry?'

'Well, don't you think if there was anything to find I'd have used it myself in the story? A picture tells a thousand words, after all. But I hunted around in here for one and found nothing. No photographs, no old reports. Zip. He's either new in town, your Count, or else he's using a pseudonym. If you find out what his *real* name is, then we're talking. That would be very worthwhile.'

Posie hadn't thought this far ahead. She had expected it to be simpler somehow, that there should be a trace, a mention of him *somewhere*.

'What about Lucky Lucy?' she asked. 'You have files, clippings on *her*, I take it?'

Sam Stubbs grinned and took them over to a white lacquered filing cabinet. 'Plenty,' he said proudly, rolling back a smart modern drawer and bringing out three fat files. 'These should keep you busy for a while.'

Posie and Len spread out the files over a shining white desk.

'We're looking for photos, or any names mentioned in conjunction with hers,' she hissed.

Len nodded and they started to work. The room was silent apart from the swishing noise of their file pages turning, and the very occasional 'snap' as one or the other of them brought out a photo or a cutting and placed it in the middle of the desk. The electric lights hummed quietly and apart from one other reader they were undisturbed.

'Oh, excuse me! Mr Irving?'

It was one of the beautiful, carefully made-up girl assistants. She approached their table with a smile.

'Hullo. I'm Pattie. Sorry to disturb you, sir,' she fawned, 'but it's the telephone for you. Apparently it's quite urgent. Would you like to follow me?'

'A call for me? Here?' Len's eyebrows knitted together in curiosity and Posie watched him follow the girl out. Two minutes later he was back, grabbing his tweed jacket from the back of the chair and stuffing his arms into his raincoat.

'Sorry, Po. It's one of my lawyer clients,' he said crossly. 'I couldn't hear him very well but apparently I've got to go now to take a photo of some Judge with a call-girl. It's a piece of evidence they've been waiting more than a year for, and apparently this evening it couldn't be easier to catch the poor devil at it. I'm sorry.'

He shrugged and swung his camera over his neck. 'It should pay very nicely, anyhow. I should be back at the Yard later, and if not, I'll see you first thing tomorrow at Grape Street.'

Posie nodded and watched him leave, swinging out of the smart glass door. She heaped the tiny pile of photos and cuttings they had collected before her and stared vacantly out of the rain-drenched window for a split-second, before a horrible thought came crashing into her mind: *How on earth could a lawyer client possibly have known where Len would be, at that exact moment?*

Nobody knew they had come here. Unless they had been followed.

Her heart jumped into her mouth and she started to run, breaking out of the Archive Room at high speed and running across Reception, though the revolving doors out onto the dark, wet pavement of Fleet Street outside. Cabs and carts crowded the wide street, and the pavement was chock-full of umbrellas and men in bowler hats crushing through the rain towards the Tube. She looked frantically for Len's tweed homburg hat sailing among the others, but she realised in desperation that she had no idea which way he had gone, or even – as he sometimes did – if he had jumped into a cab.

She had lost him.

Posie stumbled back inside, utterly defeated and on the verge of wild, hysterical tears. She crouched down at her table in the Archive Room and tried to breathe normally.

She was just gathering herself together when Pattie, the immaculate receptionist, came bustling towards her. Pattie was holding a stiff black envelope outstretched in her hands, and she waved it under Posie's nose:

'I say! It's all go for you two, isn't it? This has just arrived for you. A rather ghastly thing, isn't it? It looks like an invitation to a funeral! But you know, black is all the rage just now…maybe it's a party invite?'

Pattie laughed gaily and trooped off, but Posie's heart was hammering hard again, for the silver crescent moon embossed on the outside of the black envelope was unmistakeable.

She forced herself to rip the thing open. She read the typewritten page:

Dear Posie,

You seem very keen on finding me. That article today in the Associated Press was a nice touch, but not very subtle. Perhaps you think I am holding onto some items which you

163

consider valuable? Perhaps I am.

But you won't find me anywhere; however hard you look. Not even here among the newspapers. It is rather I who will find you.

Don't be a nuisance, there's a good girl. If you had taken me up on the offer of my drink, none of this would have been necessary.

CDR

So, he had spies everywhere. Even here; even now. But where? Was he watching her right this very minute?

And what about Len? Had he now been kidnapped too? She thought with a quick dash of surprising comfort about the service revolver Len carried with him everywhere, and how he had never failed her yet.

Heart racing, she looked around the Archive Room quickly and bundled up the photos and press cuttings into her bag, desperate to be gone.

How dare you play games with me, wherever you are, she felt like shouting aloud. *How dare you steal my cat, and my friends.* For wasn't that horrible black note surely an admission of exactly that?

And then came a surprisingly clear voice in her head, countering her fear: *I will find you.*

I will find a trace of you somewhere and I will bring you down.

* * * *

Back at Grape Street, Babe was just tidying her desk, turning the lights off and jangling her office keys in readiness for leaving. She looked up like a startled rabbit as Posie burst through the front door. All venomous thoughts of Babe had evaporated, and truth be told, Mr Minks was now the very last thing on Posie's mind.

'Gee, I was just leaving, Miss. Say, anything I can do for you?'

'Tell me, Babe. Has anyone been in touch today for me or Mr Irving? Any messages?'

Babe shook her head slowly, 'Not a soul all day. Sure has been quiet here without y'all.'

'Nothing from a lawyer who wanted Mr Irving to take photos for him?'

Again the shake of the head.

'Fine, you can go.'

Posie had half an hour to spare before she needed to leave again for Scotland Yard. To calm her shredded nerves she spread out the cuttings from the *Associated Press* on her desk, sieving the stuff frantically.

Most of it was useless, the same articles Inspector Oats had already gathered together in his file. She tossed aside photos she had seen before, rummaged through clippings she had already read. She placed them all in a big brown envelope ready to send back to the newspaper. Only one item remained.

It was a short story, no more than a paragraph really; original copy from 1915. It mentioned a counterfeiting squad who had flooded London with fake pound notes in the summer of that year, then disappeared without a trace. Lucky Lucy was mentioned as having used a fake pound note herself in an upmarket hat shop on Regent Street. When caught and questioned she had professed no knowledge of the forgery, and before any serious charges could be brought against her, she had promptly disappeared.

What was really interesting about the scrappy little piece, however, was not the story itself, but a single line in it from a character reference for Lucy, a local man who was quoted as saying, '*I can't believe it of her, and I won't believe it either. We've been neighbours these last few years and a nicer, bonnier girl you couldn't hope to meet.'*

On the back of the newspaper cutting were a few of the journalist's original pencilled notes. Posie managed to read:

Source: Harold Sharp – 9, Winstanley Mews, SW3.

Posie had no idea if it was important or not.

The story sounded too fantastic to be true; probably invented for the empty summer-season when there was little in the way of news that year, except for the horrors of the Great War.

But she told herself it couldn't hurt to chuck it in her bag, maybe check it out later.

She left the safety of her office again with a decidedly heavy heart, wondering what fresh surprises the night would bring.

* * * *

Sixteen

Both of the Inspectors looked happy in their own ways. Inspector Oats was practically rubbing his hands together in glee, desperate to share his news. With a good grace Inspector Lovelace indicated he should, indeed, go first.

'Lots has happened, let me tell you,' Inspector Oats smiled at both of them.

He explained that the trawl through the diamond sellers of Hatton Garden had been fruitless as most of them were top-notch and all above board. But then Sergeant Rainbird had had a breakthrough: he had reported that one of the shop owners, a Mr Ronald Eames, was acting 'mighty fishy' when questioned about his possible links to diamond smuggling. With no evidence to charge him, he had left Mr Eames to sweat it out for a bit. But Oats and Rainbird had returned fifteen minutes later, by the back entrance to the shop, with a full escort of uniformed policemen.

'And what do you think we found?' Inspector Oats asked, his eyes boggling. He thumped his fist on the table, grinning.

'We found Eames going down a trapdoor hidden in a tiny cupboard, carrying envelopes stuffed full of uncut diamonds and other suspect jewels, probably all stolen. No paperwork for any of it, of course! And where do you think the ruddy trapdoor led to?' His eyes glinted with triumph.

'Somewhere inside the *La Luna* club?' said Posie, certainly.

'Ay, that's right,' Inspector Oats said sniffily, some of his thunder stolen at the wrong moment. 'It turns out there are even more wretched little tunnels running under that place than we first thought…all cleverly hidden…the place is like a beehive. So Eames is sitting in a cell here, but so far he won't talk. Won't give us any names or addresses. I've even promised him a degree of leniency in his own sentencing if he testifies against anyone in Lucky Lucy's gang, or anyone else involved in this malarkey. We know there must be more.'

He went on:

'I went on to the theatre next. It was closed up, but I found some of the orchestra sitting in their so-called Green Room, looking mighty worried, all talking froggy-froggy to each other. You were right; most of them are Belgians. I asked if any of them had been at the *La Luna* club the night before, or if anyone could give me details about the owner of the theatre. Needless to say, they all clammed up. So I arrested them all.'

'What? *All* of them?' asked Inspector Lovelace, eyebrow raised. 'On what grounds? Being Belgian?'

'Withholding evidence,' said Inspector Oats, smugly. 'And those who had passports with them have surrendered them. All Belgian. Our immigration boys here are going through them now, checking dates of entry in and out of the country, comparing them with known jewel thefts both here and in Belgium. We should be able to liaise with the Belgian police about that.'

'You have been busy,' Posie said cleverly. 'And did you find anything interesting, apart from the orchestra, at the theatre itself?' She was thinking of Dolly Price and Mr Minks, and quite possibly Len now too: it had occurred to her that the theatre, with its countless hidey-holes, could be a perfect place to hide kidnapped victims.

'Not a sausage. Not a diamond either. We stripped the place clean. I tell you what though,' Inspector Oats tapped his nose confidentially. 'Your Theatre Manager Mr Blake is a bit of a secret drinker by the look of things. I've never seen so many empty bottles in one place!'

'Anything else to report?' said Inspector Lovelace efficiently.

'I'll say!'

Inspector Oats had saved the best for last.

Tasked with raiding the Soho house where Lionel Le Merle had lived, the Inspector and some uniformed bobbies had surprised the few residents who hadn't been moping around at the theatre. A tall, shabby townhouse in a seedy dark street, it had been rented for almost a year as a place to billet the theatre staff in. Twenty-odd tiny cramped rooms identical to that of Lionel Le Merle were searched, yielding up nothing but some personal effects and the odd Belgian passport. Nothing untoward.

It was as the police were leaving the Soho house that Inspector Oats had struck gold: he had noticed one of the men who lived in the house lingering in the hallway, glancing nervously backwards and downwards, as if fearful that some great secret was about to be uncovered.

'So what do you know?' Inspector Oats nodded, 'I ordered my men to re-search the whole ground floor; tear up the carpets if they had to, pull off all the pictures on the walls. And that's when we got lucky!'

Underneath a long mirror, one of the policemen had uncovered a hidden door, cut into the wall, cleverly concealed. Once opened, it revealed steps down to a cellar which, when investigated, had thrown up a few surprises all of its own.

'Not diamonds. Not guns. Not drugs. But what do you think?' Posie was just starting to guess but she didn't want to make the same mistake as last time and pre-empt the

Inspector. She shook her head dumbly.

'Long tables set up, with specialist inks and papers, and a great big printing press in one corner of the room. They'd been careful not to leave anything too incriminating lying around, but any idiot could see we'd stumbled into a forger's paradise. An illegal racket making fake money! I've no actual proof, of course, because they were careful not to leave any of the printed money at the scene; they must distribute it out from somewhere else. But I seized what I could and arrested everyone in that house too. I'll watch them squirm for a bit and see if they come up with some details for me.'

Inspector Oats was looking happier than Posie had ever seen him. She hesitated a second before opening her bag and planting the small ancient clipping from the *Associated Press* on the table.

'Oh my gawd!' gasped Inspector Oats. 'It's been going on since 1915?'

'I don't know for sure, but one of the people who could have told you was Lucky Lucy herself. She was definitely in on this. Do you remember what the Pathologist said at the Inquest – that she had callouses on her hand typically associated with writing, or printing? *A surprising amount for an actress*, he said. I bet sure as bread is bread that they were the result of printing fake notes! She was heavily involved in all of this stuff, poor girl.'

'Goodness! It's quite a racket we're uncovering here. Diamonds *and* money! Bigger than we first thought: this should please the Commissioner,' said Inspector Lovelace calmly. He pulled a list towards him. He was rather a fan of lists.

'What about *your* news?' Posie asked. The Inspector shrugged:

'Bad news first. We'll have to wait until tomorrow for the information from the Land Registry about *whose* name and information is on the lease of the theatre. And our lads have been around to No 11, St James but no joy; the management there swears they have never *heard* of a Count della Rosa, let alone having him as a member on their books.'

He continued more happily. 'But everything else has been very promising. Forensics confirmed that there *are* minute traces of diamond carbon in one of the music cases we seized, so that's a relief. Even better, the Belgian police have come up trumps: they have confirmed Lionel Le Merle as being a Belgian national, not known as having any criminal record. They have also confirmed that Georgie le Pomme was a Belgian national too, without any criminal convictions to her name, but with a decidedly racy past by all accounts!'

'Oh?'

'They have her listed as a worker at the Belgian Mint; she trained there as an apprentice from an early age. But her real love was for the theatre. She took spells as a job-bing actress in Brussels, at a number of different theatres over the years.'

'That all fits,' nodded Posie excitedly. 'So she must have found forging bank notes very easy!'

'And that's not the best of it!' laughed Inspector Love-lace, reading a police telegram. 'I found out what she was doing when she left England during the Great War. In fact, she was working for the Belgian government, of sorts!'

'Don't tell me; she was a spy?' bellowed Inspector Oats in disbelief.

'No. Even more ludicrous! She was paid by them to entertain the Belgian troops in the trenches! She was part of some fancy shindig which was basically a magician and a couple of assistants. She was one of the assistants. Very popular by all accounts, too. Can you believe it?'

Both Posie and Inspector Oats shook their heads.

'But there was something fishy there too. Apparently, although nothing was ever proven, this group of entertainers were suspected of arms-dealing. Stealing their own government's weapons and selling them to the Germans. But as I said, nothing was ever proved for certain, although the Belgian Commissioner is practically willing to bet his life that they were double-dealing and the magician's troupe was just a front. Which would make them traitors.'

Inspector Lovelace clumped his telegrams together.

'In fact, the Belgian Commissioner tells me he even has a glossy press-photo of this Georgie le Pomme as part of the magician's troupe. I'm certain it's the same girl, Lucky Lucy. He sent it out today. It will arrive first thing tomorrow.'

Inspector Lovelace went on to confirm that the Belgian police had expressed regret that the bullets from the Belgian revolver could never be traced, and that they had, as Posie had suspected, never heard of a Caspian della Rosa.

Inspector Lovelace sighed:

'Let's look on the bright side anyway. At least now we can provide the Coroner with the correct names for two otherwise unidentified bodies in the morgue. But I agree, it's frustrating about della Rosa. We really need a break… everywhere we look draws a blank.'

'He knows it too,' said Posie, biting her lip in annoyance. She produced the horrible black letter she had received earlier in the evening and thrust it forwards for them both to read, explaining her fears about Len's disappearance too.

'I don't like it,' said Inspector Lovelace, shaking his head.

'This fellow seems to have a good grasp of your movements; it seems as if he's got people on your tail at all times. And I can't work out why he cares so much, either; why harangue *you* so much? From tonight you're going to have a police escort home, Posie. No arguments. In fact, I'd prefer it if you would stay at home tomorrow. I'll leave a bobby with you outside your house all day long. I think it's safer.'

Posie exploded with rage:

'Do you really expect me to sit at home and wait while there's a cold-blooded murderer on the loose? Whoever it is has killed once already and has now taken my friend, and quite possibly my cat, and even Len! You wouldn't have got half as far in this case without my help, and now you're threatening to keep me locked up at home!'

Inspector Lovelace did his best to calm her down, muttering soothing noises and telling her how grateful they were.

'Of course I can't force you to stay at home,' he said, with the remnants of a worried frown on his face. 'It's just that we seem to be dealing with a dreadful and clever enemy here, or *enemies*. I wouldn't want you hurt, but it's up to you how you act, of course. And don't worry about Len; he's a big boy, he can take care of himself. Right, let's call it a night for now. Pick up again tomorrow. And don't think I've forgotten Dolly Price, or your, er, cat. We've put out descriptions across London. It's a priority, I assure you.'

Just then there was a loud persistent banging sound and the floor seemed to shake a little. Then came shouting and screaming.

'What on earth?' asked Inspector Oats, stupefied. He looked at the clock. It was almost eight o'clock and the station should have been sleepily shutting down for the nightshift right about now. The ruddy-faced policeman from earlier put his head around the door and grimaced apologetically.

'Sorry guv'nor. I've got some trouble down in the cells. Apart from the awful overcrowding, that is,' and here he flashed a look of pure malice at Inspector Oats.

Turning back to Inspector Lovelace he went on:

'That man Blake, the Theatre Manager. I don't know how it's happened, sir, but somehow he's blind drunk. He's asking for you. Wants to talk. You'd better come quick.'

* * * *

Seventeen

'What do you want, Blake? Make it snappy.'

Posie was observing from a side-room, through a two-way mirror. Oats had gone for the night.

Two uniformed bobbies stood sentry at the door of the interview room, and Mr Blake was sitting upright with some difficulty on one of the regulation hard wooden chairs. His green velvet jacket looked crushed and soiled, and there were horrible-looking stains over his white dress-shirt.

'What's in it for me?' he slurred, clutching at the table to steady himself.

His face looked sweatier and paler than the last time Posie had seen him, and it occurred to her that Mr Blake must be very, very drunk indeed. Even by his standards. She grinned: the moonshine Len had bought had obviously done the trick.

Inspector Lovelace sighed. He was not a man to enter into bargains, and he did things by the book. 'Nothing is in this for you, I'm afraid, apart from the knowledge that you are being a good, law-abiding citizen. Helping the police with their enquiries.'

Mr Blake squinted at him. He was having trouble focusing.

'I still don't understand why I'm here. What have I done exactly? What grounds have you arrested me on? I've been here almost twenty-four hours!'

Without knowing it, Mr Blake was asking a very good question. Posie felt Inspector Lovelace's unease. By law he only had another twelve hours to hold Mr Blake in custody, unless he charged Blake with something concrete. And there was nothing really to charge him with, so he was probably going to have to let him walk free. Inspector Lovelace remained calm, however, crossing his arms authoritatively:

'*Withholding evidence.* That's the official charge, anyway. But it doesn't look good for you, Blake, let me tell you. We picked you up at the *La Luna* club last night, where the body of one of your theatre employees was found murdered, and another employee was murdered only two days ago in strange circumstances. How do I know you're not somehow responsible for both murders? I'm looking into it now, investigating the evidence. Chances are you'll hang for this, Blake. I've got another missing girl on the cards as well – your Wardrobe Mistress, Dolly Price – remember her? If she turns up murdered too it's likely going to be the final nail in your coffin.'

'Murder?' yelped Blake, swaying slightly, growing visibly paler, if that were possible. 'Hanging? But I had nothing to do with Georgie's death, I swear it. First I knew of it was last night, on the way here in the police van. And as for Le Merle...that was damned inconvenient, let me tell you, when he went missing. Nearly had to shut the theatre down that night. It was awful! That would have been a real failure. I love that place...'

'Well, it's closed down now all right. Dead as a dodo. I've got most of your employees sitting here in the cells. So there won't be any shows on at the Athenaeum Theatre for quite some time.'

At this news Blake gasped, his face genuinely grief-stricken. Inspector Lovelace got up to go, gathering his hat and umbrella together. 'Well, if that's it? I'll be off.'

'No, no. Wait. I'll help you. But I'm no murderer. Not really much of a Theatre Manager really. What is it you want to know exactly?'

Inspector Lovelace sat down again heavily. He nodded, and pretended to consult a list in his fob-book.

'Now you're talking sense. We already know about the international diamond smuggling ring, and the counterfeit money production…' The Inspector said all of this in a blasé manner, ticking it off his imaginary list. Posie watched as Blake's jaw literally dropped open.

'So there's probably not much you can add. Or is there?'

Blake spread his hands in front of him as if to ward off traffic, and started gabbling fast:

'I swear, Inspector, I had nothing to do with any of *that* malarkey. I'm just a regular London lad, I never got mixed up in planning any of that caboodle, nor my cousin Reggie, either. It was always my fancy to run a theatre, and it seemed my dream came true at last, last year…when I was given the chance…'

'How did you meet your employer? Count della Rosa, isn't it?'

The very name seemed to change the atmosphere in the room, and Posie saw Blake nervously licking his lips. He nodded.

'I met him at a casino, I forget which one now. Somewhere in Holborn, I think. I'd been down on my luck all night and I'd lost all I had. I owed a pretty penny. I'd been hitting the sauce badly too. I was in a terrible state when the Count turned up, seemingly out of nowhere. He paid off all my gambling debts in one go and bought me a drink. He said he had a proposition for me.'

'Go on.'

'He seemed to know all about me; about my cousin Reggie too. Reggie had debts n'all. It was almost spooky, you know? As if he'd been following me, watching me. I learnt later that's what he's best at, knowing things about people: finding your weaknesses, knowing your secrets.'

Posie felt cold all over.

'He said he knew I loved the theatre. He told me he'd just acquired the lease on the Athenaeum Theatre in Piccadilly, and he needed a nice solid English Manager and a Manager's Assistant to run it for him. He said it would be a piece of cake. Almost the whole lot of them were coming from abroad; *the best of the best*, he said. Crème de la crème, he said.'

'That must have sounded tempting,' remarked the Inspector soothingly, privately thinking how naïve Mr Blake must be.

'It was. A great fat salary would be paid to me and only a couple of last-minute things needed to be sorted out; a new Wardrobe Mistress was needed and a couple of fresh stage-hands, too. Nothing I couldn't sort out in a trice. So I accepted willingly.'

'And it was all it was cracked up to be?' asked the Inspector in a friendly manner.

'At first,' nodded Blake. 'But after a while I realised it was fishy as hell. Nothing was what it seemed. The theatre was just a way to keep his gang working together legitimately in London. I mean, who's going to question a bunch of foreign dancers and musicians if they come and go sometimes? And the whole lot of them were scared of the Count. I noticed people looked in terror at him out of the corner of their eyes whenever he came past. That's when I realised he must have *something* on everybody there, that everybody there owed him in some way, people with shady pasts... I'm not saying he was blackmailing them, but he got his pound of flesh...'

'You mean at the *La Luna* club?'

Blake nodded. 'It met at his say-so, usually once a month when there was absolutely no moon. It was his little joke:

the *La Luna* club didn't really exist, legally or publicly; so it could only run on nights when the real moon didn't exist, either. He had people, spies, stretched all across London, telling people to come at the right time; celebrities, famous people, fashionable young folk. It was amazing. But it was all a cover for the diamond merchants he knew, to come and go and make their selection of whatever he had brought in that month.'

'A risky business, I'd say,' remarked the Inspector drily.

'Yes,' nodded Blake in agreement. 'But the Count told me it was part and parcel of my duties at the Athenaeum. I just helped out, transport and the like…acting as a sort of glorified bouncer. A caretaker, if you will. I wasn't in a position to argue.'

The Inspector changed tack. 'What about Lionel Le Merle and Lucky Lucy, sorry, *Georgie le Pomme*…what was the deal there? Did they know each other well?'

'They were thick as thieves. Boon travel companions. The theatre was closed once a week on a Sunday, and that's when they would take off together, go on a little jaunt to Antwerp. They were both from somewhere out there originally, by all accounts. I'd know they'd been away together because they'd bring back these little foreign cakes and share them out on the Monday night, and that's also when the Count was at his happiest…they were his best pair of runners, you see? I thought it was drugs at first; I only found out about the diamonds later.'

'Were they involved romantically?' asked Inspector Lovelace.

Blake roared with laughter. 'Not on your nelly!'

He grinned. 'Lionel Le Merle was old enough to be Georgie's father, her grandfather even! And I think that was the secret to their success: they hammed it up for the customs officers, pretending to be a father-and-daughter theatrical pair. Besides, the Count wouldn't have let anyone come between himself and Georgie. She was *his*.'

'What do you mean?' Posie watched as the Inspector seemed to tense up, every nerve and muscle twitching.

'Georgie and the Count were an item. Lovers. Crazy about each other, they were. Inseparable. Not married as far as I know, but as good as. The Count was jealous if someone even so much as looked at Georgie twice over. Obsessed.'

'So he can't have thought much of her running off with Lord Cardigeon to the Ritz Hotel then, can he?' the Inspector said, shrewdly. 'Maybe that was the motive for her murder? Pure and simple jealousy?'

Blake shrugged.

'I can't help you with what he felt, Inspector. But I *can* tell you that the stealing of the black diamond from Lord Cardigeon was the Count's idea, and it was very much pre-arranged. From what I understand, the Count knew it was locked away in a safe somewhere by the Cardigeon family, untouched.Well, one night he got to drinking in a pub with some young fellows (as I said, he makes it his business to find out about a person, their habits and such like) and they just happened to be some of Lord Cardigeon's friends.'

'Go on.'

'A simple story. He offered them a wad of money if they'd give young Cardigeon a pair of tickets to the show at the theatre the next night. And he set up Georgie le Pomme to be the bait. He knew it was a certainty that the young Lord would go crazy for Georgie. Every man lost his heart over that gal soon as he set eyes on her.'

'You're telling me she was a deliberate honey-trap?'

Blake nodded. 'That's about right. I was told she'd be away from the theatre for a couple of weeks and to organise another dancer in her place. I suppose they thought that two weeks was long enough for her to get hold of that black diamond.'

Posie sagged a little at the window and sat down in

a chair. She had always felt sorry for Rufus in all of this, but the pre-meditation behind the scale of the thing was unbelievable. In her mind she was drawn back to the folder of cuttings Inspector Oats had shown her earlier today, the many schemes and deceptions the girl had been involved in over the years, and she found herself asking the same question she had earlier: *For such a clever girl, what had gone wrong this time?*

'So, what happened?' asked Inspector Lovelace, voicing her own thoughts.

Blake shrugged. 'I'm not sure. I guess her time was up. She just needed to make her escape from the young Lord and bring the gemstone back to the Count.'

'But something went wrong?'

'I don't know. I wasn't told anything. It must have gone wrong. I'm guessing Le Merle, her old travelling companion, was sent in to find her, to remind her of their usual arrangement; their team-work, the need to come back to the Count. But something had changed for Georgie. Perhaps she had decided to strike out on her own at last? Perhaps Le Merle just got in her way...so she shot him. Of course, that's just what *I* think.'

Inspector Lovelace was noting all of this down, nodding and grimacing all the while.

Posie felt a sense of relief. At last the threads of the story were coming together, and Rufus would soon be proved to have nothing whatsoever to do with this ridiculous crime. But the relief was tempered by the knowledge that although Mr Blake's opinions were useful, and probable, they weren't exactly going to be admissible as evidence in Court.

She was aware of the Inspector's voice continuing in the interview room, but her thoughts were drifting miles away, in a frantic colourful blur of images. Could it be that a hardened, seasoned professional like Lucky Lucy had fallen victim to the famous charms (or curse) of the

Maharajah diamond? Had *she too* wanted to possess it all for herself?

'Who do you think killed the girl? If she double-crossed the Count, and she was found dead in his nightclub, it would seem he is the main suspect. Agree?'

Mr Blake shook his head resolutely.

'Not on your life. He'd never have killed that girl. Not in a million years. He loved her too much. Look somewhere else. He's not your man.'

The Inspector noted this down.

'One last thing, Mr Blake. Your employer is proving a devil to track down. Can you help me at all?'

Blake shook his head, his blood-shot eyes blinking furiously to stay awake.

'Sorry Inspector. He's a man of mystery. Likes to keep it that way. I only really saw him at the theatre and in the *La Luna*.'

Inspector Lovelace was leaving the interview room.

'I say,' Posie heard Blake saying, calling out after the Inspector hopefully.

'Have you got any more of whatever was in that thermos flask? It was jolly good.'

* * * *

181

Thursday 17th February, 1921

Eighteen

Looking back later, Posie would not be able to put her finger on the reason *why* she had woken up so confoundedly early. All she could say was that she was aware of some clear and present danger close at hand.

The pearly grey morning light was stealing into her bed-sitting room. There was no sound at all, and the silence was extraordinary. Posie reached for her bedside clock, whose luminous hands showed it was just before six o'clock. Getting up, she felt a horrible trepidation take over her, and something propelled her over to the window, compelled her to pull back the thin gingham curtains and look out at the dawn.

Nightingale Mews was empty, and misty puffs of frozen white fog were floating eerily past in clumps. The street lamp directly opposite her window was still on, flickering slightly. And then, through the tatters of swirling mist, just a few feet away from her across the cobblestones, she saw clearly what she had feared since the case had started: she was being watched.

A man, stationary under the lamplight, was carefully observing her.

Posie gulped as the mist encircled him. It wasn't her police escort from the night before, of that she was sure.

He had escorted her home and then left again: keeping watch over her from dawn onwards was not in his brief.

The man became clear for an instant again: an unfamiliar figure with a black bowler hat pulled down low to cover his face, a black overcoat, shining black shoes and then…

…what on earth was that?

Posie leant in as close as she could. Something small was pulling on a lead, a bright red lead, attached to the man's black-gloved hand. It was a small dog, more like a rat really, the sort fashionable women bought to carry in their purses when they didn't get enough attention from their husbands. It was straining hard at the red lead, prancing on its tip-toes. As if it were unused to being trapped in such a fashion…

Then she saw it clearly for a second and her heart missed a beat: it was unmistakeably Mr Minks! On a lead! With some terrible captor!

Without thinking she grabbed her coat and flung it over the top of her thick flannelette pyjamas, cramming her feet into her slippers. She hurled herself out of the room, down the stairs and through the front door…out into the cobbled street and the icy dawn fog. The cold hit her like a physical blow and she reeled, teeth chattering, looking frantically this way and that. But the man in black and Mr Minks had gone.

One end of Nightingale Mews was a dead end, so Posie automatically turned left, running as fast as she could in her slippers over the icy cobbles, out under the stone arch of the Mews entrance. She ran onto the busy Cromwell Road, with its sweep of grand museums and its busy parade of shops and cafés crammed tightly together along the pavement.

'Bring him back, you coward!'

Posie was screaming hoarsely into the frozen air, but fortunately nothing was yet open, and no-one saw her scurrying along like a madwoman, shouting wildly at someone who might or might not have been ahead of her there in the mist.

Out of breath, her slippers sodden through and her bare feet freezing, Posie came to a halt opposite the grey turrety splendour of the Victoria & Albert Museum. She bent doubled-up by a street lamp, trying to get her breath back, half-sobbing, half-panting, struck by the sheer uselessness of it all.

She turned homewards with a heavy heart, so she could begin her day over for the second time, aware that finding Mr Minks was only the very tip of what seemed like a great, dark, insurmountable iceberg.

* * * *

It was extravagant in the extreme, she knew, but she didn't care. Posie ran the chipped enamel bath with the lion's paw feet almost to the brim with hot water and poured in a whole packet of floral bath salts from Harrods.

As she lay back soaking in the delicious perfumed water, thawing her feet out, trying to stop shivering, trying to calm herself down, she heard Mrs Rapier, her landlady, out on the landing, making snide remarks about how *some people* were incredibly selfish and had no manners, using up all the hot water, and *how early* it was in the morning too to have a bath – the pipes clanking had fair woken her up – and it was not yet six-thirty! Posie ducked her head under the water, drowning out the bleats and moans.

Dressing carefully and warmly in many layers, Posie left the house as quickly as possible so as to avoid Mrs Rapier and her further catty remarks. She pulled the front door behind her as quietly as possible and set off. Surprisingly, given the butterflies in her stomach which refused to go away, Posie found she was starving.

She bought herself a hot-buttered bacon roll at the corner of Brompton Cross before boarding an almost empty bus trundling towards Victoria. Eating hungrily, she watched the sky lighten above her to an arc of pale streaky blue, rippled through with a strange golden-bronze sunlight. She watched London coming to life all around her, fascinated as ever by the hundreds and thousands of different lives and stories being played out as she sped along, each and every one with a different outcome. Posie crumpled her greasy napkin.

What would be the outcome of *her* day? Everything seemed to be spiralling horribly out of control.

The chimes of Big Ben at Westminster could be heard as they swerved past Buckingham Palace.

It was just gone seven o'clock.

****

Scotland Yard was very quiet, just stirring into life, and Posie was informed that Inspector Lovelace was not yet in.

Posie ignored the sleepy-eyed policeman in Reception, keen to be off his long night-shift, who called uselessly for her to stop as she barged on down the dark corridors in the direction of the Inspector's office. She was relieved to find Sergeant Rainbird was already in, bustling about with a mug in his hand. He simply nodded at her as if he had somehow expected her to appear, as if it were nothing out of the ordinary.

'What's new? Any progress?' she asked.

He shook his head in response and propped himself against the Inspector's desk in a nonchalant manner. He started rifling through the wire basket on the edge of the desk, marked 'INCOMING MAIL'. There seemed to be nothing of any importance there, just paper flyers; coupons and police circulars and the like.

A smartly dressed police post-boy popped his head around the door.

'Word from Inspector Lovelace. He's running late. Held up in a meeting with the Commissioner. Inspector Oats, too. You're to open the morning mail.'

Rainbird looked delighted and seized upon the thick package of papers the post-boy handed over and started ripping the envelopes open. Posie held her breath; there was something she was after in particular, but Rainbird was frustratingly heaping the opened mail all together, as if according it equal importance. He was about halfway through when he looked up at Posie suddenly.

'What you after exactly, Miss? Tell me. Put us both out of our misery.'

'Information from the Land Registry.' She smiled encouragingly. 'Please?'

Rainbird scowled, flipping through the remaining unopened papers. He passed her an envelope bearing an official-looking embossed seal. She pulled out the flimsy pink paper it contained.

'And?'

It was short. She read aloud:

LEASE GRANTED

Property: Athenaeum Theatre, Piccadilly, London.
Lessee: Poulet Productions Limited.
(Care of: *CC*, No 11, St James, Pall Mall, London.)

'Poulet Productions?' echoed Sergeant Rainbird in mixed tones of incredulity and wonder. '*What on earth*? Who are they? I thought we were expecting this Count chappie to be on the paperwork? Doesn't everyone refer to him as the owner of the place?'

Posie nodded. She chewed her lip thoughtfully and sat down on the chair nearest the desk. Silence hung uncomfortably between them.

'Does the Count really exist?' asked Rainbird bluntly after a long pause.

'Oh, he exists all right. It's just he's very careful, that's all. We'll be lucky if we find his name on a single piece of paper in the whole of London. He wraps himself up in layers and layers of protection so no-one can get at him. And *this…*' Posie waved the pink paper to make her point, '…proves just how careful he is. But he's not as clever as he thinks he is. Look at the contact address! He's let himself down there.'

Rainbird rubbed his chin thoughtfully.

'But our lads have been to No 11, St James already. It was a dead end.'

'Well,' said Posie insistently, 'You're forgetting *I* saw him there myself; mincing about as if he owned the place. There *must* be a link.'

She jabbed at the pink paper. 'But just who or what exactly is this "*CC*" referred to in the contact address? Could it be *C*ount *C*aspian?'

She held it accusingly under Rainbird's nose, as if he should know the answer. He shrugged and tipped the last of the opened letters into the wire basket for Inspector Lovelace's attention later. 'Beats me…'

'Only one thing for it, Sergeant. We'll have to get over to No 11, St James again and ask them about Poulet Productions, and just who this "*CC*" really is.'

She folded the pink paper decisively in half and put it in her carpet bag.

It was then that she looked over to the wire basket, now full to bursting with the morning's mail.

Something shiny caught her eye, poking out from beneath the various papers. It was the edge of a press-photo.

'Oh, I say! That must be the photo in from the Belgian police! Can I take a look…?' But Posie didn't wait for Rainbird's answer and pulled the photograph carefully free.

She angled the green-glassed reading lamp onto it and then gasped aloud.

'What is it, Miss?'

Posie was staring at the photo, dumbfounded.

'I said, what is it, Miss?'

She came back to earth with a bang.

'Finally we might have a break; finally, he's been caught out. On camera. Look at this! It's going to help us.'

* * * *

Nineteen

'GOT YOU!'

The photograph was large and very clear. In the bottom right corner was an inscription:

France, 1915

The focus of the picture was undoubtedly the glamorous couple at the very centre of it, drawing the eye instinctively; Lucky Lucy and Count della Rosa.

But it was actually a group photo, and there were at least three other people in the shot standing in the same line: one short man holding a ventriloquist's dummy, another tall man with an accordion, and a very fat woman with an armful of doves. They melted away into the background through no fault of their own other than not being beautiful.

Lucy wore a white ballgown with a matching feather boa, and the Count looked exactly as Posie had remembered him from Monday night: dashing, ridiculously handsome, but with something slightly menacing about his manner. He wore a black tuxedo and was grinning from ear to ear. His right arm was outstretched and he held up a squirming white rabbit to the camera. In the other hand he was balancing a wand and a black top hat. He looked as if he was enjoying himself immensely. Lucky Lucy was wrapped coyly around his waist, basking in his limelight.

Rainbird came over, taking the snap from Posie. 'So this is him then, eh? The famous invisible Count?'

Posie nodded grimly.

'Mr Blake the Theatre Manager told us that those two were lovers, but what I *didn't* realise was quite what a long history they shared. This picture was taken more than six years ago! They were real-life partners, and partners-in-crime too for a very long time. This diamond smuggling and theatre business in London is just their most recent escapade together! Look at them here, performing as magicians for the troops, whilst unbeknown to the Belgian government who were paying them, they were actually acting as traitors, smuggling guns! I had no idea the Count was out there in the trenches too!'

And under her breath Posie whispered, but mainly to herself: 'So if they had such a history together, why on earth would he have killed her? *He can't have done…*one lousy stolen Maharajah diamond can't break a tie like that. It doesn't make any sense.'

Rainbird frowned. 'But I don't understand. From Inspector Lovelace's file notes it says that he asked the Belgian police for information on the Count, and they told him they'd never heard of him! And now they're sending us handy snaps of him? It doesn't add up. The Count must have another name, surely?'

Posie took the photograph again, and stared at it.

'Good point,' she nodded. 'Can you get an urgent message to the Belgian police to ask them exactly who is who in this picture? But I'm going to keep it for now. It's our best lead yet.'

Rainbird was scribbling a telegram to the Belgian

police. He glanced up with a look of distaste etched on his face:

'Not much of a grand Count, is he? If he has to resort to working as a magician to make ends meet? No wonder he turned to diamond smuggling later on. I don't like the look of him much either, for what it's worth: nasty smile on his face, as if he was doing something really clever, when any fool knows that pulling a rabbit out of a hat is the easiest thing in the world! The trick is to make it look as if the thing has disappeared in the first place, when in reality it has been sitting there all along. Nasty rotten show-off. Magicians are the worst kind of fraudsters.'

Something Rainbird said struck Posie like a physical blow. She gasped:

'*What* did you just say?'

'I said he was a nasty show-off, that's all,' said Rainbird, slightly uncomfortably.

But she scarcely heard him: Posie's mind was working nineteen-to-the-dozen, scrambling over itself, fitting a possible solution to an unsolved problem. Could it be?

Yes! It could. She was taken aback at the ingenuity of it.

'Sergeant Rainbird! You are an absolute genius! Thank you! Thank you a thousand times! But we must leave, as soon as that telegram is sent. Never mind that Inspector Lovelace isn't here; we'll just have to move without him. This is super urgent. Can you bring a few strong men with you? Maybe with some guns? Fast as you can?'

Rainbird looked at her warily. 'Where are we off to now? Not that horrible underground nightclub again? That place gave me the creeps.'

Posie shook her head. She confirmed the location and what she expected to find there.

'Fine. I'll leave a note for the Inspector. Anything else I can do for you, Miss?' Rainbird tried to bite down the sarcastic edge breaking through his voice. In truth, he was feeling slightly frightened at what seemed a gargantuan task ahead of him, especially if it involved guns, and without anyone of a senior rank guiding him. But he felt too intimidated by this bossy girl with the determined glint in her eye to show his nerves.

'Oh!' Posie exclaimed brightly, and leant in confidentially.

'Yes! How kind of you. Speaking of *identifying people*, actually, there is something I've been meaning to ask you to do for a while now. And while the Inspector's out...'

* * * *

Twenty

They screeched around the corner of Pall Mall into St James and came to a juddering halt in front of No 11.

The police car wheezed to itself anxiously as Sergeant Rainbird climbed out, gingerly extending a hand to Posie and then brusquely ignoring the two burly armed policemen who had squeezed into the backseat alongside them.

Another police car lurched against the kerb behind them, the acidic smell of brake-fluid filling the air, and a further four policemen climbed out, their eyes scouring the hugely unlikely surroundings for what they had been told to expect as a 'first-rate crime'.

Posie led the charge and mounted the immaculate yellow stone steps. Sergeant Rainbird and the two uniformed policemen from the first car bunched alongside her in a row and she supposed they must have made an intimidating sight, because the doorman, who was exactly the same fellow she had encountered on Monday night, peeled back in an anxious show of helpfulness as they swung through the door. They were met by the smell of fried kippers and toast.

Inside the deserted entrance of the club all was much the same as on the Monday. The calm trophy-room environment was broken only by the busy murmur of voices coming from an open doorway on the left-hand side, the same door through which the Count had sailed so assuredly after Posie had declined his offer of a drink. Now it was propped open on its well-polished hinges to reveal a large but cosy common room peppered with oblong tables at which club members were sitting enjoying their breakfasts, newspapers placed carelessly on their laps. A club servant was making his rounds with a glistening silver tea-pot, and a quick closer inspection revealed the resident Butler to be bobbing solicitously over at the far end of the breakfast room.

Sergeant Rainbird looked at Posie anxiously: he hoped to goodness she knew what she was doing, but he'd give her this – she looked mightily assured – which eased the rising panic in his chest somewhat.

'Now what?' he hissed. It was all well and good, him and six bobbies standing around like lemons, but as yet he had no idea how they would go about the task at hand. They had no Search Warrant with them; nothing official apart from their identity cards and guns.

Posie was hoping she could hold her nerve, and hoping mostly that she was right in the conviction that had led her here.

The Butler had caught sight of the ominous-looking deputation gathered in the entrance hall. Looking slightly flustered, he shuffled his way through the obstacle course of dining tables to get to them.

'Can I help you?' he wheezed nervously, closing the door reverently behind him, as if to protect his precious club members from what could turn out to be some terrible peril. He stared at the sheer number of policemen, and the lone dark-haired girl standing in front of him. She looked familiar, somehow…where had he seen her before? He cast an anxious lingering glance behind him at another little wooden door, as if willing someone else to appear and help him out.

Posie opened her carpet bag with a flourish. All eyes were on her. She held up the Belgian press-photo of the troupe of magicians. She moved it into the direct view of the old Butler and tapped the image of Caspian della Rosa sharply with a scarlet fingernail:

'This gentleman, see here? He's a member here, isn't he? Do you know him?'

The policemen were silent and stared at the Butler accusingly. He seemed to be having trouble focusing under the gaze of such an unforgiving audience. He peered down at the photo in a fluster, his face turning red and rashy. He searched in his breast pocket for his pince-nez.

Sergeant Rainbird cursed inwardly: they'd already been here and asked this doddery old fellow about Count della Rosa, who he'd declared never to have heard of. If they weren't careful they'd have a complaint made against them for harassment, and to be honest, the old Butler would have a point. Posie wasn't exactly being gentle. Or subtle, come to that. Inspector Lovelace would have his guts for garters.

'Why yes, Miss. That's Mr Chicken.' The Butler nodded; pleased with himself. 'He *is* a member here, joined us about a year ago. Hails from Belgium, I believe. A perfectly charming man.'

'Mr *Chicken*?' Posie repeated incredulously.

The Butler looked faintly annoyed at her disbelief, as if she was calling him a liar. He pulled himself up to his full height and gave her a prim look from behind his eye-glass:

'Yes indeed. That's Mr Cecil Chicken standing there with that white rabbit. I'd swear on my life.'

Posie stared at the Butler, but her thoughts were miles away.

Of course! She searched in her bag again and brought out the pink paper from the Land Registry. She turned to Sergeant Rainbird and whispered frantically:

'See? It says Poulet Productions! "*Poulet*" means

"chicken" in French, which is the language these Belgians speak to each other in. So this Cecil Chicken is definitely Count della Rosa; it's his pseudonym, maybe some sort of joke. And he's been a member of this club for the very same length of time as he's owned the theatre! I expect this place wasn't chosen at random either: as well as giving him a veneer of respectability, he knew the Cardigeon's were lifelong members and he was playing the long game; establishing a connection here, in case it came in handy for stealing the Maharajah diamond. As it turned out, he had a better secret weapon closer to home – Lucky Lucy.'

'But Cecil Chicken! What a silly name to choose!' exclaimed Sergeant Rainbird. 'He could have made up a more believable one!'

Posie edged closer to the Butler. She retrieved the press-photo from him and instead she held the pink paper from the Land Registry very close to his face.

'So when post arrived for a "*CC*" to the club, as is mentioned here in this official document, that meant that you would put it aside for Mr Chicken?'

The Butler nodded, frightened now. 'I say, is he in some sort of trouble?' he faltered.

Posie ignored him. 'And where are things stored for him? Over there?' She nodded casually towards the wall of wooden pigeon-holes at the very furthest end of the lobby. This was *exactly* where she had expected to end up.

She saw the old Butler follow her gaze and a glaze of panic sheened his whole face: he had given away too much, he knew.

Posie strode across the hall and stood in front of the unguarded pigeon-holes. And now for the moment of truth.

She had stood here on Monday and searched in vain for Caspian della Rosa's name, wanting to return his packet of black matches. But of course his name had not been there.

She looked hard now, casting backwards and forwards,

up and down. All the while she repeated to herself what she had remembered not half an hour before at the office in Scotland Yard, the words Caspian della Rosa had purred to her flirtatiously when he had met her, all of which had seemed like inconsequential guff at the time:

'Sometimes, you know, the most beautiful, the rarest treasures in the world are to be found right under our very noses. They need no guarding, no protection: they exist, fabulously, alone.'

She reached forwards. Here it was.

A small typed card taped above a pigeon-hole announced that strange name:

MR CECIL CHICKEN

'I say, Miss! You've no business going through those post holes. Please wait!' the Butler was calling out to her in rising desperation. She heard footsteps behind her, coming her way, a slamming of a door nearby. 'Wait! Wait for the Manager. One second.'

Posie ignored him. She focused on the job in hand.

And there, inside the shelf itself was a clutter of letters. She closed her eyes and pushed her hand behind them, to the very back. A small, hard, tissue-wrapped item was lodged there. She closed her fingers around it, and drew a deep breath…*the rarest treasures in the world are to be found right under our very noses…*

She would never have thought to look there, and neither would anyone else: the sheer arrogance of the man, the confidence of his hiding place, the malicious teasing of the Cardigeons…it was all frankly unbelievable.

If it hadn't been for that press-photo of the magicians and Sergeant Rainbird's remark that *'the trick is to make it look as if the thing has disappeared in the first place, when in reality it has been sitting there all along*', it would never have been found.

And Posie agreed with Rainbird's assessment of the man, too. Count della Rosa was a nasty rotten show-off. He had told his side-kick in the *La Luna* club that he had hidden the thing safely; *out of harm's way*. Indeed.

She unwrapped the brown tissue paper carefully and turned in a half-circle to face the silent room. And there it was, in her hand; the black diamond, the Maharajah diamond from Gwilim. The size of a large quail's egg, attached to a slim ring of rose gold, it was brilliantly, unbearably beautiful.

As she extended her palm outwards so the others could see, the stone seemed to catch all the light in the room, gathered it up into itself and threw it out again, magnified over and over. The single stone seemed to dazzle with as much light as if it had been a many-tiered chandelier, replete with thousands of crystals. It wasn't just black, either; it threw up beams of pink and turquoise, cream and lemon-yellow and a brilliant, eye-watering white light. The stone was almost painful to observe, and Posie glanced up and saw the six uniformed policemen gaping with open mouths. Sergeant Rainbird was standing with his hand outstretched towards her as if frozen in time, and the Butler was quivering in shock.

Another man who was dressed in a smart pinstriped suit, probably the Manager himself, had joined the Butler and was looking bewildered and angry at the same time. He conferred with the Butler in low angry whispers and then leapt forwards to near where Posie was standing. At first Posie thought he was coming for her, and she darted to one side, but then she saw he had made his way to the green-curtained telephone booth at the back. He was ringing someone. She could hear his frantic, worried tones emanating from the telephone booth.

'Who are you calling?' she shouted at the man, pulling the baize curtain aside. He looked up at her, covering the mouthpiece, and she saw fear in his eyes.

Just then, she saw the looming silhouettes of the Inspectors coming through the club doorway, their hats and ubiquitous trench coats unmistakeable. At exactly the same moment the doorway to the breakfast room swung open and Rufus' father, the Tenth Earl of Cardigeon, blundered out and stood staring at the scene, thumbs looped through his braces, his mouth dropped open like a caught fish on the line.

All eyes were on the diamond.

Was it Posie's imagination or had it been growing hotter and hotter in her hand? It seemed to be burning a hole through its protective layer of tissue paper, as if it were a smouldering coal. She was desperate to be rid of the thing, this object of so much death and desire. She turned to the Earl.

'My Lord, this belongs to the Cardigeon family, I believe. I promised I would try and get it back for you and I always keep my promises. Here.' She tipped the diamond into the Earl's outstretched hands. He almost dropped it.

'What on earth? I say! Is this the…?'

The Earl seemed lost for words for once, and was breathing slowly, shallowly. Suddenly Rufus appeared behind his father's shoulder. Worry clouded his face, but when he saw the strange-coloured stone in his father's hands and Posie standing beside him, he seemed to relax a little. He smiled a watery smile, but he was still the deathly pale of a recovering alcoholic:

'What my father means to say, Nosy, is thank you. And I thank you too. From the bottom of my heart.'

'You'd better make an urgent call to Brigg & Brooks,' muttered Posie. 'Tell them you need it to be insured. Just in case anything happens to it again. You never know.'

The Earl seemed to recover himself and he harrumphed loudly.

'Yes, I'll call them now. But it's not regular insurance we'll be buying, but *travel* insurance. This little beauty is going back to India, to the Maharajah of Gwilim. Where it belongs. It's leaving on the first ship out of here. It's caused my family, and others, enough trouble to last for several hundred years. Even touching it makes me worried. I don't want to be near the wretched thing for very long, in case it infects me…'

Posie laughed. 'You *have* been near it, my Lord. At least since Monday night, and it hasn't troubled you…or infected you so far.' She explained about the hiding place and watched the Earl turn predictably red and thundery.

The Inspectors were suddenly close by at their side. Inspector Oats was looking at the black diamond with a combination of distaste and distrust. Inspector Lovelace nodded impatiently:

'Good work, Posie. I got Sergeant Rainbird's note and we hurried over as fast as we could. At least that's one mystery solved. And we didn't have to resort to violence, so that's *one* thing the Commissioner can't complain about, anyhow.'

'What do you mean?' asked Posie, her eyes widening.

'We've been in a meeting all morning with the Commissioner, and we're in trouble. Real trouble.' Lovelace threw Inspector Oats an arc of a nod, including him in the story.

Oats glared at Posie. 'Seems your little story in the *Associated Press* had more of an effect than you'd planned. And now *we're* feeling the consequences.'

'What do you mean? I didn't commission the newspaper story to spite you. I thought it would make Count della Rosa contact us!'

'Well, he's done just that!' snapped Inspector Oats.

Lovelace sighed. 'There *is* a real-life Count Caspian della Rosa. He's a respectable Swiss aristocrat and he somehow managed to catch sight of the story in the *Associated Press*. He's contacted the Commissioner at Scotland Yard and is saying we are slandering his good name by handing out his name to the press! He's furious! He says he had nothing to do with any of the events over the last few days, still less to do with the death of Lucky Lucy. He's pulled rank and sent across all of his family papers going back hundreds of years, attesting to who he is. He's also sent sheaves of fancily worded lawyer's documents: he's going to sue us if we carry on pursuing him as a possible suspect. We've been told not to investigate him further and not to mention his name again under any circumstances. *Ever*. The Commissioner has gone wild at us. It's a dead end.'

'But has anyone actually met him?' pressed Posie. 'It could all be nonsense, a load of guff. He could just be brazening it out from afar, scaring you off with legal nonsense. Have you seen him in the flesh?'

Both Inspectors shook their heads. She explained about the Belgian press-photo and Cecil Chicken. 'It's him!' she stated excitedly. 'It's the Count operating under a silly pseudonym!'

'Have you considered you've been looking at this the wrong way around?' said Inspector Lovelace carefully. 'That this Mr Chicken is using Count della Rosa's name as a cover? *That Mr Chicken really is just Mr Chicken*. Perhaps it's malicious; he has something against this Swiss Count, wants to tarnish his name? Maybe Count della Rosa really *is* the victim in all of this…'

Inspector Oats grunted. Posie stared at them both; she didn't believe that explanation at all. She was never wrong. In fact, *they* were quite wrong, she was sure. But there was no time for argument now: they needed action, a way forwards.

'Anyhow, you need to ask here for this Mr Chicken's

home address. We need to interview him. Locate him… find him. He's your prime suspect, not to mention he might now be holding Dolly and Len as hostages, or worse!'

A snarly, malicious voice wheedled beside them. It was the pinstriped Manager. He had been listening in on their conversation. He bowed and scraped and said that while he would be pleased to assist them in whatever way he could, he could not release any information on club members, especially not home addresses and such-like. If they wanted to view the Members' Address Book, the police would need an official Search Warrant.

Inspector Lovelace groaned and snapped that he would be back personally within a couple of hours with the necessary paperwork. Behind him, Posie caught sight of Rufus listening intently to the whole conversation: a look of grim determination spreading across his face. But she didn't have time to ask Rufus what he was thinking about, for they were all unceremoniously ushered out.

Outside on the pavement Inspector Lovelace clambered into one of the police cars, but not before telling Posie to take great care and to await further instructions. He instructed one of the six policemen to stay behind with Posie as an armed escort and not to leave her side. It was the same fat and ruddy-faced constable from the police cells.

Watching the police cars hurry off down the yellow stone road towards the Palace of Clarence House, Posie turned towards ruddy-face and smiled at him with a heavy heart. In truth she felt like a prisoner, but she was too polite to indicate her displeasure. Together they set off at a jaunty half-pace through the crowded streets of Piccadilly, towards the welcome haven of Grape Street.

With a stab of icy dread, Posie thought for a second that she heard footsteps tailing her again, clipping the stone pavement behind her in what was by now a familiar echo. But again, when she turned around there was no-one there.

The policeman cleared his throat:

'Looks like snow again, Miss.'

He was right: the temperature had dropped sharply and above them the clouds were darkening.

The sky was coloured by a very strange light, like a huge glittering bruise. It suddenly reminded Posie of the Maharajah diamond which she had held for perhaps two or three minutes in total.

She knew she would never forget it: all the twisted and wonderful colours it had contained, all the promise and all the terror.

* * * *

Twenty-One

Posie stared out her office window at the pigeons flying past, blurry purple smudges against the grey buildings.

She had left ruddy-face sitting in the waiting room and he had made himself busy by stoking up the fire. 'Don't worry, Miss,' he smiled. 'I'm just out here if you need me. I won't budge.'

Babe was doing heaven only knew what and Posie hadn't the energy to question her. On the way through she had had a vague impression of the girl sitting in her office, a magazine-worthy vision in parrot-green silk and satin, yet another huge sparkly piece of jewellery fastened at her throat.

Posie cooled her throbbing head against the pane of glass and bit her fingernails.

She spied her carpet bag and for something to do she tipped the contents all over her desk. At the very bottom of the bag was the scrunched-up 1915 story from the *Associated Press*. Posie turned the clipping over: she remembered that the journalist had written his source on the back, a neighbour from the time.

Yes, here it was:

Source: Harold Sharp – 9, Winstanley Mews, SW3.

Posie breathed slowly, linking what she knew so far.

Lucy had disappeared just after this story was published, in summer 1915. By the time of her departure, the neighbour had apparently lived next door to Lucky Lucy for several years already. Posie knew that Lucy's criminal activities had started in London in 1911, and so the dates worked out.

And, although she had no solid evidence for it, Posie thought it was a pretty fair bet that the man calling himself Caspian della Rosa had been here too, in London, alongside her, during the years from 1911 until 1915. In fact, Posie was willing to hedge her bets and say that Caspian della Rosa had been the mastermind behind *all* of Lucy's activities; running the counterfeiting gang, plotting her moves to steal pieces of priceless jewellery. They had looked inseparable in the Belgian press-photo. Even in 1915 theirs was not a new love.

'He was living here with her,' Posie muttered to herself, certain of it.

'And if he's as rich as he seems to be, keeping a Mews House in an expensive part of London for the last few years would be no skin off his nose. I bet he still has the same house. Why should he have moved? No-one has ever tracked him down there before. Sure as bread is bread that is where he is now.'

She dived into her desk drawers, looking for her street-map of London. She unwrapped it and flung it across the floor, thumbing through the index of postal districts on the side of the map. She found SW3, and took a pencil from her desk. She ringed Winstanley Mews. It was in Chelsea, just off Sloane Square, near the river. One of the most expensive places in town.

Irritatingly, just then there was a knock at the door.

'Miss Posie,' said Babe, poking her sleek oiled head around the door. 'I need to tell you something.' She looked guilty as hell. Posie sat back on her haunches and nodded grimly.

Babe played with her hands, twisting them over and over.

'It's about your cat,' she said, staring at the floor. 'I sure didn't mean him to be kidnapped or anything, but I kinda feel responsible for it. I feel bad.'

'Why?' asked Posie with what she hoped looked like an authoritative raise of her eyebrow. Babe stared moodily out of the window.

'A man arrived on Tuesday evening, just as I was locking up. He asked me to do him a favour; to deliver a letter to you. He told me to put it on your mat first thing on Wednesday morning, as if it had arrived hand-delivered. He was most particular about the timing. Said it was important.'

'It was the blue letter from Lucky Lucy, you mean? The threat? The one with the cat hair in it?'

Babe nodded. 'The very same.'

Posie frowned. 'So he must have already abducted Mr Minks when you were locking up then, if the cat hair was already inside the letter?'

'Guess so.'

'There's no way he could have exchanged or intercepted the letter later on?'

'No,' Babe shook her head adamantly. 'I had it with me all night, in my purse, which never left my side. It stayed right where it was. With me. At home. All night long.'

Posie stared at Babe. It pained her to admit it but the girl looked like she was telling the truth. 'And you didn't recognise the man?'

Babe shook her head and edged for the door.

'What did he bribe you with? As payment for delivering the letter?'

Babe looked shifty, but Posie stared her out: someone as mercenary as Babe could not be expected to do something for nothing.

'He gave me five pounds.'

Posie was almost speechless – this was more than a week's wages. 'Anything else memorable?'

'Oh, gee. Yes! He smelt of mints. Almost overpoweringly so.'

Posie gasped and covered her mouth. 'He smelt of peppermints? And was he short and stocky and wearing quite cheap clothes? With messy hair? Was he carrying a tennis bag?'

It all fell into place: it *must* have been the strange client who had come and gone so suddenly on Tuesday afternoon.

Babe scrunched her face up with the effort of remembering.

'No. He was wearing an expensive tuxedo, an evening suit. Wealthy clothes. I can't remember his face. Forgettable. And you're wrong about the smell. It was cat-mint he smelt of, now I come to think about it, not peppermints. Cats go crazy for it: my old Aunt Ada in Dalsto…well, anyhow, she used it and her house sure stank of it. I'd know the smell of it anywhere.'

The secretary retreated, closing the door behind her.

Posie exhaled slowly. So now she knew *who* had taken Mr Minks, and *when*. And it had been done craftily, on Tuesday afternoon, right under her nose…while she was in the office. Like a magic trick. How could she have been so stupid not to see it before? The cat must have been transported away in the sports bag, and what if the tennis racket had actually been some sort of net for catching the cat with if he had proved troublesome? Not that the visitor would have needed it, for Mr Minks had been drawn instantly to the smell of the cat-mint, worn so strongly and deliberately on the stranger's skin. It had been irresistible…a sort of drug.

Was this yet more proof that Caspian della Rosa (she would *not* call him Cecil Chicken) was involved up to his ears in this? He must have used yet another lackey. Some other associate, some willing dogsbody in his pay.

She turned back to the map.

What should she do? She wanted to leave immediately, to find the house in Winstanley Mews, but common sense for once prevailed and she knew she should tell the ruddy-faced policeman about her findings. They should then go to Inspector Lovelace, share the knowledge with him and then storm Winstanley Mews together with a professional crack-team…

Outside, the waiting room was strangely empty. Babe was thumbing through the pages of a cheap fashion magazine in her office when Posie stuck her head in:

'Where is the policeman?'

'It's lunchtime, Miss. He's just popped out to buy a packet of sandwiches,' she said righteously. 'Said he'd only be gone five minutes or so.'

'That seems strange. He was under strict orders not to leave me.'

Babe shrugged.

For some reason an ominous and unusual dread spread up through Posie's stomach. She turned and stood uneasily in her small, neat waiting room. She tidied the papers on the coffee-table. The minutes seemed to stretch on forever. She stood as if rooted to the spot, watching the heavy fresh snow hurling itself at the window. The British Museum was out there somewhere in the street beyond, obliterated under the whirling white-out. The world, and everything certain in it, was being silenced yet again. Covered up.

A loud clanging noise started up downstairs and then came the sound of the front door, three storeys below, being hurled open. Raised unfamiliar voices from the ground floor started shouting her name.

Male voices, authoritative voices:

'Miss Parker. Police! Police! Come quickly! We've been sent by Inspector Lovelace.'

In a second, Posie had grabbed her coat and bag and was heading for the glass-stencilled front door of her office.

She raced down the stairs, past the group of office workers who were milling around on the first floor, smoking. She bumped headlong into the thin lanky mass of an unfamiliar uniformed bobby who was on his way up to meet her.

'Ah, there you are! We have a lead!' he said excitedly, taking Posie's arm. 'We have to go at once!'

'Where is the original policeman who was stationed with me?' she asked as they came out onto Grape Street. A large black car with another policeman in it was parked against the kerb; the engine was running and the driver, with a waterproof hat pulled down well over his face, was busy scraping off the gathered snow from the windscreen with a small piece of black cardboard.

'Oh, we don't have time to wait for *him*!' said the lanky policeman airily. 'This is urgent.'

Posie found herself escorted up into the high leather back seat of the car, pressed hard up against the body of a second policeman. The lanky policeman swung up beside her quickly and pulled the door closed. She was sandwiched in. The driver jumped in quickly. He took off his hat and turned to face Posie. She gasped in sick fear and felt ice spread up through her veins.

Through the glass divide Caspian della Rosa winked at her and gave a treacherous sneer of a smile. She started to struggle violently, and felt a rough black hood suddenly thrown over her head. Her bag was snatched away from her and her hands were tied together deftly with a thin rope that bit hard into her wrists.

The car started to move off. She had walked right into a trap.

* * * *

Twenty-Two

The journey took around twenty minutes.

Posie had no doubt as to where they were driving to: with the police still crawling all over the *La Luna* club and the house in Soho, they were headed to the Mews House in Chelsea. The men in the car were silent the whole journey long, and Posie sensed a strained tension hanging between them in the cold air.

The car lurched all over the place: Caspian della Rosa was a very bad driver. As the car jolted suddenly, Posie sensed the change of direction and guessed they were now following the river along the Embankment, moving westwards through the town. She smelt the snow in the air, and the sharper tang of the briny river water filling her nostrils, and she knew they must nearly be there.

The car came to an abrupt halt, sending the three in the back seat nearly flying into the glass divide, and the man to her right cursed under his breath.

'I know where we are,' Posie said boldly from behind her hood. 'Don't think I don't know.' She was determined to retain the upper hand.

'Where, then?' drawled Caspian, as if enjoying a joke.

'Winstanley Mews, SW3,' she replied curtly.

There was a stunned silence in the car. The man to her

right sighed wearily. 'We must give you credit, Miss Parker. You really are very good at this detective game.'

They all bundled out of the car, and Posie was pushed forwards, blind-folded, over slippery cobbles. The air changed suddenly around her and she knew she had been pushed through a front door into a warm hallway. She was inside the very Mews House she had been meaning to visit this afternoon with the police in tow.

But how long would it take the police to get here now? She had not had the chance to share her information with anyone, and she knew that getting a Search Warrant for the club in St James could take a while; hours maybe.

She comforted herself with the knowledge that Inspector Lovelace would eventually find this address in the Members' Address Book at the club, hopefully within the next few hours: she felt sure she would be able to keep herself alive for that long, at least.

She was pushed roughly up several narrow flights of stairs and as she took slow baby steps she breathed in a warm fuggy scent which she half-recognised: the smell of zirconium, very strong here; a lingering note of cat-nip; and above it all, a sweet, heavy perfume she knew must have been Lucky Lucy's, and which, rather like a restless ghost, would not leave the place.

They went up at least three levels, and Posie realised this must be a very large Mews House indeed by London standards. She found herself standing at last on a flat, level surface and she was shoved roughly alongside a sharp-edged table, and manoeuvred backwards clumsily into a chair. Her bound hands were tied tightly to the chair behind her. A door closed somewhere and footsteps receded. She sat in the dark isolation of her black hood. Posie strained her ears for the sound of voices or for a hint of birdsong or the occasional horn of a car on the road outside. But there was only silence. She was left alone for what seemed like an age, with only the scared thumping of her heartbeat to keep her company.

The room was very hot, and the stink of zirconium was strong here. Posie started to feel drowsy, and against her will she felt herself nodding off. She had no idea how long she sat like that. She woke as the door behind her was yanked open and footsteps pounded the wooden floorboards around her.

Was that a muffled protest she could hear? Someone being dragged along? Someone struggling, shuffling along against their will? Was she at last going to be reunited with Len? With Dolly?

'Who's that?' she shouted from behind the hood. 'Who's there?'

She heard more muffled sounds; it was a girl's silenced voice, of that she was sure. She sensed someone squirming to her left, possibly at another seat, and she smelt the rancid stink of old sweat and fear. Dolly? Praise be if it was.

Suddenly she felt a familiar furry twisting motion at her feet and she heard loud purring.

'Mr Minks!' she cried with undisguised joy and was rewarded by the cat climbing against her legs, scratching her ten-denier stockings to pieces.

There was a clanking, clinking sound, as of teacups being set out around her. What sort of strange drama was taking place now?

Suddenly and surprisingly the hood was pulled off her head and she opened her eyes, expecting to blink against strong daylight, for it could only be early afternoon at the latest. But the room that met her eyes was dark; drawn with heavy curtains and blackout blinds and her eyes refocused in the dim light.

She surveyed the scene in a quick expert half-second: she was seated at one end of a long glass table and it was huge; it could have seated at least twelve comfortably. Directly opposite her sat Caspian della Rosa, smart in a dark suit, and beside him sat a smallish, plump man she had never seen before, although he seemed perhaps just a little familiar; his face was in the shadows, and he was immaculate in a pinstriped suit of an exquisite cut. Her eyes took in the shiny revolver which rested innocently on the glass table just in front of the Count's crossed arms. Her stomach lurched.

In the same half-second she looked quickly to her left and sure enough, a few seats along and looking absolutely dreadful was Dolly. Relief flooded through Posie like a surge of fresh energy, but where was Len? Would he be brought out later as some final party piece? But at least Dolly was alive, just. Tears pricked Posie's eyes at the sight of her friend, and at the memory of the disloyal doubts she had been harbouring towards her. The small girl was almost unrecognisable in her dirty and torn Pierrot costume from the night at the *La Luna* club; her small pretty face was a mask of pure terror, and her thick white and black days-old greasepaint was smeared and blurred by the tracks of many tears. She was bound and gagged and tied to her chair and she was staring at Posie with a mixture of relief and abject horror in her eyes.

'It's all right, Dolly,' whispered Posie, horribly aware that she could be heard clearly at the other end of the table. 'We'll get out of here in time for supper. Just you see.'

Caspian della Rosa threw back his head and laughed. A third man was darting around pouring coffee into fine bone-china cups. Posie recognised him as the lanky man who had been dressed up as a policeman earlier, who had convinced her to get in the 'police car'. A cup was set down in front of her and the coffee was poured, although Dolly did not get any. The lanky man then left the room.

A quick glance around told her she had been right: the Mews House was enormous; it must originally have been two houses which were then knocked together. Count della Rosa must be impossibly rich, richer than she had thought likely. The top floor of the house was one gigantic room, but it was not like a room from a normal house: its walls were covered on all sides by the same lead casing she had seen everywhere at the *La Luna* club, sound-proofed. Pieces of paper were taped up all over the metal walls. It was a workroom, a base. It had the effect of looking like a police investigation room, but more sinister.

Out of the corner of her eye on the nearest wall Posie saw maps: maps of Europe and what looked like South Africa and South America. Arrows and notes were pinned up over all of them.

'Tell me how I'm supposed to drink this with my hands bound behind me?' Posie said flatly, indicating with her eyes downwards at the coffee and then looking directly at the Count.

'First, tell me you're going to help me. Then I'll see what I can do.'

The Count smiled and played with the gun in front of him casually, like a toy. The man to his side flicked it very softly and it spun neatly out of the Count's reach and into the shadows. Dolly shrieked beneath her gag. It was the first audible noise she had made.

'*Me*? What can *I* do for you, Count della Rosa?' Posie answered, genuinely surprised.

The Count laughed again. Dolly had started squirming frantically in her seat and was flashing warning looks at Posie. She was squeaking loudly under her gag like a petrified canary.

'Be quiet, woman,' the Count barked at Dolly, his irritation showing for the first time. He smiled his wolfish smile. His eyes, even in this dim light, were blazing.

'You took something which belonged to me earlier,' he smiled. 'Now tell me where it is and I'll see about that coffee.'

'The black diamond of the Maharajah, you mean?' Posie said, head held high. She sensed both men across the table stiffen with tension. She continued assuredly:

'It isn't yours. You know that the Earl of Cardigeon has it. I expect that horrid little Manager at the No 11 club in St James has already told you. You weren't as clever as you thought you had been, were you? I managed to track you down there, through a spider-web of documents. I know all about you, Count della Rosa! You don't scare me at all. You're nothing but a lousy show-off and a murderer to boot: whatever Lucky Lucy did to you, she didn't deserve to die like that. You beast.'

Dolly was squeaking furiously now behind her gag, her eyes rolling in fear. Something Posie had said caused something in the Count to snap, and his smiles and laughter were now gone. He stood up angrily. His eyes flashed violently:

'Tell me *where* he will put it. Back in the bank vault in the name of his idiot son?'

'Sorry. I'm not telling you,' Posie replied tartly. 'And where is Len exactly?'

The Count looked faintly amused for a second, then thumped the glass table furiously. He clawed to his right and searched for the gun in the shadows. For some reason he couldn't locate it. Instead, he marched around the table empty-handed, furious, and untied Dolly from her chair, pulling her upwards by her short crop of bleached hair. She screamed behind the gag.

He pulled Dolly along, behind where Posie was sitting. As he passed Posie's chair he leant over and hit her coffee cup deliberately, causing it to smash. Splinters of china and scalding hot coffee ran across the table-top, and cascaded down over Posie's lap. Mr Minks mewed in terror and leapt away. Posie could only twist and turn, trying to avoid the hot liquid as best she could, feeling her good tweed coat absorbing the worst of the flow.

Suddenly there was a CLICK, and the area next to their glass table was brightly flooded with harsh electric light.

Posie twisted her body around to look at what was

happening. The Count had marched Dolly over to a long rough-wood trestle table which had previously been hidden in the shadows, and Posie now saw that the room was used, among other things, as a developing studio for photography. Shallow trays ran the length of the trestle table containing shimmering liquids and dark viscous solutions. No wonder the air in here was so noxious.

A pile of finished photographs were stacked neatly at the end of the table. With one hand still gripping Dolly's hair, the Count grabbed at the top photograph.

'Recognise yourself?' he sneered and threw it at Posie. The photo was a blurry snap of Posie at the Ritz Hotel, stepping over the body of Lionel Le Merle, on her way to find Rufus on the Monday afternoon. So then: she had been trailed by this lunatic since this whole sorry mess had started.

'Or these?' Caspian della Rosa was throwing others her way in a manic rush: a photo of Posie standing petrified, arms outstretched on the top step of the club at St James on Monday evening; a picture of her squatting near the body of Lucky Lucy at the *La Luna* club on Tuesday night, among policemen and photographers; a snap of her walking in the street, among crowds and umbrellas, turning around, looking nervous. That had probably been taken yesterday, after the Inquest.

'Still not scared? You see, Miss Parker, I know all about you, too. And there are more. Many more.'

She looked at the Count full-on and did her best to shrug as if it meant nothing to her.

'You don't frighten me.'

'Don't I? Oh, but I should. Oh, dear. I seem to have misplaced my gun temporarily. But there is more than one way to skin a cat, Miss Parker, is there not?' he smirked. 'If you will forgive my choice of words.'

He grabbed Dolly's head and pushed her face almost fully into one of the trays on the table, holding her just centimetres above the gloopy liquid. He emitted a manic burst of laughter. Was it possible the man was actually deranged? Dolly was whimpering like a dog who knows its final hour has arrived.

'Do you know what this chemical is, Miss Parker? It is pure liquid cyanide. If I hold your little friend's face under for just a couple of seconds the show will be all over. Don't believe me? I've had lots of experience. Most recently here on Monday afternoon when Georgie, who you know as Lucky Lucy, took a little bath in the stuff. I think it took about three seconds for her to die. Not much of a curtain call for an actress, would you say?'

Posie gasped, her heart was thudding like a hammer against her chest.

'So tell me about the diamond.'

'Of course!' she stuttered, her words running over themselves, her horrified gaze never leaving Dolly's stricken face.

'The Earl doesn't want it in his family's possession any longer. It will be returned to the Maharajahs who originally owned it. It will leave on the first boat out of England, on course for India.'

'When?' snapped the Count. Posie shrugged:

'Look up the newspaper listings. Perhaps as early as tomorrow? Now let Dolly go.'

For a second the Count looked across to where he had been sitting before, at the glass table in the far corner.

'Good, I will track it down. Thank you. It should not be difficult.'

Posie exhaled in relief as she saw his grip on Dolly loosen, and she saw a blind moment of panic in the girl's eyes as she too looked over to the glass table where Caspian had been sitting, where the silent second man still sat alone in the shadows. Posie had forgotten all about him.

She twisted her head back again suddenly as the Count started to laugh again. His laugh chilled Posie to the bone and she saw that he was indeed a man unhinged. He grabbed at Dolly again and with his free hand pulled off her gag, forcing her face downwards again into the tray of liquid cyanide.

'Worthless little wretch!' he shouted just before Dolly hit the pan of liquid. 'Did you *really* think I would let you live?'

'No! No! What are you doing!' Posie screamed. 'That's not fair! I've given you the information!'

But at the same time she was conscious of a sudden movement in the corner of the room, in the shadows. Someone was standing up, a low voice resonating through the room, filled with a quiet authority:

'No. Enough now.'

And at the same moment she heard the soft click of the trigger of a gun, a whizzing sensation and a bullet passing within a hair's breadth of her face, skirting past Dolly and coming to rest in the lithe chest and treacherous heart of Count Caspian della Rosa.

For a second the Count looked shocked, disbelief etched across his handsome face, before collapsing backwards onto the wooden floorboards. Dead as a doornail.

Dolly stood wide-eyed and totally silent. She didn't look at the dead man at her feet at all. She glanced instead into the corner at the second man who had saved her.

Posie wished she could stand up, take the girl in her arms. She felt sick to the bottom of her stomach but she had to be strong. 'Dolly, come here, untie me. We're safe now. Caspian della Rosa is dead.'

Dolly covered her mouth and trembled.

'You've got it all wrong, lovey. I was tryin' to warn you,' she whispered. 'He's not dead at all. You should be very, very scared. Everyone else is.'

Posie tried her best to laugh – the body on the floor was not moving at all. Was poor Dolly delusional after her traumatic ordeal?

CLICK.

More lights flicked on and the whole glass table was suddenly harshly illuminated. The head of the table was now occupied by the small, stocky man in the pinstriped suit; the man who was such a brilliant shot. An expert killer in fact.

'Your friend is right,' the man said in a melodious, foreign-lilting voice, tilting his head to one side in slight amusement, playing with his coffee cup.

'*I* am the real Count Caspian della Rosa; the Swiss aristocrat who contacted the police today to complain about my invasion of privacy. I hoped to put them off my scent. They swallowed it too. Hook, line and sinker.'

He smiled reassuringly. 'Have no fear. I can assure you I am one hundred per cent the genuine article.'

* * * *

Twenty-Three

Posie swallowed. 'I don't understand. How can it be that this dead man here has been posing to everyone as Count della Rosa?'

'Oh, but he didn't. Only to you.'

The man took a calm drag of his coffee, and wiped his lips with an immaculate strawberry-pink handkerchief.

'But *why*?' Posie stammered.

'Because I told him to, of course. He always did everything I told him to. Well, until recently anyway. He was my wingman. My mouthpiece.'

'But why did he lie to me? Why did this man pretend to be *you*?'

The man smiled briefly. 'I needed you to fall just a little bit in love with a glamorous idea…' The man trailed off into silence: he seemed to be hundreds of miles away.

Posie had no idea what he was on about. She decided on a more concrete tack:

'You don't seem very upset now he's dead…'

The man shrugged easily. 'Cecil was a paid thug. A useful one; a handsome one. But he was a thug all the same, and just lately he was becoming reckless in many ways. Dangerous for me. He had to go.'

'Cecil? So the Inspector was right…and I was wrong…

he *was* Cecil Chicken?'

'The very same. It was his *real* name too! A laughable name, is it not? But sometimes, you know, the truth is far better than fiction. All of my workers are required to work under their own names, unless of course I instruct them otherwise. It makes things easier; more plausible if they are ever questioned.'

Posie exhaled. She stared at the man seated in front of her. He seemed personable enough, but was he just another crank, some madman? She hoped to goodness that the police would arrive soon. The gun, she assumed the Belgian revolver so reverently spoken of by the Forensics Officer, Mr Maguire, still lay horribly close to the man's plump little hands.

She looked at the man narrowly. 'Who *are* you? Be straight with me.'

'I've told you already. I am a Swiss Count. I can trace my family back at least six hundred years, in fact. I could show you my papers and my passport but I sent them across to Scotland Yard, to that nice Commissioner, first thing this morning. Just about now one of my associates will be picking them up for me. They are one hundred per cent genuine. But I see by your face that you still don't believe me, Miss Parker?'

'I don't know what to believe anymore,' she said flatly, struggling with the new and doubtful information.

She shrugged. 'I know I never came across any evidence for a Count at all. It seemed at points that he was just a myth. But people speak of him as if he really does exist, and usually in tones of fear. Are you saying all of that was *you?*'

'Yes. And you have observed accurately that in my business dealings I am always very discreet. That is how we Swiss are; masters of secrecy. By necessity. I run an empire with connections stretching out all over the world, mainly run by Belgians; a clever people, with a great expertise in jewels. Hardly a soul outside of my staff at the Athenaeum Theatre would recognise me or know exactly who I am. Not one piece of paper will link me to anything, but here I am all the same: the most powerful man in all of Europe.'

Posie was certain now the man was deranged. She had to play this carefully. She kept an eye on the gun.

'Of course you are,' she smiled insincerely. Behind her, next to the body of Cecil Chicken, Dolly was silent and had not moved once. It was as if she had been turned to stone.

'I will show you evidence if you will not believe me. But you know, Miss Parker, I am slightly disappointed in you. I thought you were a great detective…We have met before. Several times, in fact. Do you *really* not recognise me?'

Just then Mr Minks jumped up onto the man's lap and started purring happily, unfaithful cat that he was. He looked cosy sitting there on the strange man's lap. The scene reminded Posie of something. Just then the man looked over at Posie and laughed. He changed his parting and then slicked his hair forwards messily and when he spoke it was with a perfect English middle-class accent.

'And now?'

Posie took a sharp intake of breath – it was the man who had visited Grape Street and pretended to be a client in order to take away Mr Minks! But what a difference a gesture, an accent made! These slight adjustments and he was another person entirely.

'You should have been an actor,' Posie said with what she hoped sounded like admiration rather than sarcasm. Behind her she heard Dolly stifle a yelp of fear.

The man spoke again in his normal voice:

'Ah! Now you have hit the nail right on the head, Miss Parker! I knew we would get along fabulously. When I was a small boy all I could dream about was acting, and owning a theatre. But alas, in a noble family such as mine, I was told to forget all about my dream. There were other, grander plans laid out for me. But I continued acting off and on, over the years, even though it was almost always offstage. And this last year I finally got to realise my dream of owning a theatre.'

He turned and smiled widely. 'And just this last week, what a lot of chances you have given me, Miss Parker, for acting! I have followed you around in all manner of disguises.'

Posie stared at the man in horror. So it was *he* who had been tailing her in his brogues and taking snaps, not the man she now knew to be Cecil Chicken.

He stood up and sauntered across to the wooden trestle table, carrying Mr Minks in his arms. He kicked the body of his wingman out of the way. He reached for the remaining stack of photos which Cecil Chicken had not thrown at Posie. He sheaved through them, smiling to himself:

'I was busy on Monday: I was a photo-journalist at the Ritz, hungry for news of a murder. And then I followed you along Whitehall in the evening, and then I played a club servant at No 11, St James. And I was kept busy on Tuesday too: I was a shoddily dressed client with a fondness for tennis and stealing cats in the afternoon, and later on at my own nightclub I played a police forensics photographer. The next day I was an old Catholic priest. And today I have been a dawn cat-walker, and then a policeman! And I'm secretly thrilled you didn't recognise me as being one and the same person. Quite a compliment.'

Posie's head was spinning. He was right: she had not thought for one minute that *one* person could possibly be all these different people, some of whom she had noticed and others whom she had barely glanced at. But it made sense: what was it Len had said recently when he had slipped under the police tape at the closed *La Luna* club in search of Mr Minks?

'*That's the thing with photographers…we're almost invisible.*'

And it was the same thing with a club servant, a priest…
these people had been almost invisible somehow, blending
into the background. Bit parts. Insignificant parts.

It was the same too with this strange man here who
seemed so proud of himself. He was forgettable. He was
like a blank canvas and if Posie had tried to sketch his
face later on today she would have found it very difficult.
It wasn't that he was ugly; just that he didn't register much
of an impression. A perfect character actor, in fact, but
one who would never, *ever* be a leading man. Not like the
stunning man lying dead at their feet.

'And it turns out you've been carrying a photo of me
around with you all of today. I suppose without realising it.'
Across the man's face flickered the merest glimmer of hurt.
Then came the slow smile again.

'Miss Price, please open Miss Parker's bag and put the
only photograph you will find within it on the table in
front of her.' He was whistling now, straightening photos
and instruments on the wooden table as if he didn't have a
care in the world.

Dolly fumbled with the catch on the carpet bag, breathing raggedly. She found the Belgian press-photo and put
it on the glass table, avoiding the pools of still-wet coffee.
She waited at Posie's side.

Posie gulped and scanned the photo. The brightness of
Lucky Lucy and the man she had thought of as Caspian
della Rosa was undimmed, and she had trouble focusing
on anything else. She forced her eye along the group, and
now she saw him where she hadn't even bothered to look
before. The man who claimed to be the real Count della
Rosa, the man just a couple of feet away from her now was
the man with the ventriloquist's dummy.

'Oh!' she gasped. She looked up. 'So you *all* knew each
other a long, long time, then?'

Posie looked again at the photo and now she noticed
tiny, tiny details she had missed at first. She saw now that

this man's eyes had been locked firmly onto Lucky Lucy, and that he was wearing the same cool, calm smile that he wore right now; his grip on his ventriloquist's dummy tight. Posie knew then that he had been wildly in love with Lucky Lucy. And she realised that somehow he had been the brains, the power behind the whole posed picture. He had stage-managed it. He had *wanted* it to look like this.

She knew in that instant that the man was telling the truth, that he *was* who he claimed to be.

'The war years were happy times for us,' he smiled. 'We were forced to leave England for a while, but we all got the chance to act. They were productive days.'

'I heard a rumour you were trading in weapons,' Posie shot at him.

'Productive days,' he repeated mildly, ignoring her taunt. 'Do you know what I called my ventriloquist's dummy?'

Posie shook her head.

'Cecil!' he sniggered, kicking the body at his feet lightly. 'It humiliated poor dear Cecil of course, on a daily basis, but then I pulled his strings in real life too, and paid him handsomely, so he couldn't complain too much. And he received other benefits.'

'Like what?'

'Helping to run my vast empire, of course. And as you can see from that photograph, he got to pose around the place with my girl, my greatest love. Although it was just an act.'

'Why did you let him?'

The man looked up at Posie directly and with a look of sheer incredulous surprise on his face.

'Why do you think? A girl like Lucy was so beautiful that she lit up any room she walked into. Do you really think people would have believed she was *my* girlfriend? A man like *me*?'

For the first time Posie felt a tiny stab of pity for the man. He went on:

'To all the world, Cecil was her perfect, beautiful match. Besides, too much attention on me in public would have exposed me. People would have questioned who I really was. It was always paramount that I was never centre-stage. Cecil was my shield.'

The man had crossed to the other side of the room and flicked on another light-switch. Yet more boards covered in maps were revealed. Boxes wrapped in brown paper and string were stacked neatly along the far wall. The man seemed preoccupied, and nestled his chin in Mr Minks' fur as if for comfort. He was standing looking at a map, consulting his wristwatch. All this time Dolly stood in silence.

Just then the strange atmosphere of the room was broken by a penetrating ringing noise. It sounded like a telephone, but could it be? Who on earth had a telephone in their *own* house? Posie tried to catch Dolly's eye but the girl was watching her boss in silent stricken fear. The man crossed the room, past the brown-papered parcels. He released the cat and picked up the receiver and took the mouthpiece.

'Yes, I'll accept the call,' he nodded. He waited a few seconds before speaking to someone he obviously knew quite well. He sounded irritated.

'Which one? Kimberley, you say? I've transferred the money already, you fool. Get on with it. You know the score. Sign the papers. Get the place opened up and get mining.' He slammed the receiver down and returned to look at a map.

Posie swung herself around as much as she was able to. Her fear had begun to ebb a little. She wanted to know the full story, and the man seemed talkative enough.

'So why did you kill her, Lucky Lucy?'

The man stepped back into a shadow, and didn't speak for what felt like a long time. When he spoke at last it was in a soft and resigned voice:

'I didn't kill her. I would never have been able to do that. I loved her too much. From the very first moment I set eyes on her on stage in Belgium, years ago. I loved her even though she betrayed me, and everything we had worked for. I didn't see it coming: it was just a normal job for us, although the prize was very special.'

'You mean the Maharajah diamond?'

He nodded. 'I had been after it for years, ever since I had heard about it as a boy. We knew she had it at last. I had spies watching her. It was on her finger! All she had to do was get into our waiting car. I was sitting watching her in the Palm Court at the Ritz, unobserved as usual, drinking a soda-and-lime behind a newspaper. I had brought along a few men from the theatre as I suspected there might be trouble. I had seen something different about her in that last week; a brightness, a strange energy. Something told me she was going to steal that black diamond from right under my nose and run away. I was in danger of losing them both.'

'The curse was at work again, you mean?'

He shrugged in the shadows. 'I don't believe in that really. But when she made a run for it I wasn't surprised. I *was* surprised she had a gun on her, and I *was* surprised she shot poor old Le Merle. But I told Cecil to go after her and catch her up and I would try and sort out the mess she had left behind, clean up a little. That's when I first saw *you*, tripping up the stairs…'

He tailed off into silence.

'Cecil was good at his job. He caught Lucy and brought her back here. Home. But I had no idea he was going to kill her. And you were right: she didn't deserve to die like that. I couldn't forgive him. He had to die sooner or later. I had given him too much power, you see. At heart, he was always a magician. You were right about that too – he was a show-off, and he liked to live dangerously. When I told him to get rid of Lucy's body I had no idea he would simply throw it in a cupboard at my own nightclub and make it look like a suicide, albeit shoddily done. It must have appealed to his sense of humour, to try and ruin her beautiful face and make it look like she had taken the cowardly way out too: he and Lucy had come to despise each other; they were always rivals in a sense, competing for my attention. He was simply delighted she was out of the picture.'

He sighed. 'And likewise, when I told him to store the Maharajah diamond somewhere secure for the next few days, I had no idea he would do something as reckless as storing it in a pigeon-hole, unguarded!'

Posie stared at the man. Everything fitted together now, and yet somehow, she still didn't understand.

'Miss Price, please untie Miss Parker from her chair. I want her to come over here.' The Count gesticulated loosely at the board he was standing in front of.

Dolly darted forwards and Posie felt her trembling, fluttering hands at her back, untying the rope. Dolly bent near her and made a show of having trouble with the knots, stalling for time, whereas Posie knew the bindings were already unfastened.

'Be careful, lovey,' whispered Dolly under her breath. 'I've seen him in action, don't believe his mild manners. He's a devil of a man. He's much more dangerous than his horrible side-kick the Chicken ever was.'

The telephone was ringing again. Under cover of its noise and the Count answering, Posie rose from her seat, whispering urgently:

'And Len? Where is he? Have they got him bound up in some cupboard here too?'

Dolly shook her head almost imperceptibly: 'No, you're wrong, Posie. He's not here. Never has been.'

A great shuddering wave of relief rippled through Posie and it was with a much lighter heart that she trotted across the wooden floorboards to the corner with the maps. The

Count had finished on the telephone and looked pleased with himself.

'I said I was going to show you my empire. And here it is,' he waved expansively. 'Some of it anyhow. The most important bits to me. See these? These are my diamond mines in South Africa.'

Posie stared at a map of a country she had never been to, a huge expanse of green. The green was studded with black pins, and in places they were so close together that it looked as if a great swarming mass of horrible insects were crawling over the paper. Tiny white paper inserts with incomprehensible details in miniscule writing were attached to each pin. The Count rubbed his hands together gleefully. In a few places, no more than ten or fifteen places perhaps, a bright red pin was attached to a slip of paper. Posie raised her eyebrow inquisitively.

'These red pins are mines I do not yet have. But I want them. They are next on my list. In fact,' and here he drew out one red pin and replaced it with a black one, 'I have just acquired another. You probably heard me earlier on the telephone. A beauty.'

Posie looked down at the man. She realised for the first time that she was taller than he was, a good couple of inches taller. 'But what I don't understand is, if you own so many mines and you smuggle stolen jewels too, why on earth are you stealing the Cardigeons' diamond, when you could obviously afford to just buy it from them yourself?'

The man laughed and his dull brown eyes were suddenly lit up with an incomprehensible fire.

'I love everything about diamonds, everything. I collect rare treasures. And the black diamond of the Maharajah – it is perhaps the most famous in the world – do you really think it could be *bought*? That the Cardigeons would sell it to me? Of course not! To steal it is the only way. Even now my spies have located it. They have just telephoned me. It is to be sent out tomorrow on the *HMS Endeavour*. My associates will make sure it never leaves the country.'

Posie realised she had been wrong again. The man was mad, but it was a particular kind of madness, a driven sort of madness she had not encountered before. A wild, craven possessiveness.

'This is just the tip of the iceberg,' the Count said, his face becoming serious again. 'I have more: castles in France and Belgium; mountain lairs in Switzerland; ranches in South America; nightclubs and speakeasies in New York. And money, *my* money, flowing everywhere.' He tapped one of the brown-paper bundles stacked next to the skirting-board.

'You mean counterfeit money? Produced in Soho using your photographic equipment and using Lucky Lucy's forgery skills acquired at the Belgian mint?'

'How astute of you,' he half-bowed. 'Although I am a pretty good forger myself, you know.'

The telephone rang again. He had been expecting the call, it seemed, and after the Operator had connected the caller, the Count simply nodded.

'I understand,' he said quietly and replaced the receiver. He turned to Posie and smiled. 'Whilst I dearly love London as my headquarters, I fear it is time to be on the move again. For a while at least.'

Posie shrugged. Why on earth was he telling her all of this? Surely he knew she would go straight to the police and tell them all she knew? Why was he being so reckless? They stared at each other.

'What do you want with me?' she said in a half-whisper.

He laughed indulgently.

'Oh, come, my dear. Surely you know the answer to that?'

She shook her head. Behind her she felt Dolly slip her tiny clammy hand into her own in a show of solidarity.

Count della Rosa moved to the very end of the wall and flicked another spotlight. A baize screen was set up there, and what was illuminated made Posie sick with shock. Dolly gasped behind her. It was covered entirely in photos and newsprint. Everything was about Posie.

At the very centre was the recent photograph of Posie which had been printed in the *Associated Press* the day before. Red pins and tiny slips of paper covered the board in a seething mass. The board was the plotting of a madman, a crazed mind at work. An obsessive. Posie turned, open-mouthed.

'You want *me*?' she whispered, although her voice did not sound entirely her own.

Caspian della Rosa tilted his head to one side and nodded.

'Yes. I told you I collect rare treasures. I found one once in Lucky Lucy and I was fortunate enough on Monday to find you at the Ritz, sauntering in out of the snow as fresh as a daisy. I knew Lucy had betrayed me and I needed a replacement. I couldn't believe my eyes when I saw you! And so I tracked you down, and I tricked you, and I lured you into my web, my world; the mysterious and glamorous world of the *La Luna* club. Why else do you think I made Cecil pretend to be me and invite you for a drink? He was a honey-trap; designed to get your attention before you met the real 'me.' But you declined and played hard to get! So then I instructed him to drop the matches as a clue; I knew you would find the club…And why else would I tease you on with my clever little notes from "Lucky Lucy" to whet your appetite? I knew you were the kind of girl to rise to a challenge and try and uncover the truth! The only fly in the ointment was your finding Lucy's body at *La Luna* – for which, my apologies: I would not have wished that on you a thousand times over. Oh, and you were not supposed to find the diamond, of course. That forced me to move pretty quickly today, let me tell you! I *need* it, almost as much as I need you.'

He laughed shrilly. 'We will be a great team, I know it.

You are resourceful and brave, and I have already watched you play one part with conviction. I was watching you every minute at the nightclub; you made a spectacular Countess Faustina! We will disappear, and then return again in a few years. Build up the theatre again, the business…it will all be fine, my darling. Don't worry about a thing. But we must go. That telephone call was my man at the club in St James. The police had arrived, so they will have this address by now.'

He looked at his wristwatch. 'We have approximately seven more minutes, by my calculations, until they get here. Let's go, my darling. I have an escape route. It's fail-safe. We use it for distributing the packages of money.' He looked at her expectantly, his brown eyes dog-like in their adoration.

Posie remained rooted to the spot. Dolly's hand, now cold with fear, was still locked in her own. She was torn between great fear and impossible outrage. She stamped her foot suddenly like a small child, a feverish toddler:

'What if I don't *want* to go with you?'

But immediately Posie saw her mistake: there was no choice in any of this. The Count, smiling as usual, had picked up Mr Minks again and was rubbing his head with the smooth butt of the revolver. He took a step forwards.

'Now, Miss Parker, don't spoil things when we were getting on so famously.' He pulled the gun properly out now, and rather than aiming it at the cat, his eye and his gun were both trained on Dolly.

'Ah! My Wardrobe Mistress. So disposable, don't you think? If your answer is still "NO" in five seconds, Miss Parker, I will shoot her. After that, I will shoot your cat. And if your answer is still a negative, I will have no choice but to shoot you too, my darling. It will be a shame. Remember. Time is of the essence. So. I will begin. FIVE. FOUR. THREE…'

Posie drew a great breath, and released her hand from

Dolly's grip. She put both hands up as if in surrender and stepped forwards. She began to speak:

'No…it's fine. I'll come…'

Just then, and as Dolly screamed, there was a movement behind them and to their left. A perfect shot, like a deadly reprimand, whistled past Count della Rosa's ear, the bullet lodging itself with pin-point accuracy into the centre of the board covered in pictures of Posie behind him.

A second shot whipped through the air and narrowly missed the Count's outstretched arm. Surprised, the Count dropped his revolver and ducked. Mr Minks squealed and jumped away. Turning, her heart in her mouth, Posie expected to find Inspector Lovelace or the boys from Scotland Yard, but both she and Dolly yelped in surprise.

It was Rufus.

****

Twenty-Four

He strode forwards into the room, the gun which had nearly been his undoing earlier in the week trained firmly on the Count.

Rufus looked in control, totally calm and collected. There was not a whiff of the drunkard about this man, and everything about the hero, the man who had won not one, but *two* Victoria Crosses in the trenches in the Great War, saving his men.

'What ho, girls!' he said from behind his Webley. He smiled and it was a smile of pure triumph, but his gaze was steely, and it remained fixed on the Count:

'I know who you are, della Rosa, but you don't scare me. All I know about you is that death and violence follow you about like a bad smell. I know that somehow my girl died because of you, or your stupid foolish friends.' He looked contemptuously for a second over to the body of Cecil Chicken.

'And now here you are, at it again. But I'm not going to be cheated out of happiness a second time by a fellow like you.' He darted a look of concern over to Dolly, who promptly burst into tears.

Rufus turned his focus back on the Count:

'But see here, old thing; I'm the kind of fellow who

can't abide violence. So how about we do this peacefully? You confess everything to the police and we'll go quietly. They'll be here any minute. I stole a look at that Members' Address Book at the club before the police managed to get to it. Seems you're not the only one able to bribe a crooked club Manager, eh, old chap? Now, put your hands above your head, where I can jolly well see them.'

The Count did as he was told, his gaze lingering expressionlessly and calmly on Posie's face. She was worried. Surely it couldn't be this simple? A man like the Count would have a few tricks up his sleeve, she was sure of it.

And here it was.

A loud crashing sound, subtle as a bull in a china-shop, was filling the room and flooding the house. There were shouts and shrieks from downstairs and a violent thumping of boots on the narrow stairs. Was this possibly the whole of the Count's gang? The rest of the Athenaeum orchestra, now released from jail and come to help him? Were they masters of perfect timing, or just lucky? Either way, there were sure to be more guns involved, and Rufus was, after all, just one man against what sounded like an army... Posie screwed her eyes shut as she anticipated the ruckus. The door flung open, and crowds seemed to flood the room. She opened her eyes and dared to look.

Mercifully, it was Inspector Lovelace, and behind him came Sergeants Rainbird, Binny and what seemed like twenty other uniformed bobbies bustling into the room. Inspector Oats came lurching in too, his eyes darting this way and that; taking in the body, the maps, the trays of developing solution. Yet more policemen were swarming up the narrow stairs and through the small door.

The police turned *en masse* and saw the Count, his hands still above his head, his face a calm mask of surprised contrition. Inspector Oats was already taking a pair of silver handcuffs out from his pocket, his face set in a hard but satisfied line. Posie breathed more normally, and noticed that Dolly had slunk behind Rufus, who was still training his gun on the Count with determination.

'Okey-dokey, let's be 'avin yer, Mister der-la Row-sa!' said Oats, advancing.

It was then that it happened. The oldest trick in the book.

The whole room, previously floodlit, was plunged into sudden darkness with the click of just one light-switch.

'Don't let 'im get away!' shouted Oats.

Screams and the sound of people falling over followed. The telephone started to ring again, urgent among the chaos. Beside her, Posie sensed swift movement and heard the scraping and thudding of something heavy being pulled along, the whispering of low voices. Then a sharp bang.

'Don't shoot! Don't anyone DARE shoot!' She heard Inspector Lovelace shouting.

People were fumbling for matches, torches, for switches. For anything. After what felt like an age someone worked out that one entire side of the room was covered in black-out blinds and they started to rip them down haphazardly. The room was instantly flooded with natural daylight. All eyes were trained on where the Count had been standing.

But of course he was gone.

So too were the packets of brown-paper covered money, and so too were the South African mining maps and the scrap-book cuttings of Posie on the baize-covered board.

In fact, the entire wall behind the pin-board, familiar as it was to anyone who had been to the *La Luna* club due to its strange metal casing, looked different. It was revealed as a vast door, swinging open just a crack.

'It's a door! He's escaped that way!' shouted Sergeant Binny and ran over to it. Half of the policemen scurried past and followed him through.

Inspector Oats was loitering near the huge floor-to-ceiling windows, and Posie saw for the first time that the house looked straight out onto the river Thames, its garden ran down directly to the river bank. The brown pulsing waves could be seen flowing beneath the swirling snow-clouds.

Posie saw instantly that this was Caspian della Rosa's escape plan. Perhaps there was a genius lurking in the man after all? For while the police had bottle-necked themselves into this high-up room in the Mews House, blocking the stairs and sealing off the road outside with their cars and road-blocks, she was certain no-one had thought of the river outside, of an anonymous little motor boat parked ready as a getaway, loaded up with precious cargo.

'Oh my gawd!' shouted Inspector Oats at the window. 'He's on the river! He's sailing off! Let's be 'avin him, boys. Get down there now! Put alerts out!'

Inspector Lovelace was standing in the middle of the room, stock-still. He knew the uselessness of pursuing the Count. He was already too far ahead of them, in many ways.

The Inspector came over to Posie who had started to shiver uncontrollably. He put his arm around her.

'Did you see that?' The Inspector nodded subtly towards the empty baize-covered board, where one tiny piece of paper was pinned in the very middle, stuck with one red pin.

'I think it's meant for you.'

Posie advanced. She took the paper down and read it before screwing it up into a tight ball as if it meant nothing in the world to her.

But they were words she knew she would never forget:

**I WILL COME FOR YOU.
I AM YOUR NEMESIS.**

****

Outside on Winstanley Mews the police were milling around with that now-familiar defeated stance, lounging against the parked cars. Inspector Oats and the two Sergeants had managed to beg a neighbour's boat and had tried to pursue the Count upstream, but no-one held out much hope of their success. Dolly and Rufus were sitting in the back seat of a police car, huddled together like survivors of a shipwreck.

Posie stood blinking, quite alone in the street.

She found she didn't have a single thought in her head. Mr Minks was nestled warmly in her arms.

Then, at the far end of the Mews she saw a familiar lone figure advancing, running, in fact. She screwed up her eyes against the London snow, and then she saw she was right. It was Len.

'Po, what on earth?' He was breathless, doubled-over, wheezing and gasping for air. 'Are you all right? I found your map on the floor of your office with the pencil-marks ringed around this street. I thought you had left me a clue! I thought the worst. That you had been kidnapped or something! Crazy, right?'

Posie scrunched the ball of paper in her hand hard.

'Where have you been?' she demanded, furious all of a sudden. A late white knight is no knight at all.

Len looked up in surprise at her angry face.

'Why, I've been on a job, you noddle. I told you yesterday! Turns out the lawyer who instructed me saw us on our way into the *Associated Press* building on Fleet Street! A case of good timing! It was a very well-paid job too. But it took me almost twenty-four hours to get what I needed. Besides, I've sent several messages and even a telegram to Grape Street, telling you not to worry. Didn't you get them?'

Posie shook her head and pursed her lips together. Babe needed to go; double-dealing little madam that she was. But that could all wait until tomorrow.

First, home. A long hot bath was in order. And she didn't care if Mrs Rapier screamed the house down about it.

* * * *

Friday 18th February, 1921

Twenty-Five

The Maharajah diamond had been insured for travelling by Brigg & Brooks, and was entrusted into the care of one Captain Grace of *The Galactic*, an ocean-going liner bound for Bombay, which had not been advertised for sailing in any of the newspapers.

It was due to leave shortly after the *HMS Endeavour*, and policemen had swarmed the decks and checked the passenger-lists of both ships to try and hunt down Count della Rosa or any of his possible associates who might have been deployed to steal the jewel. Happily, they had drawn a blank.

The Earl of Cardigeon had personally accompanied the jewel to the London Docks, and, as he stood on the scrubby concrete side of the vast berth at Poplar, he had breathed a huge sigh of relief as the lumbering bulk of *The Galactic* disappeared off into the distance.

It would arrive in Bombay in around two and a half month's time, and he had already written to the Maharajah at Gwilim to inform him to expect the arrival, and to ensure he or a trusted servant would be able to receive the jewel from the hands of Captain Grace.

* * * *

All charges brought by Scotland Yard against Rufus Cardigeon were dropped, and the bail money of five thousand pounds was in the process of being returned.

The Earl of Cardigeon had already had his valet pack up his things. He had had enough of London and was looking forward to returning to the fields and freedom of his stately home at Rebburn Abbey in the north. He was leaving that very evening, and had told Rufus that he would be delighted if he would join him. Rufus, clear-headed and full of purpose, had agreed, but he had begged a few days alone: he had things to sort out first in town.

The police had kept searching the river-ways for Count della Rosa and in mounting desperation had informed all British ports and airports to be on the look-out for him. But no-one reported a sighting. It was as if he had disappeared into the very air or earth itself.

The cells at Scotland Yard were almost empty again, as the orchestra players had all been released without charge: murky though some of them were, there were not enough or certain enough grounds to hold them for any longer. Mr Blake and his lackey Reggie had also been released without charge, turned out to face an uncertain future without the theatre featuring in it. At least without the Athenaeum Theatre, anyway.

But Scotland Yard were still holding onto Mr Eames, the dodgy diamond-dealer, and they were still combing the ghostly shell of the *La Luna* club for further traces of diamonds or smuggling activities, hoping for a possible lead.

The bright young things of London were already talking about some new and hopefully illegal hotspot for dancing and celebrity-spotting. It was over near a power-station, on the other less famous side of the river, in thrillingly unknown territory…The furore over the *La Luna* club was almost forgotten about in the excitement of this new next thing…

* * * *

Late on Friday morning, Inspectors Oats and Lovelace had found themselves pleasantly surprised to be invited to a slap-up celebration lunch at Simpson's on the Strand by none other than the Earl of Cardigeon himself. They accepted readily.

The other guests at lunch included the Earl, Rufus, Posie, Len, and Dolly Price. Over coffee and chocolate mint-thins at the end of the meal Posie asked Inspector Lovelace what the real chances of finding Count della Rosa ever were. He replied in a half-whisper, so only they could hear:

'Needle in a haystack territory, Posie. I dare say he was out of the country and on course for another destination by the time we were all tucked up in our beds last night. One thing's for certain: we won't be seeing him again on our shores for a while. But it wasn't all bad. At least one of the biggest crime and smuggling rings in London has been broken, and one of the ring-leaders, this Mr Chicken, will be troubling us no more. We're still investigating the nightclub, and maybe there'll be some new leads there… we'll certainly be kept busy anyhow.'

'Good!' said Posie decisively. She was still thinking about how close she had come to becoming the next Lucky Lucy, and how she had stood staring at the scrunched-up note Count Caspian had left for her last night in her bed-sit, for hours after she should have been fast asleep.

It was time to go. It was still snowing outside and

people lingered in the warm porch of the restaurant: Dolly and Rufus were murmuring sweet nothings at each other; Len was looking bored, and somehow the Earl and Inspector Oats had to be prised apart, having found an unlikely common interest in chub fishing. Inspector Lovelace helped Posie on with her coat. He pulled on his hat, and smiled.

'As usual, Posie, it was a pleasure working with you. Not bad for a week's work, eh? I may have leaked a story of my own by the way, so don't be surprised if you have a rush of new clients off the back of it. Hopefully that will make up for the fact you're probably not going to get paid by the tight-fisted Earl for all your hard work this week and for finding his flipping diamond. Oh, I almost forgot!'

He scrabbled in his inside coat pocket and drew out an envelope.

'It's from Sergeant Rainbird. He said you asked him to find the answer to something yesterday. I'm not even going to ask what it is. Good-day!'

Out on the street Posie and Len found themselves alone at last. It was a ten-minute walk up through the narrow dark lanes of Covent Garden back to the Grape Street Bureau.

Len had seemed tightly wound since yesterday, and was obviously very put out that he had arrived late on the scene, and that Rufus had managed not only to get there on time, but to play the part of the hero so convincingly that Len couldn't even risk bad-mouthing him. Len was unusually quiet. It didn't suit him.

As they crossed the Strand, avoiding the horse-carts and motor taxis, Posie started to laugh. She felt a huge sense of relief, and after all, Len was here and unhurt, and surely that was the biggest gift of all? She took his arm as they started to wind up the cobblestone streets. He suddenly darted over to a news-stand where the lunchtime edition of the *Associated Press* was being sold.

He paid his penny, and shook out his copy in disbelief:

'Thought so! Look at this! Your name on the *front page*! Your photo too! Says you found and broke an international jewel smuggling ring! Single-handed!'

Posie nestled in, reading. She smiled. The Inspector had been as good as his word. He had even contacted Sam Stubbs to write the piece. Len put his arms around Posie, and looked down into her eyes, his green gaze intense:

'Say, shall we go and celebrate someplace, Po? Champagne? Just the two of us?' he smouldered.

'My feelings for you haven't changed, even if you nearly did run off with a Count yesterday! We need to pick up what was interrupted on Tuesday, remember?'

'How could I forget?' she whispered back.

'But first, we need to do something really quite horrible.'

* * * *

Twenty-Six

The papers from Sergeant Rainbird lay spilled on her desk between them. However many times they read the contents it didn't get any better: they had been taken for fools. Used and abused.

'I'm so sorry,' Len said, dragging his fingers through his hair. 'It's my fault we ever took Babe on. You had misgivings at the start and yet I told you it was all nonsense! This is worse than we ever could have imagined.'

Posie nodded. What he said was true. And worse, he had made her doubt her usually impeccable judgement. Outside in the outer office, Babe was beavering away, making it look as if she were busy typing up Len's invoices for his lawyer clients.

Posie looked at her watch. It was almost three o'clock. 'Let's get this over with. It's almost time.'

She had used a telephone in an office on the way back to call Scotland Yard. And now Sergeant Rainbird was due here any minute. Posie didn't really like confrontation: she was a peace-maker at heart, it had been embedded in her by her father. It had even been written over her the night she was born, when the stars spelled out a Libra sky.

But they had no choice.

'Babe! Can you come through for a minute, please,'

250

Posie trilled calmly. The girl loomed sulkily in the doorway after a couple of minutes, a wad of typing in her hand, as if to illustrate the point that she was too busy to see them. She took the chair indicated and looked from Posie to Len, who sat together in a row opposite her, behind Posie's desk.

'Why do you think you're here?' Posie said flatly.

Babe shrugged. 'Gee, I'm sure I dunno. Am I in trouble? Something to do with that cat, I'm thinking? But I told you everything I knew.'

She pouted and played with a bracelet. Today it was a delicate, sparkling affair set with red stones and shimmering white dew-drops. To be honest, apart from the Valentine's Day pearls Babe had worn at the Athenaeum Theatre earlier in the week, Posie had never given much thought to the extraordinary way the secretary dressed herself. Now Posie stared very hard.

There was no use beating about the bush.

'I'll come straight to the point. For some time now I have questioned your motives in working for us here. A beautiful girl like you, you could have been working for a fashion house, or a big firm who could pay you big bucks. Why work for a tiny Detective Agency stuck in a dusty street in Bloomsbury? Time and time again in the last couple of months I have doubted you, and each time you were gallantly defended by Mr Irving here. We decided to trust you, and you have abused our trust. Today we have found out the extent of that abuse.'

Posie waved the police reports vaguely in Babe's direction.

Babe looked from one to the other, eyes like a rabbit-in-the-headlights, and made to move from her chair. Posie had no idea if Rainbird was here yet, but she hoped so, otherwise she would have to bluff this one out:

'There's no point in running, Babe. Policemen from Scotland Yard are here now. Just like yesterday. Did that scare you, then, too? Having a real-life policeman sitting in our waiting room? Did you think I was on to you already then? That I knew your *real identity*?'

Panic filled Babe's face but she remained silent.

'Is that why you sent the policeman out on an urgent false errand when those other men asked you to do so? To keep the coast clear so they could kidnap me? Did they pay you again? How much was it, another five pounds?'

Babe coloured first red, then a dark beetroot purple.

'And all the other bad things you've done, to deliberately thwart me in my business: *not* sending telegrams I dictated; losing incoming telegrams; lying about receiving messages. And in all of this you were simply obeying instructions! You were trying to ruin me, to ruin my business.'

Posie's voice was getting higher and higher, tighter and tighter. Len decided it was a good time to take over. He picked up the papers from Sergeant Rainbird.

'You are not an American from New York called Babe Sinclair,' he said quietly. 'No such person exists. We have the intelligence from the police here. The immigration logs have all been checked. You are Nellie Foster, of Dalston, London. You have been impersonating someone else, and you were good at it too. And now we know why. You were an actress for years, bit-parts mainly, but you were sometimes on the London stage.'

Posie was near to tears. Babe continued to stare stupidly, risen half-up from her chair.

'And I thought at points that you might be working for Count della Rosa this last week,' Posie added. 'But I was wrong. It was worse than that.'

The door to Posie's office opened and Sergeant Rainbird came in. In the waiting room other uniformed men were hanging around. The Sergeant clipped across the room, handcuffs outstretched.

'Thank you, Miss Parker,' he smiled. 'It's not every day a mere Sergeant gets to arrest a criminal and gets his hands on some of the world's most valuable stolen loot at the same time, is it?'

'We know who you are,' he smiled grimly at Babe, clicking the handcuffs into place. 'You are the sister of Bernie Foster, the mastermind behind the theft of the jewels of Countess Faustina Carino in the Burlington Arcade at Christmas.'

He grinned from ear to ear. 'And while your brother and his pals were put away in jail for a good long time because of Miss Parker's investigations, we had no idea where the jewels had ended up. Now we know! They were turning up at Grape Street nearly every day, being paraded about; flaunted by the woman whose brother probably told her to look after them and keep them safe!'

'And he also told you to get his revenge on me, out of sheer spite,' added Posie. 'Which you have tried to do, on a daily basis. Oh, just take her away! I can't bear it!'

Babe didn't struggle. She hung her black head and moved off with the Sergeant meekly. But at the door she turned and stared at Len and Posie and then gave a horrible throaty cackle.

'But I very nearly got away wiv' it, din' I?' she said in a broad cockney accent, and gave Len a horrible lecherous wink before heading out of the door.

The quietness in the offices after the last policeman had hob-nailed his way downstairs was strange. Neither of them moved from their chairs.

'I'll find someone else. A good secretary this time around,' Posie said in a soft, quiet voice. 'I think we're going to need help with all the extra work which will hopefully come our way now. But *I'll* interview her, if you don't mind.'

'What about Dolly Price?' asked Len, sweetly. 'She'll be out of a job now the theatre's closed down, and you two get along together like a house on fire. That might work?'

Posie laughed aloud. 'You've changed your tune!' she said. 'You thought she was a bad hat before, and now she's the best thing since sliced bread?'

'Maybe I was wrong. It happens,' Len said contritely.

'No,' Posie shook her head. 'It would be lovely, but something tells me Dolly will have bigger fish to fry than working at the Grape Street Bureau.'

Len laughed too. He stood up and got his hat. 'Tell me over a drink. Where shall we go? Come on. We deserve it after that ordeal.'

There was a loud rap at the outside office door.

'I'll go,' Len said, as Posie dived for the glamour attack and was already applying her lipstick. Posie heard the familiar friendly tones of a girl from the office downstairs, and then the girl's retreating steps on the stairs.

'Just a telegram!' he said cheerfully, coming back into the office, ripping the paper open.

Posie sprayed herself in parma violet and mussed her hair. She was almost ready. She would come back later to feed Mr Minks.

Just then she looked up and her heart skipped a beat as she saw Len, stricken-faced, crumple into a chair.

* * * *

Twenty-Seven

For a tiny second she thought she saw Len's hands tremble, the telegram flicker uncertainly in his hands.

'All okay?' she asked, but she didn't need to wait for his answer to know that it would not be good news. His face had gone white.

'It's the old man,' he said quietly. 'He's not in a good way, Po. Not good at all, in fact. Very ill. He says he's only got a matter of weeks... He wants me to go to him, help him out. I must leave England immediately.'

'Of course,' Posie said, shaken at the news. She hadn't heard Len speak about his father in an age, and hadn't liked to ask. 'But *where* is he exactly?'

Len laughed. 'Didn't you know?' he smiled, a shadow of his usual light-hearted self returning. He nodded at the wall behind her desk:

'*There*,' he smiled. 'He went to the Cap d'Antibes two years ago. He was so impressed with your painting up there that he left straightaway. He sends me postcards now and then. Apparently it's even better than he expected: warm, glamorous, an easy-going pace of life. He even has a French lady-friend down there, I believe. Imagine! Poor blighter.'

Posie nodded, 'I'm so glad he's had a good time.'

'I'd better get going, pack a bag and book a train,' Len said, standing and grabbing his tweed jacket, glancing at his watch.

'Who knows? I might even be able to get a third-class berth from Calais on the Blue Train if I'm lucky. It'll take me there direct.'

Posie felt her heart beating very fast against her rib cage. She wanted to stop Len, to jump in his way and keep him here in London just as it had seemed that he might become hers at last. And now all this talk of the glamorous Blue Train, the easy life in the South of France with French lady-friends: what if he didn't come back?

'When will you return?' she said, almost whispering the words, chiding herself for her selfishness as she spoke them aloud.

Len came close to her. He stroked her cheek tenderly.

'Soon, my love. I promise. I can't tell you when exactly, but I'll come back. Will you wait for me?'

Posie nodded. Of course she'd wait. What a question! Even with all the uncertainties still hanging between them, the unanswered questions. The girlfriend, for example… He kissed her hand and reluctantly let it go.

'I'll write,' he called over his shoulder. And then he was gone.

She watched Len's retreating back as he almost ran out of the Grape Street Bureau, and she felt as if the wind had been blown out of her sails.

She felt a soft rubbing sensation at her ankle, and saw Mr Minks was busily looping himself backwards and forwards, making a fuss of her, purring loudly.

'You want feeding, don't you, sir?' Posie said, bending down and scooping him up, grateful for the distraction. She thought briefly of Count della Rosa, and how the cat had seemed equally comfortable in his arms, oblivious to any danger.

She wondered where he was right now…

And then she banished the thought from her mind, and stepped through into the kitchen.

* * * *

Three Months Later

Epilogue

It had been a late spring that year, and the flowers had taken an age to come through. But now they were more than making up for it, and as Posie strode bare-foot through Bloomsbury Square Gardens with her glacé sandals clutched in her hand, the smell of the roses and freshly cut grass drifted past in a summery May-time bliss.

Lunchtime was nearly over, and workers were reluctantly shouldering their way back to dark, uninviting offices, vying for dusty pavement space with the crowds of tourists who were milling around outside the British Museum, waiting for the guards to open the doors for the afternoon visiting slot.

Posie slung her shoes back on and headed back to the office on Grape Street.

She decided to treat herself to a penny ice at the news-stand, and just as she was choosing the least garish colour on offer, her eyes caught sight of the headline of the lunchtime edition of *The Times*:

GALACTIC SINKS!
ALL SOULS LOST! DOES THE CURSE OF THE
MAHARAJAH DIAMOND STRIKE AGAIN?

She gasped and took the slippery ice-cream and a copy of the newspaper at the same time, gobsmacked. She stood rooted to the spot, reading the details.

It was incredible: the boat had sunk only five hundred nautical miles off the coast of Bombay. There was no obvious reason for the disaster, although the ship was running behind schedule and it was thought she was trying to make up for lost time by taking a perilous short cut.

All three hundred souls aboard had drowned. A rescue mission was not being attempted, and no foul play was suspected. The Maharajah diamond, in Captain Grace's possession, was now buried somewhere at the bottom of the Arabian Sea.

The rest of the story was given over to lurid details about the history of the curse of the Maharajah diamond and its string of tragedies, including a brief mention about Lucky Lucy and Count della Rosa, who had, as yet, evaded capture by the police and was top of police wanted-lists across all of Europe.

Posie folded the paper carefully, and licked the raspberry ice thoughtfully. *So this is how it ends*, she thought to herself.

She sighed: poor Captain Grace and his crew, and all those poor passengers. But somehow she was pleased that the wretched diamond, which she had held for a blistering few minutes, was now out of human reach and couldn't cause any more heartache.

She got into her office on the strike of two o'clock. A client was coming in half an hour and she wanted to prepare in good time.

The new secretary, Prudence Smythe, was busily folding invoices and licking stamps in her little office. She was a conscientious girl, and a very good secretary. She had a nice prim telephone manner too, and that was important. The telephone, which Posie had installed with the money which Len had been paid for his last job, rang all day long.

Inspector Lovelace had been right: the crazy week in February and the article in the *Associated Press* had done wonders for business at the Grape Street Bureau. Posie was more in demand than she could ever have wished for, and it felt good to know that she could keep the place running virtually single-handed, not comfortably perhaps, but adequately. Gone were the days of worrying about selling her last few nice bits and pieces to pay for rent and firewood, and gone too was the guilt she felt about relying on Len's shadowing work.

Just as well she was in demand: Len had been gone now for three long months, and with no definite fixed date for his return, Posie's earnings had had to keep the whole place afloat.

He wrote infrequently, but his letters when they came were filled with a longing for London, for Grape Street and for Posie. It seemed Mr Irving Senior's health had miraculously turned a corner, and French doctors were hopeful for a full recovery. At the bottom of every letter Len had written:

Yours, my love. Soon. X X

Posie wrote every week to the boarding-house address Len had given her and fed him tit-bits of news.

She took her scissors now and started to cut out the article about the sinking of *The Galactic*. She would send it to him with a short note. She missed Len terribly, but she didn't want to press him in the letters, to ask when exactly 'soon' might be.

Just then Prudence knocked and came through. There was a telephone call for Posie and the caller wouldn't speak to just a secretary. He had demanded Miss Parker in person.

Posie took the earpiece. The booming tones of the Tenth Earl of Cardigeon met her ears. He sounded in a surprisingly good mood:

'Parker?'

'The very same, sir.'

'You seen the news about *The Galactic*?'

'I have, sir. A tragedy. I am afraid the Arabian Sea is a bit far for me to get to, sir, if you were going to ask me to find the diamond for you a second time. Besides, I can't swim.'

The Earl laughed a great belly-laugh.

'Not why I'm ringing, Parker. I've been in touch with the insurers. They're going to pay out and the Maharajah has decided he will split the proceeds in half with me. Jolly nice fellow, what?'

Posie gulped, surprised. 'Yes, I'd say so, sir. You can get the roof fixed now at Rebburn, can't you?'

Again came the belly-laugh.

'Perhaps. But I wanted to thank you properly for helping us out back in February. It all looked a bit of a lost cause at one point. I've decided to give you some of the insurance monies by way of thank you. I know you're in a bit of a tight spot since all your family died. I'm going to send you a cheque for ten thousand pounds. That should see you right, what?'

Posie couldn't remember the conversation ending, but she had floated through the waiting room in a blur. Ten thousand pounds! A small fortune! Certainly enough to buy her own flat, *and* pay the rent upfront on the Grape Street Bureau for several years to come... Was she dreaming?

Prudence bobbed in. 'Your client is here, Miss. The one about the missing husband? And these arrived for you by the afternoon post.'

Prudence laid a thick cream envelope embossed in silver on Posie's desk. It could only be one thing. A wedding invitation!

Posie tore it open and sure enough, enclosed within was a silver-lettered card inviting her *and a partner* to the September wedding of Lord Rufus Cardigeon and Miss Dorothea ('Dolly') Price. The wedding would be at St

Bride's Church in London.

'Oh! How lovely!' Posie smiled to herself, imagining the day ahead, the chance for a new dress for the first time in years, and at her side...she hoped against hope that he would be back in time...

Dare she mention her recent good news *and* the wedding invite in the letter she would write to Len today?

'And these came, for you too,' Prudence mumbled shyly, passing across a bunch of bright yellow mimosa. The dry dusky scent took over the room, filling it with sweetness.

'I'll get a vase for you. The florist who delivered them said they were from the South of France. He said the gentleman who sent them was most particular about you knowing that. Said they would remind you of him, while he wasn't here...'

Prudence had gone a deep shade of pink and bowled out of the door backwards. Posie laughed and burrowed her face in the sweet soft buds of the mimosa and inhaled.

It was going to be a lovely summer.

* * * *

Thanks for joining Posie Parker and her friends at the Grape Street Bureau.

Enjoyed *Murder Offstage*?
Here's what you can do next.

If you loved this book and have a tiny moment to spare I would really appreciate a short review on the page where you bought the book. Your help in spreading the word is invaluable and really appreciated, and reviews make a big difference to helping new readers find the series.

Posie's second case, *The Tomb of the Honey Bee* **(A Posie Parker Mystery #2)** is now available in e-book and paperback formats from Amazon and other e-book stores, as well as in selected bookstores in the UK.

http://www.amazon.co.uk/dp/B00Q9BLYHC
http://www.amazon.com/dp/B00Q9BLYHC

More Posie Parker books will be released in 2015, including *Murder at Maypole Manor* **(A Posie Parker Mystery #3) and a Christmas novella.**

You can sign up to be notified of new releases, pre-release specials, free short stories and the chance to win Amazon gift-vouchers here:

http://www.lbhathaway.com/newsletter

Historical Note
and 1920s Money

The historical timings, dates, background and detail described in this book are accurate to the best of my knowledge, save for the following exceptions:

Locations

1. The *La Luna* club never existed, although it is based very roughly on a club (*The Cellar Door*) in Aldwych, London (http://www.cellardoor.biz).

2. The Hatton Garden I have created is entirely fictional. In reality it is a world-renowned centre of excellence for diamonds.

3. The Athenaeum Theatre does not exist, neither does No 11, St James.

4. Nightingale Mews, SW7 and Winstanley Mews, SW3 do not exist.

5. *The Galactic* (and its sinking) is entirely fictitious.

6. The *Associated Press* is fictional.

7. The story of the Maharajah diamond is fictional (as are both the Maharajah and the city-state of Gwilim itself,

although timings with regard to the rebellions and the period of the Viceroy in India are accurate).

8. I have taken the liberty of including the wonderful art-deco Bush House on Aldwych, London, WC1 (as background detail in chapter six) although in reality it was a building site in 1921 and not opened officially until 1925.

9. The famous Blue Train, *Le Train Bleu*, (which Len takes in chapter twenty-seven) was already in service in 1921 (running from Calais to the fashionable hotspots of the South of France, including the Cap d'Antibes) but was not known by such a nickname until 1924.

Grape Street in London, WC1, really does exist, although you might have to do a bit of imagining to find Posie's Detective Agency there.

Characters

The characters in this book are all fictitious, save for the appearances in chapter nine of Ivor Novello, the famous composer (1893–1951) and Kitty La Roar, who kindly appears as a historical version of herself (see www.kitty-laroar.com).

A Short Note on Money

Very roughly, the 1921 figures for money given in the book equate to:

1. Five Pounds = a 2014 value of £207 or $346

2. Five Thousand Pounds = a 2014 value of £207,187 or $346,760

3. Ten Thousand Pounds = a 2014 value of £414,375 or $693,495

4. Seven Hundred Thousand Pounds = a 2014 value of £29,000,000 or $48,531,923

Acknowledgements

I would like to thank Wendy Janes for her invaluable comments on the manuscript in draft, especially concerning the geography of 1920s London. Any mistakes remaining are, needless to say, my own.

Thank you to Red Gate Arts for producing such a beautiful and original art-deco cover design, and to Jane Dixon-Smith for her wonderful formatting and layout design.

My biggest thanks are reserved for Marco, for helping Posie Parker's adventures to get onto the page and become more than simply a figment of my imagination.

About the Author

Cambridge-educated, British-born L.B. Hathaway writes historical fiction and contributes to a number of popular history magazines and websites. She worked as a lawyer at Lincoln's Inn in London for almost a decade before becoming a full-time writer. She is a lifelong fan of detective novels set in the Golden Age of Crime, and is an ardent Agatha Christie devotee.

Her other interests, in no particular order, are: very fast downhill skiing, theatre-going, drinking strong tea, Tudor history, exploring castles and generally trying to cram as much into life as possible. She lives in London and Switzerland with her husband and young family.

The Posie Parker series of cosy crime novels span the 1920s. They each combine a core central mystery, an exploration of the reckless glamour of the age and a feisty protagonist who you would love to have as your best friend.

To find out more and for news of new releases and giveaways, go to: http://www.lbhathaway.com

Connect with L.B. Hathaway online:
  (e) author@lbhathaway.com
  (t) @LbHathaway
  (f) https://www.facebook.com/pages/L-B-Hathaway-books/1423516601228019
  (Goodreads) http://www.goodreads.com/author/show/8339051.L_B_Hathaway

Further Reading

If you are looking for some further historical reading on London during this time, see the following (all great reads and all easily available on Amazon and at good bookshops):

Singled Out: How Two Million British Women Survived Without Men After the First World War, Virginia Nicholson (Oxford University Press, USA, 2008)

Bright Young People: The Rise and Fall of a Generation 1918–1940, D J Taylor (Vintage, 2008)

Vile Bodies, Evelyn Waugh (Penguin Classics, New Edition, 2000)

Made in the USA
Middletown, DE
10 June 2021